Praise for **Kate Bateman**

THIS EARL OF MINE

"Bateman's scintillating first Bow Street Bachelors Regency is full of intense emotions and dramatic twists. Intelligent, affable characters make this fast-paced novel shine, especially for fans of clever women and the men who sincerely admire them. Future installments will be eagerly anticipated by Regency readers." —*Publishers Weekly* (starred review)

"A book that begins with a Regency heiress seeking a bridegroom in Newgate Prison promises daring adventure, and Kate Bateman gives readers just what they're looking for in *This Earl of Mine*. . . . Pure fun." —*BookPage*

"Genuine romance that shines through . . . delightful leads and sexy capers." —*Kirkus Reviews*

"Romantic, suspenseful, heartwarming, this book was absolutely delightful, and I'm already counting down the days to the next story set in this world."

—*Natasha is a Book Junkie*

"Delicious, witty, and ripping good fun! Kate Bateman's writing sparkles." —*USA Today* bestselling author Laura Lee Guhrke

A Reckless Match

Kate Bateman

St. Martin's Paperbacks

This is a work of fiction. All of the characters, organizations, and events portrayed in this novel are either products of the author's imagination or are used fictitiously.

First published in the United States by St. Martin's Paperbacks, an imprint of St. Martin's Publishing Group

A RECKLESS MATCH

Copyright © 2021 by Kate Bateman.

For information, address St. Martin's Publishing Group, 120 Broadway, New York, NY 10271.

www.stmartins.com

ISBN: 978-1-250-80156-2

Our books may be purchased in bulk for promotional, educational, or business use. Please contact your local bookseller or the Macmillan Corporate and Premium Sales Department at 1-800-221-7945, ext. 5442, or by email at MacmillanSpecialMarkets@macmillan.com.

Printed in the United States of America

St. Martin's Paperbacks edition / October 2021

10 9 8 7 6 5 4 3 2 1

To my Mum and Dad, Ron and Jan
Bateman; I told you I'd write a book set
in Wales! *Cymru am byth!* And for the
Marvelous M, Monsters #1, #2, and #3,
and Monty—scourge of squirrels and
destroyer of socks. I love you all.

We say it's exhausting to compete,
But we shine for each other.
It's still our favorite game.
                    —ART GARFUNKEL (ON PAUL SIMON)

The Legend

It started with a pig.

According to the Montgomerys, the pig was stolen. According to the Davies clan, it got lost.

Whether the pig was stolen, or simply wandered across the much-disputed boundary between the medieval Davies and Montgomery domains, very much depended upon which side of the feud you happened to be on.

The Montgomerys demanded it back. The Davies clan had already eaten it. The Montgomerys stole another pig in retaliation. Things escalated from there.

Some said it wasn't a pig at all, but a woman—and that she'd run off quite willingly with her forbidden lover—but whatever the truth of the matter, centuries of bad blood ensued.

Scarcely ten miles separated the Davieses' monstrous Welsh castle from the Montgomerys' equally large English manor, but the lush fields and green valleys between the two estates became the most contentious border in Britain, and probably in Europe too.

A decent-sized river provided a natural division, and since

the bridge that spanned it was so narrow that only a single horse and cart could cross at a time, large-scale attacks from either side were impossible. Individual instances of murder and mayhem, however, were rife.

It was occasionally suggested that the two families should build a wall, like the Roman one Hadrian had constructed between England and Scotland, but both sides strenuously disagreed. A wall would spoil the fun.

Finally, King Henry the Seventh, tired of the bloodshed between two of his most powerful houses, and inspired by tales of similar warring factions—the Medici and the Borgia in Italy—devised a truly Machiavellian solution: a royal decree that bound both houses, on pain of death.

A strip of no-man's-land was delineated between the two estates, belonging to both families, equally. Every year, on the day of the spring equinox, one representative from each family had to present themselves on the dividing bridge and shake hands in a gesture of goodwill. If either side failed to send a representative, ownership of the land would default to their bitter rival.

The thought of losing to the opposition was a powerful motivation. What was death, compared with shameful defeat? Neither side *ever* missed a meeting—although most of the handshakes were accompanied by muttered threats of obscene violence.

With open warfare thus actively discouraged, the two families devised new and creative ways of boosting morale, since baiting each other was everyone's favorite occupation. If the Montgomerys supported one particular faction, the Davieses, naturally, supported the opposition, and the mutual animosity survived years of upheaval and strife. Catholics and Protestants. Tudors and Stuarts. Roundheads and Cavaliers. They became experts at political backstabbing, sneering across crowded meeting halls, and fleecing one another at dice and cards.

By the late seventeen hundreds both sides considered themselves fairly civilized; now they traded sarcastic barbs in opu-
lent ballrooms, stole one another's wives and mistresses, and
met in the occasional hushed-up duel.

Montgomery males went to Oxford. Davies men attended
Cambridge. And while both sent sons to fight Napoleon, the
Montgomerys chose the cavalry, while the Davieses joined
the fusiliers and the navy.

And still the spring equinox deadline endured . . .

Chapter 1

"Nobody's coming."

Madeline Montgomery squinted down the empty road as a thin bubble of hope—a foreign sensation of late—rose in her breast. She checked her silver pocket watch. She hadn't mistaken the day. It was six minutes to noon on the spring equinox, and the road was deserted. There wasn't a single, dastardly, devilish Davies in sight.

"*Galahad!*" she whispered incredulously. "*Nobody's coming!*"

Her ancient gray mount twitched his ears, completely indifferent to the historic significance of the moment. Maddie sank onto the low stone parapet of the bridge. She hadn't felt this optimistic for months, not since her father had made his shocking revelation about their "unfortunate financial situation."

"It's a miracle!"

Galahad began to crop the dandelions at his feet. Maddie lifted her face to the sun and pushed back the brim of her bonnet. She'd get even more freckles, but who cared? Experience had shown her how fragile life could be: She'd once been struck by lightning out of a blue sky just like this. It had been a freak accident, a one-in-a-million chance, the doctors said. But now an even *more* unlikely event was about to occur. Five hundred years of history was about to be swept aside. The proud and illustrious name of Montgomery—and, by extension, Maddie herself—was about to be saved!

By an unkept appointment.

Excitement tightened her chest. Sir Owain Davies, the old Earl of Powys, would *never* have given her father the satisfaction of ceding the land. Baiting each other had been their main source of amusement for over fifty years.

But Sir Owain had died last summer, and the new earl, his eldest son and heir, Gryffud, hadn't set foot in his ancestral home since he'd returned from fighting Napoleon six months ago. He'd stayed in London, busy—according to the scandal sheets—setting the ladies' hearts aflutter and enjoying every possible pleasure offered by the metropolis.

Not that Maddie had been keeping track of *his* whereabouts, of course. Gryff Llewellyn Davies was her nemesis, and had been since they were children.

An echo of his wicked laughter trickled through her memory, and she fanned herself with her hand, then untied the ribbons of her bonnet and tugged it off, along with her gloves. Her hair, always too heavy for its pins, surrendered to gravity and fell in a messy cloud around her shoulders.

If the thinly drawn references to Gryff's exploits in the papers had caused an annoying, burning sensation in her chest, it was certainly *not* yearning, or jealousy, or anything else remotely emotional regarding the awful man. She didn't give a fig what he did. Truly. He was an irresponsible rakehell who'd neglected his duties and the affairs of his estate for far too long. Indeed, his debauchery was about to work to her advantage. While *he* was enjoying himself in any number of disreputable ways, here she was, virtuously saving her family from ruin.

A small, anticipatory smile curved her lips. There was simply *no way* he'd remember to get back here in time to shake her hand. Hadn't the *Gazette* reported his involvement in an illegal duel only last week? He'd probably been shot dead by some angry, cuckolded husband.

Maddie expelled her breath in a huff. No, she'd have heard if the wretch was dead. More likely, he was celebrating his undeserved victory with a glass of brandy and a thoroughly unsuitable companion.

She checked her watch again. "Three minutes to go."

Galahad, intent on his dandelions, ignored her. She sent another glance up the deserted road, hardly daring to hope.

Neither of the other three Davies siblings could possibly be coming. Rhys and Carys were both with Gryff in London, and the youngest brother, Morgan, was away at sea.

As the blue steel hands of her pocket watch crept toward the number twelve, Maddie choked back a giddy feeling of euphoria. She glanced around at the peaceful green valley and repressed the urge to leap about and twirl like a madwoman. Neither Davies nor Montgomery had ever owned this piece of land outright, so its natural riches had remained untouched for centuries.

"There's coal under here, Galahad. Maybe even gold! If we mine for it we'll have money again and I won't have to go anywhere near that awful Sir Mostyn—let alone *marry* the old letch!"

The horse wrinkled his whiskery nose and Maddie let out an incredulous laugh.

"And you know what's even more amazing? I am *finally* going to get the upper hand over that insufferable Gryffud Davies!"

Galahad flattened his ears and bared his teeth, as he did every time her opponent's name was mentioned. Maddie nodded approvingly.

"Do you think Father will let me write and tell him he's forfeited the land? Just *imagine* the look on his face!" She sighed in anticipated rapture.

The symbolism of having this meeting on the spring equinox was not lost on her. Equinoxes only happened twice a year, when the tilt of the earth's axis was inclined neither away from, nor toward, the sun. They represented equality. Day and night: twelve hours of each. A reminder that the Davies and Montgomery clans shared this strip of land between them, equally.

Her stomach gave an excited flip. *Not after today!* Today was the start of a glorious new—

A gust of wind snatched her bonnet from the low wall of the bridge. She made a desperate dive for it, missed, and the hat went sailing down into the river below.

"Oh, blast!"

Galahad lifted his head and snickered. And then his ears swiveled toward the rise in the road and Maddie turned to see what had caught his attention. She listened, praying it was nothing, but then she heard it too: the unmistakable drumbeat of approaching hooves, like distant thunder.

"No!" she groaned.

A lone horseman appeared on the crest of the hill, a plume of dust billowing in his wake. She shielded her eyes with her hand and squinted. Perhaps it was one of the village boys—?

But of course it wasn't. That broad-shouldered silhouette was unmistakable. Horribly, infuriatingly familiar.

"Oh, bloody hell."

Galahad's whinny sounded a lot like a laugh. Disloyal creature.

It had been almost four years since she'd set eyes on Gryffud Davies, but nobody else in three counties looked *that* good on a horse, as if they'd been born in the saddle. And who else exuded such arrogant, effortless grace?

Maddie's pulse began to pound at the prospect of a confrontation. Perhaps, if she was lucky, he'd have lost that unholy appeal, that teasing glimmer in his eyes that suggested she was the butt of some private joke. Gryff Davies always looked as if he couldn't choose between strangling her or ravishing her. She'd never quite decided which would be worse.

Her stomach swirled with excited dread, but she smoothed her suddenly damp palms against her rumpled skirts and set her face into an expression of polite indifference.

He rode closer, and she cataloged the changes three years had wrought. It was worse than she'd feared; he was as sinfully good-looking as ever. Curling dark hair, straight nose, lips that always looked on the verge of curving up into a smile, but usually hovered in the region of a smirk whenever he was looking at her.

And those wicked, laughing green eyes, which never failed to turn her knees to water and her brain to mush. They still held that fatal combination of condescending amusement and smoldering intensity.

Maddie clenched her fists in her skirts and lifted her chin to a haughty angle, choosing to ignore the fact that her hair was doubtless a windblown mess, and her hat was floating off downriver. She didn't care what Gryffud Davies thought of her.

He probably wouldn't even recognize her. She hardly resembled the skinny, freckled eighteen-year-old she'd been when he'd left for war. Perhaps he'd mistake her for one of the village girls.

Please God.

He slowed his mount as he neared the bridge, his eyes raking her in a thorough, devastating inspection that dashed any hope of staying incognito. Maddie straightened her spine and glared at him.

Those lips of his widened in a smile of pure devilry.

"Well, well. Maddie Montgomery. Did you miss me, *cariad*?"

Chapter 2

Gryff gazed down at the gorgeous, angry woman on the bridge and felt his spirits soar. Madeline Montgomery, the infuriating, tart-mouthed thorn in his side, was glaring up at him with murder in her eyes. It was a marvelous sight.

Her delicate brows twitched in obvious displeasure. "Don't call me that."

"What? *Cariad*?"

"No, *Maddie*." Her tone was decidedly prim. "My name is Madeline. Or better yet, Miss Montgomery."

"*Cariad* it is, then."

A muscle ticked in her jaw, and he just knew she was grinding her teeth.

"Not that either. I'm not your darling."

"Admit it. You missed me," he teased. "You've been pining for a good fight ever since I left. Did none of the locals oblige you?"

Her bosom rose and fell in silent indignation and Gryff bit back a delighted chuckle. The world—so long off kilter thanks to the madness of war—settled into place like a dislocated shoulder clicking back into its socket.

"Of course I didn't miss you."

She muttered several more things under her breath; he definitely caught the words "insufferable ass" and "blockhead." He bit his lip and tried not to laugh as a fierce sweep of exhilaration burst in his chest. The world beyond these valleys might be unrecognizable, thanks to Bonaparte's limitless ambition, but some things never changed. Miss Montgomery's antipathy toward him was blissfully undimmed.

What *had* changed—in the most delightful way—was her appearance. Years of playing cards had granted him the ability to mask his expression, but it was still an effort to conceal his shock at the changes that had occurred in his absence.

Three years ago he'd been an arrogant twenty-three-year-old, desperate for glory and adventure. She'd been a skinny tomboy with barely any feminine curves. That hadn't stopped him from fancying her, of course. His youthful self had found her quick wit and unladylike temper utterly irresistible.

The fact that they were sworn enemies had only added to the charm; it was only natural that her flashing eyes and tempting lips should have been the stuff of his filthy, moon-drenched fantasies.

Despite what the gossip rags said, he wasn't a rake, but he had ample experience of the female form. And while he'd spent countless hours wondering how she might have blossomed in his absence, the reality far outstripped his feverish imaginings. Maddie Montgomery was magnificent.

A pink blush stole across her cheeks as he inspected her, and he suppressed another chuckle.

Her face hadn't changed much. The freckles that had peppered her nose and cheeks had faded, but he could still make out a few stubborn survivors. Not surprising, considering she still didn't seem to be in the habit of wearing a hat. She'd scorned them at eighteen too.

Her hair was the same wild mass: riotous waves, the color of newly shelled horse chestnuts, shot through with a hint of rose-gold. Her lips were a luscious pink that made him think of the inside of seashells, and her eyes were that striking shade of not-quite-blue, not-quite-gray that pierced his soul.

But God help him, her body. She'd been a scrappy hoyden before, all elbows and knees. Now she was a *goddess*—albeit an enraged one. His fingers itched to trace the inward curve of her waist, the rounded perfection of her hips. It took everything he had not to vault from the saddle and touch her face to make sure that she was real. To seize her in his arms and kiss her until they were both breathless and panting and glad to be alive.

He shouldn't be goading her, of course. It could only lead to trouble. But teasing her was a pleasure he'd missed out on for three long, miserable years. The memory of her face was something he'd fallen back on when times were particularly hard. Wounded, exhausted after battle, he'd often reminded himself to stay alive, if only to spite her. To tease her just one more time.

To do more than tease.

To taste.

No. Bad idea. The worst.

He took a calming breath and lifted his brows in a manner he knew would drive her to distraction.

"My goodness. Whatever happened to the filthy little hoyden I used to know? The last time I saw you, you were covered in mud from head to toe."

"Because you and your dreadful brother had pushed me into the stream and—"

With a visible effort, she bit her lip and subdued her fury. The breath she took expanded her chest and made her breasts swell within her formfitting riding habit in a way that Gryff approved of immensely.

"No," she said, exhaling slowly. "We're both adults now. We can be civil. I refuse to let you rile me."

"But it was always such fun."

Her stormy gaze met his. "Do you really want to know what happened to me?"

He nodded.

She crossed her arms over her delectable bosom. "Very well. I was struck by lightning."

She hoped to shock him, of course, but he'd heard all about her accident as soon as he'd arrived back in London. The whole world knew a Davies would want news of a Montgomery misfortune, and the *ton* had gleefully provided him with the details.

For one terrible moment he'd thought she'd been killed, and his heart had seized in his chest. A world without her in it, opposing him, was unthinkable. His pulse had only resumed its natural rhythm when he'd realized she'd survived the freak accident.

They said she'd suffered burns to her body, although nobody had seen them to verify; her dresses concealed any damage. She'd missed her first London season, recuperating, but not the next, and by all accounts she'd been a popular addition to the various balls and amusements held in the capital in his absence.

The fact that she'd made a full recovery filled him with inexplicable relief. As had the news that she was still unwed. Gryff cast a surreptitious glance at her left hand, searching for an engagement band, just in case his information had been wrong, but her fingers were conspicuously bare.

It wasn't that he wanted to marry her *himself*, of course. He wasn't remotely ready to commit to something as drastic as matrimony, even if it was expected of him, now that he'd gained the title. After risking life and limb in the army, he'd promised himself a year of fun before bowing to the duties of the earldom.

But the thought of Maddie Montgomery married to some-one else—and therefore less able to continue their mutually satisfying tradition of prickly adversity—just didn't sit right with him.

"Lightning, eh?" he said brightly. "It suits you."

"I almost died!"

"Well, obviously you didn't, or you wouldn't be here now, awaiting my arrival with bated breath." He raised his brows in haughty inquiry. "Unless you're lost?" He gestured behind him, back the way he'd just come. "Montgomery land is six miles that way."

She jabbed a finger in the opposite direction. "And the Davies boundary's that way. We both know to the inch where our lands begin, Davies."

"So you *are* here to meet me. How lovely."

She threw her arms out in pure exasperation. "Of course I'm here to meet you, you dolt! It's the spring equinox. You didn't think a Montgomery would forget such an important date, did you?"

Her disgruntled expression was so full of outraged pique that he let out a delighted snort. "You didn't think I was coming!"

"*Hoped* would be a better word," she muttered crossly.

"You thought I'd forfeit the land!" Gryff shook his head and sent her a pitying look. "Oh, *cariad*, I hate to disappoint you"—his laughing tone said the precise opposite—"but I'd never give up anything that brings us both such satisfaction."

Her accusing glare warmed his blood almost as much as the thought of all the other activities he could show her that involved "mutual satisfaction." He gave himself a mental cuff around the ear.

Stop it.

"You deliberately waited until the very last minute to raise our hopes," she fumed.

He didn't bother to deny it. "*Our* hopes?" He glanced around the deserted valley. "You seem to be the only one here, sweeting. In fact, why *are* you the representative this year? Where's your father?"

Her eyes darted away. "He's not been well. I offered to come in his place to shake your hand."

"Because you didn't think anyone would be coming."

Her guilty flush showed the accuracy of his guess. He chuckled and dismounted.

"Well I must say, you're a damn sight easier on the eye than your father."

He dropped the reins, confident Paladin wouldn't stray. He took a step toward her, but an incongruous splash of color in his peripheral vision caught his attention and he peered over the side of the bridge. A bedraggled straw bonnet was caught in the reeds.

He turned back and eyed her riotous hair. "Yours?"

Her sigh was resigned. "Yes. There's no point trying to recover it now."

Even as they watched, a fresh surge of water freed the bonnet from its temporary prison. It floated off down the river, ribbons swirling gaily in the current, and disappeared out of sight.

She made a low growl of annoyance and turned to him, tilting her head back to glare into his face. She hadn't grown much since he'd seen her last; her chin still only reached his shoulder.

She thrust an ungloved hand toward him. "All right then, Davies. Let's get this over with."

Gryff glanced down. Her hand was so small in comparison with his own—dainty, with pale skin and neat oval nails. His own were huge and tanned. Soldier's hands: The calluses from hefting a rifle and supplies halfway around Europe had yet to disappear.

At his brief hesitation, she said, with some asperity, "Come on. You know the terms of the decree. We must shake to ensure another year of peace."

"Very well."

Gryff tugged his leather riding glove off with his teeth, then removed the other glove in the same manner. Her gaze lingered on his lips for a moment, then rose to clash with his own. A simmering heat warmed his blood.

He enfolded her hand in his.

A jolt of tingling energy shot through him as their skin pressed together, as if she still retained the charge from that lightning strike of hers. She sucked in a breath and tried to back up, but it was too late; a wicked idea had seized him and refused to be denied.

As she tried to extricate her fingers, he tightened his grip and tugged her forward until she took a stumbling step into his chest.

"Shaking hands is so *formal*," he murmured. "I think it's time we started a new tradition."

Before she could utter a word of protest, he dropped his lips to hers.

Chapter 3

For the briefest of moments Maddie registered the shocking sensation of his mouth on hers: a flash of banked heat. Then, as quickly as it had started, it was over.

She blinked in stunned bemusement as he stepped back and released her hand.

Gryff Davies had just kissed her.

Kissed her!

Maddie frowned. Considering she'd spent the best part of a decade imagining precisely this moment, it was somewhat of an anticlimax. She'd dreamed of something more prolonged. More—dare she say it?—*thorough*.

Yet despite its brevity, there was no denying that the dizzying brush of his skin had been enough to leave her own lips tingling, and her cheeks burning with heat.

She was fairly certain she ought to slap him. Not because he'd offended her maidenly sensibilities, but because he hadn't done a decent job of it. The man was supposed to be a rake. If he was going to ravish her, he could at least do it *properly*.

As if sensing her violent thoughts, he took a step back, out of reach, and sent her an unapologetic grin.

"No need to hurt yourself, *cariad*. I'll consider myself slapped."

Before Maddie could formulate a response, he strode back to his horse—a huge, handsome bay that made poor Galahad look like a knock-kneed donkey in comparison—and mounted in one fluid movement.

Maddie realized her mouth was hanging open. She snapped it shut, and strove for something pithy to say. Unfortunately, all that came out was, "Ohhh. You—"

He held up a hand. "I know, I know. Cad. Scoundrel. Libertine." His cheeky smile did something funny to her insides, and the way his gaze lingered on her lips caused an unwanted flutter in her stomach. "Let's add rake and reprobate as well, just to be thorough."

He pulled on his riding gloves with brisk efficiency, controlling the huge stallion with just the power in his thighs, and Maddie did her best not to stare at the lean muscles that rippled beneath his tan breeches.

"So, that's the pact sealed for another year." His lips twitched in amusement. "If you'll excuse me, Miss Montgomery, I'll bid you good day."

He sent her a jaunty salute, fingers to eyebrow, and urged his mount forward. She had to press back against the low side of the bridge to avoid being trampled.

Maddie finally found her voice. "Will you be taking up residence at Trellech Court?"

His broad shoulders lifted beneath his dark jacket. "For a while. There are plenty of estate matters that require my attention."

A stab of sympathy pierced her. "I'm sorry about your father."

He shrugged again, but his smile dimmed. "We rarely saw

eye-to-eye, but thank you. I wasn't able to attend the funeral. It took three weeks for the news to reach me in Portugal."

Maddie nodded. "My father attended."

"To gloat, no doubt." His lips quirked in cynical amusement.

"Not at all. He wanted to pay his respects to a worthy adversary. You know how much they loved annoying each other. He hasn't been the same these past months."

"I'm not surprised. They'd turned mutual animosity into an art form."

That was true. The two men had celebrated each other's losses, whether with money, women, or cards, for at least fifty years. In recent times they'd taken to outbidding each other at auction, on everything from thoroughbreds at Tattersalls to the rare books they both collected at Christie's. But that gleeful one-upmanship had ended with the old earl's death.

Maddie frowned. She'd initially attributed her father's bad mood to the demise of his longtime rival. The thrill of outfoxing his adversity was gone. He was miserable without someone of equal cunning against whom he could plot and scheme.

And of course he missed Tristan. Her older brother had taken himself off on a Grand Tour of the Continent as soon as Napoleon had been exiled on Elba, to study the art and architecture he so admired. He'd been away for months.

But those hadn't been the only reasons for her father's uncharacteristic brooding. Six weeks ago he'd finally admitted the truth: The Montgomerys were teetering on the verge of bankruptcy. He'd invested—and lost—an enormous sum in the great stock exchange scandal that had consumed the capital last year.

The debts were crippling. Not even the sale of Newstead Park, the seat of the Montgomery clan for countless generations, would cover the losses. Still, his outrageous suggestion that Maddie save them all from ruin by marrying their ancient-but-wealthy neighbor, Sir Mostyn Drake, had come as a nasty shock.

Maddie had always thought of herself as a dutiful daughter, stoically prepared to make any sacrifice for the good of the family. But the idea of marrying the lecherous, twice-widowed Sir Mostyn was simply too much.

Unfortunately, in the weeks since Father had made his pronouncement, she hadn't come up with a better solution.

The grim reality of her position chased away any lingering glow she'd felt from Gryff's outrageous kiss. For a few brief minutes, before he'd arrived, she'd thought her problems were over. Now she was back in the same hopeless predicament as before.

Her misery must have shown upon her face, because Gryff's brows lowered in what, on any other man, might have indicated concern.

Maddie choked back a bitter laugh. Gryff was a Davies. He didn't care about her happiness; he'd laugh himself silly if he knew how low his foe had fallen. He'd relish the thought of them penniless and destitute.

Shame and impotent frustration made her clench her jaw, even as the prick of tears threatened behind her eyes. She swallowed hard.

"Sweeting, what's wrong?"

She shook her head and turned away. There was more chance of her being struck by lightning again than of revealing her troubles to *him*.

She caught Galahad's reins, and by the time she'd gained the saddle she had herself firmly under control. She sent Gryff Davies a haughty, withering glance.

"Nothing's the matter. Nothing at all. Good day, my lord."

"Nothing's the matter, my arse," Gryff muttered, glaring at her stiff-backed retreat.

How could she deny it, when he'd watched all the delight-ful confusion he'd sparked with his cheeky kiss disappear be-neath a sudden tidal wave of misery? Her eyes had darkened with the shadow of pain, and he'd had to quash the instinctive urge to dismount and comfort her.

He shook his head at his own foolishness. "Lunacy."

Madeline Montgomery's problems were none of his con-cern: He had more than enough troubles of his own. His re-cent duel had come to the ears of the Prince of Wales.

Dueling was still strictly illegal, and even though Gryff hadn't killed his opponent—hadn't even *wounded* him, actually—Prinny's moods were so mercurial that he was as likely to have Gryff thrown in prison as an example to others as he was to laugh about it at the club. Gryff had deemed it prudent to leave London and rusticate in Wales for a few weeks until all the fuss had died down.

God, it was going to be dull, especially without Rhys, Morgan, or Carys to relieve the monotony. No gambling, no boxing matches, no operas or plays. Apart from the servants, the only living creatures in residence at Trellech would be the bizarre collection of animals in the menagerie—a remnant of his father's passion for collecting exotic animals from around the globe.

While Gryff didn't actually mind the motley bunch of feathered and furred inhabitants—except that bloody peacock, Geoffrey, whose shrill cry never failed to incite him to vio-lence—they were no substitute for human company.

He took a deep breath and made a conscious effort to relax, to let the unspoiled beauty of the place ease the ten-sion in his shoulders. Wales always did this to him; it peeled off the layers of civilization, the invisible armor he wore in London. He could feel himself becoming more primitive, less restrained, with every mile he put between himself and the city.

He didn't *want* to be primitive. He'd lived that way as a soldier for the past three years, reduced to the most basic, animalistic level of kill-or-be-killed. He wanted fun, risk-free adventures, meaningless flirtations.

His gaze strayed ahead of him, to the haughty, irritating little baggage riding away. *Not with her, though.* What had possessed him to kiss her? She was the quintessential forbidden fruit, and he really couldn't afford another scandal.

But teasing her had always been his favorite hobby, rousing her ire impossible to resist. Unfortunately, her ire wasn't the only thing he'd roused; he was still shockingly hard in his breeches, and his temperature was nothing short of roasting.

He frowned at her stubbornly straight back and the alluring sway of her hips that followed the gait of the horse.

"Why doesn't the foolish woman have a chaperone?"

Paladin tossed his head, picking up on the tightening of his hand on the reins, and Gryff clucked his tongue in a soothing response.

English society hadn't changed that much in his absence. A woman, even one as formidable as Madeline Montgomery, shouldn't be gallivanting all over the countryside alone.

True, she'd be back on Montgomery land after a mile or so, but that was no excuse. This corner of the world might not be as crime-ridden as London, but smuggling and thievery were still rife this near the coast.

Gryff let out an irritated sigh. She probably didn't have any idea of how to defend herself if accosted.

"The woman can't even control her own hat," he growled.

Witness how easily he'd stolen a kiss. A less gentlemanly assailant could have stolen far more. A shudder passed down his spine as he remembered with vivid clarity the horrors that could befall an unprotected woman. He'd seen more than enough in Spain, the results of the withdrawing French army's rape and pillage after Vitoria.

Miss Montgomery might be his family's sworn enemy, but he should at least make sure she got home safely. She couldn't very well go on annoying him if she was dead.

With a sigh, he turned Paladin and set off in her wake.

Chapter 4

Maddie was in no mood to go home. Instead, she turned Galahad off the path and guided him through the trees to one of her favorite spots: a secluded valley, home to one of the many ancient holy wells that littered the countryside.

The Welsh called it Ffynnon Pen Rhys—Pen Rhys's well. The English, naturally, had their own name for it: the Virtuous Well, presumably for some chaste saint or virginal martyr. Maddie hadn't been here since before her accident, when she'd sneaked over the boundary in search of adventure, intrigued by local tales of mystery and magic.

A tangle of ancient trees ringed the clearing, dulling the sound and giving the place a tranquil, spiritual feel, like a natural cathedral. Scraps of ribbon and colored fabric had been tied to the lower branches of several of the trees, evidence of previous visitors' offerings to whatever spirits dwelled in this mystical place. Bleached by wind and rain, the bright reds and rich blues had faded to pale rose and periwinkle.

She dismounted and picked her way across the mossy clearing toward the curved stone wall that protected the well. On the surface it was scarcely knee-high, but a set of shallow steps descended about six feet down into the earth and opened into a tiny stone-flagged courtyard, open to the sky. Once she was inside, the walls rose higher than her head.

The well itself was housed in a small, arched enclave, surrounded by a lip of flat stones. After heavy rain it often overflowed, filling the courtyard with several inches of water, but today the stones were dry beneath her boots.

Local tradition had it that a coin or metal offering tossed into the waters would make any wish come true. If the resulting bubbles that formed on the object rose quickly, the wish would be granted with equal speed. If slow to rise, the wish would take longer to come true. If no bubbles came at all, the wish would not be granted.

Maddie was naturally skeptical of such an inexact system. The last time she'd been here, years ago, she'd wished for Gryff Davies to either die an excruciating death or fall madly in love with her—either of which gruesome fates would serve him right. Clearly, the bubbles rising off her sixpence *that* time had been in error.

But desperate times called for desperate measures.

She fished around in the pocket of her riding habit for a coin, found nothing, and almost laughed in self-derision. The Montgomerys scarcely had two pennies to rub together, if Father was to be believed.

The only metal thing she could find was her folding knife, but it had once belonged to her mother, and she was loath to part with it.

Struck by sudden inspiration, she patted at her wayward hair and found a stray hairpin, clinging stubbornly to the strands behind her ear. She approached the circle of stones.

"Please, well," she muttered, feeling slightly foolish at

having to voice the thought out loud, even with only Galahad to hear. "Save me from having to marry Sir Mostyn. Help me find some other way to restore the Montgomery fortunes."

With a final kiss for luck, she tossed the hairpin into the open mouth of the well and listened for the corresponding splash.

None came.

Maddie leaned forward, expecting to see the dark ripple of water below, but to her astonishment all that greeted her was a dark, gaping hole.

"Good Lord!" Her shocked whisper echoed back to her from the darkness.

"Do you know, I'd forgotten this place was even here."

Maddie spun around with a yelp, one hand pressed to her pounding heart. Gryff Davies's handsome face peered over the parapet, his dark brows raised in interest.

"What are you doing here?" she scolded. "Are you *following* me?"

His expression was innocence itself—and she didn't believe him for a minute.

"Why would I be following you? I thought you were headed home. I was just refamiliarizing myself with my land."

"*Our* land. This particular bit belongs to both of us, remember?"

He sent her an angelic smile. "How could I forget?"

Sure that her cheeks were pink with embarrassment, and uncomfortable with his elevated position giving him the advantage, she hastened back up the steps until she was back on an even level with him.

His horse stood happily beside Galahad, cropping the grass at the edge of the clearing. He leaned back, settling himself casually on the low wall, and Maddie became acutely aware of the fact that they were alone. The thick trees and dense ferns muffled even the sound of birdsong.

She cast around for something to say. "The waters here are supposed to cure everything from scurvy to colic."

The corner of his mouth twitched. "Do you have one of those?"

"Of course not. I'm neither a sailor nor a sheep. I'm in excellent health."

His gaze slid down her body, and his lips twitched again, but all he said was, "I should say so. You look remarkably hale and hearty, Miss Montgomery."

A new flush rose on her skin. She probably looked as if she had a fever.

"If you're not here to be cured of some hideous ailment," he said, "you must be here to make a wish. Unfortunately for you, I've never heard of these waters fixing a wicked tongue or a fiery temper."

She sent him a withering glare.

"And I'm pretty sure they've never provided anyone with a husband, either."

Obnoxious man. "You couldn't be more wrong. I wasn't wishing for a husband at all." *Quite the opposite.* She wanted to escape an engagement, not attract one. "And even if I *was*, it's of no concern of yours."

He rose to his feet, and she took a wary step back.

"So what *do* you desire? Come now, I'm all agog to hear it. What could the spoiled, pampered Miss Montgomery possibly want or need?"

Freedom, she almost blurted out. *And a fortune to assure it.*

"You'll never know. Besides, this well is dry."

His eyes danced with teasing merriment. "Is that a euphemism?" He shot her a mock-sympathetic look. "Just because you're a twenty-two-year-old spinster doesn't mean you're a dried-up old prune *just* yet."

She glared at him, and his smile turned wolfish.

"You're clearly not meeting the right kind of men. Why, I'd be willing to bet that I could—"

"It was *not* a euphemism," she sputtered, desperate to stop his provocative words. She didn't entirely understand what he was talking about, but just the *way* he said it made her sure it was something he shouldn't be discussing with a lady. "I meant that the well"—she waved vaguely behind her—"is literally dry. As in, 'without water.'"

He glanced at the lush greenery around them, from ferns to moss to grasses.

"Are you sure? This place doesn't look like it's lacking rainfall." He stretched his arms above his head and inhaled deeply. "There's nature blooming everywhere. I can practically feel all this clean air doing my lungs good. God, I miss the smog of London."

Maddie turned away from the sight of his broad shoulders flexing beneath his jacket and started across the clearing.

"It is odd. We haven't had many days without rain. Certainly not enough to have caused a drought." She tramped over to the far side of the glen and began to pick her way over a heap of lichen-speckled rocks. "Perhaps something happened to divert the course of the underground spring that feeds the well?"

"Why does it matter?" he called from behind her, sounding bored. "I'm sure it's not the first time a well has dried up."

"I've never heard of it. Not around here."

"You're an expert on wells, are you?"

"No, but I'm used to looking at the surface of the land to determine what lies beneath."

"Ah yes. I remember your passion for scrabbling around in the mud, looking for treasure."

"It's called archaeology," she said primly. "And there's a lot more to it than 'scrabbling around in the mud.'"

"Yes, like luck. Which you don't seem to have. I bet you've

never found anything more exciting than a few Roman coins and bits of old pottery, have you?"

His accuracy was extremely irritating. She'd dreamed of unearthing some vast treasure ever since she'd been a girl. This particular part of the country had an ancient, checkered history—everyone from the Celts to the Romans had left their mark. Who knew what riches might be hidden beneath their feet?

For the last few summers she'd overseen her own digs, hiring local men to do the strenuous work, and fantasizing about finding some impressive Viking hoard. When she'd learned about her father's financial troubles, she'd spent hours in the fields, looking for anything that might be sold to the British Museum or to a private collector.

Maddie shook her head at her own naïveté. Hoping to find buried treasure was as silly as expecting a wishing well to restore their fortunes.

But how else could they avoid ruin? She'd already researched all the paintings in the house, hoping one might have been wrongly labeled COPY OF REMBRANDT instead of BY REMBRANDT, but no such luck. She and cousin Harriet had moved on to scouring the library, in case any first-edition folios of Shakespeare's plays were lying about in there, dusty and forgotten.

Her only other option was to marry a rich man, because according to society her only real attributes were her noble family lineage and single status. Perhaps she should just sacrifice her pride, go to London, and try to snare a rich husband?

The idea was extremely distasteful, even if it was common enough among the upper classes, and it was unlikely to yield results. Maddie was too odd, too opinionated. Hardly the meek little mouse most men seemed to want for a wife. The only ones who showed her any interest were widowers and letches, like Sir Mostyn.

"It's not luck," she said, belatedly remembering her unwanted companion. "It's making an educated guess, based on scientific observations."

Behind her, Gryff gave a skeptical grunt.

A strange, sunken indentation in the earth farther on drew her attention, and she started forward to investigate. "There must be a logical explanation for the lack of water. A rockfall farther up the source, for example."

The grassy hollow looked as if some giant hand had taken a scoop out of the earth. She reached the edge of it and turned to see if Gryff was following, but at that very moment the ground beneath her seemed to buckle and sink, as if she'd stepped on a feather mattress.

She flung her arms out, trying to catch her balance, but it was too late. Before she could do more than give a panicked cry, she was falling—down, down in a terrible blur of earth and rock. The roar of falling stones and ripping roots filled her ears and the last thing she heard was Gryff's voice, bellowing her name.

Chapter 5

Maddie landed on her back with a painful thump that knocked the air from her lungs. She sucked in a shocked breath, then coughed in the dust-filled air. Her ribs spasmed in protest. When the sound of falling stones trickled to a stop, she opened her eyes to darkness, half amazed that she wasn't dead.

Her eyes adjusted slowly to the dim light. Above her—at least ten feet above—was a patch of blue sky with clouds scudding overhead.

Gryff's face appeared in the opening, his handsome features twisted in an expression of concern. "Christ! Are you hurt? Don't move a muscle!"

Maddie almost snorted. He was probably worried that if she died, *he'd* be blamed. She wouldn't be the first Montgomery to have been sent to meet her maker by a murderous Davies.

She made a brief inventory of her body, rotating her ankles and wrists, and started to rise.

"Don't sit up!" Gryff immediately shouted. "Stay right where you are. I'm coming down."

"No, don't! We'll both be stuck down here."

He ignored her objection. His head disappeared, only to be replaced by his booted feet as he carefully lowered himself into the hole and slid his way down the rock slope that now slanted to the floor. A flurry of loose stones cascaded in his wake, settling all around her, but he was soon at her side.

"Are you hurt?"

Maddie ignored his outstretched hand and sat up on her own. He sucked in a disapproving breath at her rebellion, then squatted down in front of her and caught hold of her ankles. She gasped and tried to push his hands away.

"Stay still," he growled.

Maddie was still too shaken to object when he pushed her petticoats up to expose her stockinged shins and ankle boots. His strong fingers gently squeezed her ankles and she stared down at his tousled hair in wordless astonishment.

He shot her a smile from under his lashes. "Before you start haranguing me, I swear I'm not taking advantage. We need to make sure you haven't broken anything." His eyes twinkled. "Just pretend I'm old Doctor Williams."

Maddie suppressed a snort. Gryff was *nothing* like the white-haired, stoop-shouldered village physician. Doctor Williams's liver-spotted hands were always cold, no matter the season, whereas she could feel the heat of Gryff's fingers through the cotton of her stockings as they slid confidently up her shins to her knees.

Her stomach contracted in alarm. How high was he planning to go? She shoved her skirts back down and drew her knees up to her chest to prevent his exploration from going any further.

"Nothing's broken. Truly."

He released her with a chuckle and sat back on his haunches. "Spoilsport. Still, it doesn't look like there's any serious damage. How's your head?"

"Still attached," Maddie snapped. "Stop fussing. I'm fine."

He held up two fingers and leaned forward, peering deeply into her eyes. Maddie's breath hitched. In the semi-darkness his mossy-green eyes appeared almost black.

"How many fingers am I holding up?"

He was far too close. She could feel the warmth of his breath on her cheek. "Green," she murmured.

His brows drew together. "What?"

She swatted his hand down. "Nothing. Two. Two fingers."

He nodded, apparently satisfied, and stood. The move put the flap of his breeches—and the manly bulge contained therein—right in front of her eyes. Maddie blinked again, to clear her swimming senses. Perhaps she ought to remain sitting for a little longer?

"Can you stand?"

"I think so."

He offered his hand again, and she ignored it—again—and got stiffly to her feet. She felt like a ninety-year-old woman. "I'm fine. Really. Just a little shaken. It was no worse than taking a tumble from a horse. I was just winded, that's all."

Her ribs ached in protest but she bent and brushed at her skirts to dislodge the remaining dirt. A flurry of debris fell from her hair.

"How's your bottom? Bruised? Want me to take a look?"

She sent him a narrow-eyed look.

"Maybe you should loosen your bodice?" he said, straight-faced. "Let yourself breathe."

"You seem full of helpful suggestions to undress me."

He sent her a wicked grin, utterly unapologetic. "Is it working?"

"Not in the slightest."

He gave an exaggerated sigh of disappointment and stepped closer. She took a cautious step back.

"Stay still," he commanded softly. For a bizarre moment she thought he was going to cup her cheek or stroke her face, but his hand detoured at the last moment. She felt a tug as he plucked at a stray hairpin dangling near her shoulder, and held it up in front of her nose.

How mortifying. She must look a complete wreck. So much for appearing a cool, mature, sophisticated woman. What was it about him that made her feel as gauche and as scrappy as the eighteen-year-old she'd been when he'd left?

She snatched the pin from his fingers, then flinched as he pushed her hair back from her forehead. She registered a brief sting.

"You've hurt your head."

She tested the painful lump with her own fingers. "It's just a graze."

"Let's hope it knocked some sense into you."

"What do you mean?"

His expression darkened. "What were you thinking, scrambling about up there like a mountain goat?"

Her mouth fell open. "Are you blaming me? For an unavoidable accident?"

"Yes, I'm blaming you," he scolded. "You shouldn't have been risking your neck. What if I hadn't followed you? You could be lying down here with a broken leg, or worse. Nobody would find you for weeks."

Unwilling to admit that he had a point, she went on the offensive. "Why *were* you following me?"

"To make sure you got home safely, of course."

His angry confession knocked the wind out of her sails. "Oh."

He lifted his brows. "Yes, *oh*. Contrary to what you might believe, Miss Montgomery, I do have a shred of chivalry within me. Anytime you want to thank me—"

She opened her mouth to curse him, but he didn't appear to expect an answer because he placed his hands on his hips and swung around, away from her, peering into the darkness. "Looks like this is some sort of cave."

Maddie squinted into the gloom. The single shaft of light from the hole above only illuminated a small area, but she could make out a rocky wall off to her left. A chill, damp breeze and the sense that the darkness extended much farther than this little patch of light raised the hairs on her arms.

"There must be a series of them that bring the water to the well," she said. "But we're only about ten feet down. The well is much deeper than that."

"So the cave system must continue beneath us." He strode a few feet away, out of the puddle of light, and she bit back the urge to call him back. "It's too dark to see how far it goes. I'll come back another day with lanterns. Find out how big it is."

He stepped back into the light, and the look on his face was a mixture of excitement and devilry. Maddie wondered if it was the same look he wore when his horse was winning at Newmarket, or when he'd been dealt a particularly good hand at cards.

"Why are you so interested in exploring?"

"I've been desperate for an adventure ever since I got back from France. This fits the bill nicely."

"Wasn't your duel with Lord Sommerville excitement enough?" she asked sweetly.

He gave a careless shrug. "Didn't even wing him."

She waited for him to say more, but he remained infuriatingly tight-lipped.

"Well, you're not doing anything without me," she said finally. "This is shared land, remember? I have just as much right to explore as you do. Besides, what if you discover something interesting?"

"I suspect your idea of interesting is rather different from mine," he said drily. "But God knows, this is probably the best entertainment a man can hope for around here."

She ignored his grumbling. "We might be the first people to set foot in these caves for thousands of years. Maybe the first people ever. What if we discover something of archaeological importance? Like human bones? Or artifacts?"

"This may surprise you, Miss Montgomery, but finding human remains isn't high on my list of fun things to do. But I promise to tell you if I find any. How's that?"

"Not good enough. You'd probably walk right past them, oblivious. Or you'd find something exciting and not tell me, and hog all the glory for yourself."

He rolled his eyes heavenward. "Fine, Little Miss Suspicious. You can come—if you think you can keep up."

He tossed the challenge down so lightly, and even though Maddie knew it was a deliberate taunt, *knew* it was a mistake to have anything to do with Gryff Davies, she couldn't help but rise to the bait.

"Of course I'll be able to keep up. When do you want to meet?"

He sent her an appraising look. "Think you'll be recovered enough by tomorrow?"

"Of course."

"All right then. Meet me back here at noon."

He started to scale the tumbled slope and she scrambled up after him, her sore muscles protesting. He didn't even attempt to help her, this time. When they finally stood back in the clearing she took a grateful lungful of air, glad to have escaped from the pressing darkness below.

The horses were still grazing peacefully together by the trees. Since there was no mounting block nearby, she used a moss-covered boulder to mount Galahad and sent Gryff a stiff nod. He gave her that mocking salute again.

"Until tomorrow, *cariad*. I can hardly wait."

Chapter 6

Maddie's attempt to sneak in from the stables unobserved was foiled when she encountered her cousin Harriet in the back hall.

Harriet's father, Uncle John, was brother to Maddie's father. Harriet lived most of the year in London, helping to run Uncle John's mapmaking business, but she always spent a good part of the summer at Newstead Park. Only a year younger than herself, Maddie considered her the sister she'd never had.

Harriet's eyes widened as she took in her bedraggled appearance. "Lord, whatever happened to you? Did you fall off Sir Galahad?"

"No, I lost my hat in the river. And then I fell into a hole. And that wasn't even the *worst* thing to happen to me today."

"The Davieses sent a representative, I take it?" Harriet surmised drily.

"The dreadful Gryff Davies himself."

Harriet lifted her brows. "Really? I thought he was still in London. Being scandalous."

"Sadly not. He made a concerted effort to ride down here

in person, just to thwart us." Maddie hobbled stiffly along the corridor and entered her bedchamber. Harriet followed.

"I suppose it was too much to hope that he'd actually forget to come," Harriet said reasonably.

Maddie collapsed on the bed with a groan. "Our problems would have been solved."

Harriet knew all about the family's dire financial situation. Unfortunately, Uncle John was in no position to help. The mapmaking business had been slow since the end of the war; he had no money to spare.

"What was he like?"

Maddie threw her arm over her eyes. "The same. Worse."

Harriet chuckled. "Those Davies boys were always terribly attractive."

"Terribly annoying, you mean."

Harriet nudged her hip and Maddie felt a flush warm her cheeks. "Is Gryff Davies the reason you fell down the hole?"

"No. Well, yes. Indirectly."

Harriet was wise enough not to try to decipher that cryptic remark. She pleated the bedcovers between her fingers. "I don't suppose he mentioned his brother?"

Maddie almost laughed at her cousin's studied nonchalance. Harriet had been obsessed with Morgan Davies, the younger of Gryff's two brothers, for years.

"Who, Rhys?" she teased, keeping her expression blandly innocent.

"No, the other one. The one who went to sea."

"Oh, you mean *Morgan*. No, I don't believe he discussed either of his brothers, now that I think of it. Nor his sister. He was too busy being insufferable. Why do you ask?"

"No particular reason."

Maddie sent her a comical look of disbelief.

Harriet gave her a haughty, superior look back. "If you must know, I heard the admiralty were using some of our maps for navigation. I was just wondering how he was getting on. Whether he was satisfied with the accuracy. That's all."

"A purely professional interest," Maddie said, straight-faced.

"Of course." Harriet's ears were turning pink. "But, you know, I've been checking the admiralty reports in *The Times*. Morgan's ship hasn't been heard of for months."

"Don't tell me you're *worried* about a Davies," Maddie scoffed. "They're like bad pennies. Always turning up."

"Of course not," Harriet said, too quickly. "No more than I'd worry about any other living creature on this earth. Like a snake. Or a toad."

"Out of basic human kindness," Maddie added, her eyes twinkling. "I understand. But Gryff didn't mention him, I'm afraid."

She rolled on the bed and winced as her body protested. She was going to be covered in bruises by tomorrow, and doubtless as stiff as a board, but there was no question that she wouldn't let Gryff go adventuring without her. "Have you seen the Aunts today?"

"Not since breakfast. They've gone to see Lady Brassey, over at Raglan Grange."

Maddie nodded. The Aunts, as they were collectively known, were Prudence and Constance, her mother's older sisters. The two of them had occupied Newstead's east wing for as long as anyone could remember. From what Maddie had heard, they'd come to visit thirty years ago, and had never left.

Her father grumbled about them constantly. He referred to them as "a two-woman coven" and "those gossiping harpies," and generally left them to their own devices. But ever since scarlet fever had taken her mother, mere days after Maddie's tenth birthday, they'd been an unfailing source of comfort and support.

"Your father was asking about you," Harriet said.

"He'll want to know which Devilish Davies dared to show

his face." Maddie gave a weak smile. "Actually, I was rather surprised he let me go in his stead. This meeting used to be the highlight of his year. He loved squaring up to the old earl."

"Maybe the new earl will start some project he can oppose, just on principle?"

Maddie sniffed. "If anyone has a God-given talent for annoying people, it's Gryff Davies. I'm sure he'll aggravate us all in countless ways until he slopes back to London." She pushed off the bed and unfastened the row of buttons that secured the top part of her riding habit. "I should change. Father hates it when I come down all muddy from one of my digs."

Having donned a cotton day dress and tamed her hair into a bun, Maddie descended the main staircase and sought out her father in his study. She found him seated behind his desk, wire-rimmed spectacles perched on his nose. Piles of papers were scattered all around him.

He glanced up as she entered. "Well?"

The hopeful expression on his face was enough to make her stomach swoop in misery. She hated to be the one to dash his prayers of financial deliverance. She shook her head, and his features dropped back into their previous cast of morose dejection.

"They managed to rustle up a representative," he surmised. It was more statement than question. "Some second cousin, twice removed. Some lazy fop with just enough Davies blood in his veins to stop the land coming to us. Am I right?"

"Not exactly. A Davies *did* come. But it was the new earl. The oldest son, Gryffud."

Her father grunted. "The soldier? Your uncle John wrote that he was safely tucked up in London, drinking and whoring himself into an early grave."

Maddie pursed her lips. "I'm sure he was. But he still managed to ride down here to honor the agreement."

Father's bushy eyebrows waggled like a pair of hairy

caterpillars. "Are you sure it was him? I don't put it past those devils to send an impostor. Did you ask for proof that he was a Davies?"

"I didn't need proof. He looks exactly the same as he did when we were children."

Well, not exactly the same, Maddie amended silently. He was broader. Wilder. More rough around the edges. And with a new air of cynical experience that only added to his charm.

Damn him.

"A preening cockerel, I'll warrant," Father muttered.

"It was definitely him."

He sank back in his chair. "Blast it. Still, I never really doubted they'd come. Every last Davies would have to be moldering in his grave before they'd cede an inch of land to us."

Maddie tried not to roll her eyes at his dramatics. She gestured at the mountain of papers strewn across the desk. "What's all this?"

A spark of his old excitement flared in his eyes. "I'm reviewing the old earl's plans to dig a canal across the common land. I've no doubt the son will prove as demented as his father and try to push it through again. I need to speak to my solicitor, lodge a new objection."

"That sounds expensive," Maddie warned. "And besides, the new earl might not have any interest in building a canal. Why not wait and see what he does?"

Father, of course, ignored this perfectly sound advice. "But you object to it too, Maddie."

"*I* have good reason. A canal would destroy anything of archaeological significance in its path. What's *yours*?"

He gave a huff. "I don't need a reason. Any plan conceived by that Welsh scoundrel is bound to be a bad one. We haven't needed a canal here for hundreds of years. Why start tearing up the countryside now?"

Maddie took a deep breath. They'd discussed this before.

And while it pained her to suggest that their beautiful valley be disfigured, their urgent need for funds might have to take precedence over aesthetic and historical preferences.

"The world is changing. Maybe a canal isn't such a bad idea. We'd get a portion of the toll levied on every barge that used it."

Father's brows lifted. "Why are you suddenly playing devil's advocate, eh?"

"Because any plan that doesn't involve me having to marry Sir Mostyn Drake should be seriously considered," she said tartly.

"Now, Maddie—"

"I can't do it," Maddie blurted out. "He's dreadful."

"Well, I admit he's not anyone's first choice of husband, but he's rich," Father cajoled. "And a shrewd businessman. Once you're married you hardly need to see him—"

"Do you think he'll let me continue my excavations?"

Father opened his mouth, but she forged on without letting him interrupt. "He would not. He curls his lip every time I mention it. He told me 'the wife of a justice of the peace shouldn't make such a spectacle of herself, tramping about the fields.'"

Father's face fell comically. "Ah."

"Even if the man I eventually marry doesn't share my hobby, I hope he'll at least allow me to pursue it. You had such a wonderful marriage to Mother. I want something like that."

Father slumped lower in his chair, and Maddie knew that she'd won.

"Ahh, Maddie," he sighed. "Of course I want that for you. I only thought that you might . . ." He trailed off and ran his hand through his hair. "He offered to pay me, you see."

"Who? Sir Mostyn?" Maddie stilled. "To marry me?"

Father nodded.

"How much?"

"Two thousand pounds."

Maddie blinked.

"And he said he'd waive your dowry. It would go a long way toward settling some of the more pressing debts," Father said dejectedly.

"How much did you lose, exactly?"

"Close on six thousand pounds."

The room wavered in front of her eyes. Good God, she'd known they were in trouble, but not to such an alarming extent. Six thousand pounds was an exorbitant sum.

"Two thousand from Sir Mostyn would keep the worst of the creditors at bay," her father muttered. "It would give me time to raise the rest of the money from other ventures. We wouldn't have to sell the house."

Maddie swallowed a ball of guilt and despair. Was she being unreasonable? Was it childish fantasy to expect a loving union like the one her parents had shared? Was her personal happiness more important than that of the rest of the family, whom she loved with all her heart? What if her refusal saw the Aunts thrown out of the house they'd lived in for years? A house that had been defended by countless generations of Montgomerys.

But the thought of marrying Sir Mostyn was utterly abhorrent.

Things would have been different if he'd been a decent man. He wasn't handsome, but looks weren't everything. She might have been able to accept a kind, if elderly, squire. Someone who would respect her opinions and see some value in her archaeological work. Someone who would view her as a partner in their marriage, with whom to share confidences, discuss problems, and offer mutual support.

None of that would happen with Sir Mostyn. He reminded her of an undertaker. Or a crow. His sallow skin was accentuated by his perpetual choice of dark clothing, and his watery blue eyes were always lingering on her bosom . . .

Father's resigned sigh brought her back to the present.

"Ah, well. I told him we'd give him a final decision at Squire Digby's dance on Saturday. If you truly can't bear the thought of marrying him, then I won't force you." He sent her a valiant smile, but Maddie's heart was heavy as she returned it with one of her own.

"Thank you. We'll find another way to raise the money, you'll see."

He brushed off her gratitude with another gruff harrumph and she decided to change the subject. She pointed at the latest copy of *The Times* that was perched on the corner of the desk. "I hear Napoleon's reached Paris. They say he already has a hundred and forty thousand men."

The ploy worked. Bonaparte was another of her father's lifelong foes. His brows twitched in outrage. "That scoundrel! He won't rest until we're all humming the Marseillaise."

It had been almost three weeks since the deposed emperor had escaped from his island prison of Elba, and the newssheets had followed his inexorable progress toward the French capital with breathless dismay.

"I hope Tristan hasn't been caught up in all that madness," Maddie said. Her older brother had an uncanny knack for becoming embroiled in the most unfortunate escapades.

Father rubbed his forehead. "I sent a letter to his last address, some unpronounceable place in Austria, but I haven't received a reply. You know what he's like. Always moving about."

Maddie nodded. What else was there to say? "The Aunts are out for dinner with Lady Brassey."

"I thought the smell of brimstone had dissipated."

Father's lips twitched into a smile and she sent him a chiding look. "Be nice. You know we'd be lost without them."

"If wishing made it so," he muttered. "I tell you, Maddie, your dear mother was the best of the bunch." He sent her a brief, regretful smile, and they shared a moment of bittersweet understanding. Then he cleared his throat and made a shooing gesture with his hands. "Well now, off with you. I'll see you at dinner."

She left him to his brooding. Heaven only knew what he'd say if she told him she was meeting his new nemesis tomorrow. Still, the possibility of finding some interesting archaeological treasure to sell was more than enough incentive to meet up with a Davies.

Alone. In the dark.

Chapter 7

Gryff was already at the entrance to the cave when Maddie arrived the next day.

He'd dressed sensibly, in buff breeches and scuffed riding boots, and a jacket that was less fitted than the one he'd worn yesterday, although it still did an admirable job of accentuating his broad shoulders. His white shirt was secured at the neck with a loose, informally tied cravat and she couldn't help but smile. He looked like an amiable country squire, instead of the seasoned soldier or darling of the *ton* he was rumored to be.

Looks, however, could be deceptive. Was she being foolish, coming here alone? What did she know about the man he'd become? Years of warfare could have had all manner of negative effects on his character.

What if he'd turned into some raving lunatic since he'd been away? He could strangle her down there and nobody would ever know.

She should have told Harriet where she was going. In fact, she should have asked her cousin to accompany her. But some wicked part of her had wanted this adventure—and Gryffud Davies—all to herself.

Just for one day.

She couldn't explain it, but despite his undoubted physical superiority and their history of antipathy, she'd always felt safe with him. He was a known entity, reassuringly constant in his role as her relentless tormentor. He might have teased her mercilessly when they were younger, but he'd never done anything that put her in actual physical danger. Rogue he might be, but honor was as ingrained in him as the seams of coal were embedded in these Welsh hills.

He sent her a smile of challenge from across the clearing as she dismounted.

"Afternoon, Miss Montgomery. Ready for adventure?"

"Always."

His gaze flicked over her and she repressed the need to check her hair to see if it was still contained. After yesterday's debacle, she'd tamed it into submission with a ruthless series of plaits and pins. Nothing short of an earthquake could dislodge it.

Not wanting to flatter him into thinking she'd made an effort with her appearance, she'd dressed in the same practical work clothes she used when on a dig: a blue serge day dress, a matching spencer, and her worn leather ankle boots. Father always joked that it made her look like a washerwoman. Still, she wasn't going to ruin a perfectly nice dress tramping around in the muck, especially when they currently had no means to buy a replacement.

She cleared her throat. "Before we go down there, Davies, I want your word that we've called a temporary truce."

His lips curled up. "A truce? Where's the fun in that?"

"Don't think I've forgotten all the mean tricks you and your brothers played on Harriet and me when we were younger."

"Childish games."

Childish games that had left her strangely restless and hell-bent on vengeance. This was not the time to restart such foolishness.

"A truce," she repeated sternly. "For as long as we're in these caves. That includes no leaping out at me from the darkness and trying to scare me witless."

He clapped his hand over his heart as if he'd received a mortal blow. "Would I?"

"Absolutely. For all I know, you could be planning to strangle me and leave my body down there to rot."

He gave a comical lift of his eyebrows. "There are many things I'd like to do to your body, Miss Montgomery, but believe me, strangling is not one of them. Besides, a dead enemy's no fun—just ask your father."

"Well, that's true," she conceded, desperately trying to ignore the swirling heat his suggestive comments had created. "So you agree to a cessation of hostilities?"

"I do. Would you like to seal our bargain in the same manner as yesterday?" More heat scalded her skin as his wicked green gaze flashed to her mouth.

"No thank you," she said primly. "I'll accept your word on the matter."

"How disappointing." He eyed the small bag she'd lifted from the saddle with a cynical lift of his brows. "What have you got in there? A clean pair of gloves? Monogrammed handkerchief? You women carry all sorts of ridiculous things about with you."

"I'm not such a peahen. I have candles and a tinderbox. A compass. My folding knife."

He gave a grunt that might have been grudging respect and slung his own satchel across his chest, bandolier-style. "You can leave the candle. Open flames are a bad idea in enclosed spaces like mines."

"This isn't a mine, it's a cave."

"Better safe than sorry."

He pulled a cylindrical brass lantern from a pannier on his saddle. The top section had a clear glass shade and a little pitched circular roof. He lit the wick on the burner inside and replaced the glass cover over the flame. "This is the very latest in mining technology—a new type of lamp designed by a chap named Stephenson. It doesn't give out as much light as a candle, but it's safer."

"Safer how?"

"When you're underground you have to be careful to watch for damps."

She wrinkled her nose. "Damps?"

"It's what miners call the gases apart from air that can build up in pockets and potentially poison you. Or explode." He gave a boyish grin, as if such a dangerous prospect delighted him. "Little sparks can't ignite damps, but a naked flame, such as from a candle, can."

"Good Lord," she breathed. "How do you know this?"

"I know you think me a shameless dilettante, Miss Montgomery, but my father did actually insist that I learn about the Davies coal mines, since I would one day inherit them."

He passed the lantern to her, then lit another for himself and approached the hole through which she'd fallen. He peered downward. "And for all his faults, he did try to improve conditions for the workers. He provided all our men with these lanterns last year."

Maddie suppressed a shiver as she looked down into the yawning hole. The darkness did not seem inviting. Undeterred, Gryff started down the loose rock slope.

"There are several kinds of damps, you know," he continued cheerfully. "Firedamp is a potentially explosive mix of methane that collects in pockets in the coal seams. It can cause an explosion if it comes into contact with a naked flame. Such a thing happened three years ago at Felling mine, up near Newcastle. Ninety-three people died."

"How dreadful!"

"Then there's blackdamp." His voice echoed strangely below her. "That's a poisonous mixture of carbon dioxide and water vapor, with no oxygen in it at all. Makes it impossible to breathe."

Maddie's own breath caught unpleasantly in her throat. The beast was just trying to scare her off, to make her change her mind about accompanying him. Well, she wouldn't be so fainthearted. She forced herself to follow him down the jumble of stones, sliding a little in the loose scree.

"Whitedamp, on the other hand," he said as she reached the bottom, "is carbon monoxide mixed with other gases caused by combustion, and stinkdamp—"

"Stinkdamp!" Maddie glared at him. "Now I know you're making it up. There's no such thing as stinkdamp."

"There really is," he said, and in the half-light of the lanterns she couldn't tell if he was joking or not. "Stinkdamp smells of rotten eggs, thanks to its sulfurous elements."

She rolled her eyes. "What's next? Blue-damp? Yellow-damp?"

He ignored her mockery. "And of course, there's the lethal *after*damp, which you get after an explosion of firedamp or coal dust."

"Of course," she said, with faint sarcasm.

He hefted his lantern higher. "That's why we need these."

She gave a put-upon sigh. "Very well, no candles."

"It's good to know you can see sense when it's presented to you, Miss Montgomery."

"You make it sound as if I would argue with you just for the sake of disagreement."

His lips quirked. "Isn't that what Montgomerys and Davieses *do*?"

He strode away to inspect the far walls and she found herself hoping that the cave would only extend a few feet in either direction. Unfortunately, he made a sound of surprised delight. "Look at this! A tunnel. I knew it."

She sent a fearful glance into the darkness. "Wait. What if there's bats? Or rats?"

"Or cats, wearing hats?"

She rolled her eyes at his childish teasing. "I'm beginning to think you took a blow to the head during battle."

"Several," he agreed. He sauntered back to her and placed his lantern on a nearby rock. "But it's not the bats or the rats you need to worry about. It's the dreaded cravat snake."

"Cravat snake," she echoed drily, amused despite herself. "Do tell."

"It's a relative of the garter snake."

"Of course it is."

"The cravat snake is so called because it wraps itself around its victim's neck, like a cravat."

Without warning, he stepped up close and wrapped his hands around her throat and Maddie suppressed a squeak of shock. His skin was warm and his hands were so big they encircled her neck with ease. His fingers tangled in the hair at her nape, while his thumbs gently caressed her chin.

She swallowed, feeling the muscles of her throat contract beneath his touch. Her pulse fluttered beneath his palm; he must be able to feel it, but she strove for cool indifference.

"Round and round it twists," he murmured, his gaze fixed on where he touched her skin. His thumb traced a featherlight caress down the front of her throat, and Maddie suddenly knew exactly how the poor mouse felt as it was suffocated by a python. She couldn't move, drained of all will.

"And then it tightens. Slowly," he whispered. "Until it steals its victim's last breath."

She was already feeling faint, just from his nearness.

He increased the pressure, just a tiny amount, and heat and dark confusion pooled in her blood. Her nipples tightened inside her bodice, and a strange heaviness gathered in the pit of her stomach. And lower still. She shivered, appalled by her reaction. Oh, he took a ghoulish delight in frightening her.

"Stop it." She batted his hands away, breaking the spell, and he released her, stepping back with a chuckle.

"Fear not, Miss Montgomery. There are no cravat snakes in England. Or Wales. The worst thing you'll encounter in these caves is me."

That's what she was afraid of.

He reclaimed his lantern and set off into the gloom. "Come along, boots."

"Boots?"

"It's an army term for the youngest, newest recruit in the regiment. A Johnny Newcombe."

Maddie frowned. The thought of having him as her superior officer, bossing her around day and night, was truly horrifying. She rummaged in her satchel, withdrew a stick of chalk she'd found in the schoolroom, and drew an arrow at waist height on the wall.

He glanced back over his shoulder. "What are you doing?"

"Marking our route so we don't get lost. If the cave goes some distance, we can follow these back."

"Good idea. You could have brought a ball of string too, and unwound it."

"Like Theseus in the Minotaur's labyrinth?"

"Yes." He sounded surprised that she'd caught the classical allusion and she sent him a serene smile. She'd had plenty of time to read while she was recuperating. She'd probably read more Homer than he had.

"It was Ariadne's idea. Most of those big strong Greek heroes needed a clever woman to help them out."

He sent her an amused look. "If you're the brains of this expedition, *cariad*, we're doomed. We'll be down here forever."

She glared at his retreating back.

The cave was, as he'd said, more like a tunnel. It rose at least ten feet above them and was almost the same distance wide. A horse and cart could have fit inside with ease. The floor seemed quite smooth—perhaps it had once been a riverbed? A few puddles glistened in the indentations of the rock; the faint sound of dripping could be heard ahead. Gryff was already some way ahead of her, and Maddie scurried after him, one hand extended to the wall, not wanting to be left alone in the darkness.

"And to think I thought I'd be bored," he said, when she caught up with him. "You don't get this kind of thing in London."

"From what I hear, you found plenty of excitement in London. I heard you had to leave because of that duel with Sommerville."

"That's true enough."

She lifted her brows, hoping he'd elaborate, but he seemed determined to disappoint her. Irritating man.

They'd ventured so far that the circle of light where she'd fallen through the roof was now scarcely visible behind them. She scraped a new chalk arrow on the wall as a cold blast of air from up ahead stirred the hair at her temples and she gave an involuntary shudder.

Gryff glanced over at her. "Afraid of the dark?"

"Not the dark, exactly. But you must admit, it's not a very pleasant sensation, knowing you have several hundred tons of rock above you."

His lips quirked. "Having an entire French regiment bearing

down on you isn't a very pleasant sensation either, let me tell you. I'll take rocks over bullets any day. Are you cold?"

"A little."

His eyes turned wicked. "In the army they teach you to share body heat when it gets chilly."

A flush crept up her cheeks, and she thanked the heavens for the concealing darkness. She certainly wasn't cold *now*. Just the thought of him being that close to her, of pressing his body to hers, was enough to make her burn.

"I'm fine, thank you."

His amused chuckle, as if he knew precisely the effect he had on her, echoed around them.

"I should have invited Harriet to come along," she muttered.

"Your cousin? She's not in London?"

"No. She's here for the summer, as always."

Did Gryff not remember the numerous occasions he and his brothers had stumbled across them during the summer months? Maddie had always cursed their uncanny ability to predict where they would be—whether catching butterflies in the meadow, fishing in the stream, or searching for treasure in one of the abandoned castles that littered the countryside. She frowned. *Had* it always been purely coincidental? Or had they deliberately sought them out, just to make mischief?

"Harriet's a mapmaker now, you know," she said. "She could have come and drawn these tunnels."

"I suspect underground mapping would be quite difficult. It's hard to gauge distances without any points of reference. A compass might not even work down here."

"Why not? Isn't the earth's magnetic field the same wherever you are?"

"It is. But there are iron deposits in the ground, which might lead to incorrect readings. Iron's been mined here for centuries, just like coal. Gold too, in small amounts."

The roof of the tunnel had become lower and Maddie prayed

that they'd reached the end, but Gryff just ducked down and carried on.

"Low bit here. Watch your head."

Since she was almost a foot shorter than him, she didn't even have to hunch. The warm glow from her lantern illuminated the broad expanse of his back and the tight curve of his rear. She really *didn't need to be noticing his rear.* Especially not in a confined space like this. What was wrong with her?

Maybe that lightning bolt really *had* addled her brain. The symptoms had just taken a few years to manifest.

Chapter 8

Maddie lifted her lantern, intrigued by the strange shadows cast on the walls as Gryff forged onward.

"This is like starting at a new dig site," she called after him. "So many exciting possibilities. What if we find King Arthur's resting place? Legend says he held court only a few miles away from here, at Caerleon."

Gryff snorted. "We're more likely to find dragons, asleep in an underground lake." He glanced back and frowned at her look of confusion. "What? You don't know the tale?"

"No."

He shook his head in disgust. "That's because you're English. Every Welshman's heard it from the cradle. Very well, I'll tell you. There was once a warlord named Vortigern, who wanted to build a fortress at Dinas Emrys, to the north of here. His men would build the walls, but every morning when they came back to work they found they'd been destroyed. Merlin, the wizard, told him that two dragons—one white and one red, representing the English and the Welsh respectively—lived in a lake beneath the hill. It was their fighting that was destroying the towers. So Vortigern dug up the mountain, found the lake, and woke the dragons, who began to fight. The white dragon was defeated and fled, and the red dragon returned to his lake."

"Of course you'd remember a story where the Welsh beat the English," she sniffed.

"I doubt we're going to find much down here, though. Not this far underground. If any ancient people used these caves for shelter, they'd have stayed near the entrance."

"Ah, but they might have *hidden* things down here. This would be an excellent place to leave valuables."

He sent her a look of mock horror. "Why, Miss Montgomery, you're nothing but a treasure hunter. Like that chap Belzoni over in Egypt."

"That's not true!"

He lifted his brows in teasing disbelief and she bit her lip as a flash of guilt snaked through her. She had no claim to such moral outrage. Her digs might have started out with scholarly intent, but finding some miraculous hoard now would undeniably help her finances.

"I won't deny that it would be nice to find something of monetary value," she clarified, "but that's not my primary motivation."

Liar.

"Of course it isn't." He stepped around a lumpy rock formation hanging from the ceiling. "You're a Montgomery. You have plenty of money."

Her spirits plummeted, but pride kicked in and she pasted a cheerful smile on her face. "Exactly."

"I hear you've been digging the place up ever since I went away."

"This whole valley is littered with historic ruins. There are Roman remains at Caerleon, and ancient standing stones— Harold's Stones—just outside Trellech. If I can find something significant, the whole area will benefit."

"How so?"

"We'd become a spot for tourists, which would generate employment. There are scores of ex-soldiers returning home who can't find work. It's no wonder some of them have turned to smuggling and thievery to make ends meet. People already flock to see Tintern Abbey, just downriver. They'd visit here too if we had something worth seeing."

"They visit Tintern because Wordsworth wrote a poem about it," Gryff said drily, "and because Turner immortalized it in paint. A picturesque ruin is far more interesting than a lumpy mound of earth."

She frowned at his broad back. "That's why I've been looking for artifacts. *Treasure*, as you put it. People are always impressed by shiny baubles. We need a hoard of Roman jewelry, or an ancient burial site. I know they're here."

"You're looking for a needle in a haystack." His hair glinted as he shook his head. "How can you—of all people—be so optimistic? You were *hit by lightning*, for goodness' sake."

"That's precisely why I *am* so optimistic. I'm living proof that unlikely events can happen. According to the doctors it was nothing short of a miracle." Maddie smiled into the darkness. "To tell you the truth, I rather hoped I'd gain some magical powers, like being able to light a candle with my bare hands, or the sudden ability to play the piano, but nothing. Not even a spark."

"Oh, you have a spark, Miss Montgomery."

Heat rose in her cheeks at his teasing tone. "Hopefully not big enough to ignite one of those damps you were talking about."

He chuckled, a deep sound that echoed around the rocky walls and did strange things to her insides. "It is a shame you didn't retain any of that lightning energy. It would be very useful right now if you glowed in the dark."

"I probably wouldn't be able to touch anyone. Think how

awkward it would be if everyone I shook hands with received a shock."

Like the one she'd received when he'd kissed her.

No, she wasn't thinking of that. She certainly hadn't spent an inordinate amount of time replaying it in her head last night. *Liar.*

He sidestepped another lumpy outcrop. "Do you remember what happened? When you were hit?"

"I wasn't struck directly. At least, I don't think so. I was out at a dig site, in the middle of a field. The sky was clear and I didn't hear thunder or see any lightning. The men I'd hired had gone home and I was about to leave myself, so I stuck my spade into the ground and started to walk away. I was about six feet from the spade when there was a blinding flash and a tremendous crash of thunder.

"I think the lightning struck the spade handle. I must have lost consciousness for a while, because when I woke, I was lying flat on the ground. My heart was pounding and I had a dreadful ringing in my ears and a burning sensation in my arm. Thankfully, Sir Galahad hadn't bolted, so I managed to ride home.

"I felt sore all over, and when I removed my clothes there was a strange pattern of burns coming up on my skin. All down my arm, and over my ribs, were marks that looked like swirling ferns or streaks of lightning.

"Father sent for Doctor Williams. He was fascinated; he'd never encountered anyone who'd suffered a lightning strike before." She snorted with wry amusement. "He began taking copious notes and drawings; I'm sure he was imagining the paper he would present to the Royal College of Physicians."

"You laugh now," Gryff said, his voice oddly serious, "but it must have hurt at the time."

"Like the devil," she agreed. "The red marks turned into raised blisters that took weeks to heal, and the redness didn't fade for months. Even now, years later, you can still see them.

I don't think they're ever going to disappear completely. I have such fair skin, you see."

"Do they still give you grief?"

"Occasionally I get an intense pain that shoots up and down my arm, but it never lasts for more than a few minutes. And really, it could have been far worse. I'm just thankful it didn't scramble my brain."

"It was pretty scrambled before, as I recall," he grunted. "You were always getting into some scrape or another."

Maddie scored another chalk arrow on the wall. "No thanks to you and your brothers."

Her legs were beginning to ache. They must've covered at least half a mile already. Maybe more. The tunnel was sloping gradually downward; perhaps it ran all the way to the sea?

Surely he didn't intend to follow it *that* far? Then again, he'd been a soldier. He was probably used to marching twenty miles a day without complaint.

She hitched her satchel higher on her hip. Well, he certainly wouldn't hear a Montgomery complaining. She'd go wherever he led.

Chapter 9

"You know," Maddie said as they trudged onward, "The fact that I could have died gave me a great deal to think about. What if I'd never woken up? What would people have said about me?"

"They'd have said you were a hoyden who never wore a hat."

She ignored his levity. "No, really. What had I achieved? The sad truth is, very little."

"You were only eighteen. Nobody would have expected—"

"Exactly! A well-born woman like me isn't *expected* to do *anything*. Nothing interesting, at any rate. We're supposed to live quietly, speak politely, marry where we're told. It's only you *men* who are expected to make something of yourselves. You're given an education to help you make advances in science or literature. You become lawyers and landowners, soldiers and clergymen, artists and doctors. Just look at Tristan; he's followed his passion for architecture—he's having a wonderful time gadding about the Continent."

She sucked in a breath, astonished that such a vehement diatribe had come out of her mouth. She'd never articulated her frustrations before, never even known she harbored such feelings, other than a vague sense of dissatisfaction, but they must have been simmering inside her for months. Years, even.

"Joan of Arc led the French to victory over the English when she was eighteen," she said, more levelly. "Cleopatra became a queen."

She scratched another chalk arrow on the wall. "It's not as if I want to do anything spectacular. Just something I can look back on and be proud of. Something that leaves the world a better place, with a little more knowledge or beauty. Is that so much to ask?"

Gryff grunted, and she held her breath, afraid that she'd said too much, revealed too much. This darkness was dangerous; it created a false sense of intimacy, it made her feel like she could tell him anything.

Ridiculous.

"It's a noble goal," he said finally, and she let out a surprised little huff of relief that he wasn't mocking her ambition out of hand. "When you think of it, I haven't done much for the past few years either, except march around the Continent fighting. That's hardly an achievement."

She opened her mouth to remind him that he'd risked life and limb to defend his country, but he cut her off with another question.

"So what did you do when you recovered?"

"I went to London and did all the things I'd always wanted to do. I visited the theater and the opera. The British Museum, the Tower, and the Royal Exchange."

She'd enjoyed the social whirl, the excitement of being courted and flirted with, but no particular man had caught her fancy and she'd been in no hurry to choose a husband.

"But there are only so many routs and balls one can go to before it becomes tedious," she finished.

"Surely you jest?" he gasped, mock-scandalized. "I thought

you ladies lived for dancing and shopping. Who was it that said, 'When you're tired of London, you're tired of life'?"

"Samuel Johnson. But I must be the exception, because after a few weeks, all I wanted to do was come back here and start digging."

"Where did this fascination with archaeology come from?"

She shrugged. "I've always been interested in history. It's hard *not* to be, living around here. Wales has more castles per square mile than anywhere else in Europe. But I suppose my serious interest began when father's old school friend Sir Richard Hoare came to visit. He and a man named William Cunnington had been investigating a site near the stone circle of Stonehenge, near Glastonbury. They discovered the Bush Barrow treasure, an ancient burial that contained jewelry, gold, and weapons. Sir Richard believes there are similar hoards buried all over the country."

"Forgive me for playing devil's advocate," Gryff said, "but isn't that just grave robbing? You wouldn't dig up someone who was buried last week and steal their wedding ring. So why is it acceptable to dig up someone who died a thousand years ago?"

Maddie frowned. She'd never really thought of it like that. Trust a Davies to come up with an irritatingly logical argument.

"Well, I mean, the *bones* are never disturbed. It's just the artifacts that are removed. Besides, it's not just barrows and tunnel graves that yield discoveries. Plenty of times a hoard has been hidden by someone who meant to come back and retrieve it, but they were killed before they could. So it just stays there, waiting for someone like me to find it."

Gryff halted and Maddie breathed a silent sigh of relief.

"Oh, thank heavens. Have we reached the end?"

"Not at all. There are side tunnels that branch off. Which way shall we go?"

"Don't you think we've gone far enough?"

He sent her a chiding look. "Where's your sense of adventure? Listen, I can hear rushing water. I think we're about to find that underground stream you were talking about." He pointed to the narrowest of the available routes. "This way."

Maddie eyed the slim crack in the rock with apprehension. "I don't think so. What if it gets even narrower? I'm not getting wedged in there."

"You won't. I'll go first, and I'm bigger than you."

"What if *you* get stuck?"

"Then I expect you'll just leave me down here to starve," he said, grinning. "You'll be glad to see the end of another Dastardly Davies."

"Don't tempt me." Maddie drew a new arrow on the wall and gave a sarcastic flourish of the hand for him to precede her. "After you."

He turned sideways and started to push himself through the narrow opening. After a few moments the glow from his lantern disappeared completely and Maddie felt a rush of alarm.

And then his voice echoed back from between the stones. "Come *on*, Montgomery. Stop dawdling."

With a sigh, Maddie followed. She lifted her lantern high and sucked in her stomach to edge sideways through the narrow crack. Her skirts snagged on the uneven walls and she mentally cursed Gryffud Davies with every breath, but after about ten feet or so the crevice widened out again and they carried on.

"My father had his own plan to grow the local economy, you know," Gryff said suddenly. "But it was doomed from the start."

"Why?"

"Because it needed Montgomery cooperation."

"Ah." Maddie wrinkled her nose. "The only time a Davies ever cooperated with a Montgomery was to hand him a poi-

soned chalice, or to give him a helpful push off the battlements. Legend has it Queen Elizabeth once told Shakespeare
that our families made his Montagues and Capulets look like
amateurs."

"Good to know we're maintaining tradition."

"What was your father's scheme? Are you talking about that
canal?"

"I am."

"Then you're right. It *is* a lost cause."

"I expect your father refused it on principle."

"I won't deny that thwarting a Davies would have given him
a great deal of pleasure, but there's logic behind his opposition too. He refused because I asked him to."

Gryff stopped dead, and she almost bumped into him as he
twisted around to glare at her.

"You! You're the reason? But why? You'd get a percentage
of the tariffs. Why would you have an aversion to making
money?"

"I don't have an aversion to making money," Maddie coun-
tered irritably. "Far from it."

God knew, *any* income would be a blessing right now, even
if it derived from a deal with the devil. Or a Davies, which was
tantamount to the same thing. But a girl had to maintain *some*
moral principles.

"What's your objection, then?" Gryff ground out.

"Those plans had the canal cutting dangerously close to an
important tunnel grave near Newchurch. I asked your father
for permission to dig there for the past three summers, and
he always refused. He wouldn't even allow me to dig a test
trench to see how far the site extends."

Gryff frowned. "So it's as I said earlier: You think people
who've been dead for hundreds of years should take precedence over people living right now."

"It's not as simple as that. The past and the present should be given equal consideration. And since when did you become interested in this project? You haven't even been here for the last few years."

His eyes narrowed in displeasure at her accusatory tone, and his brows rose in a haughty, forbidding expression that instantly put her hackles up.

"I became *interested* when I became Earl of Powys," he said curtly. "Everything that happens on these lands is my business. My father chose that particular route because it was the shortest distance from the pithead to the river. A straight line is always the cheapest. It would cost a great deal more to avoid the burial site. Why are you so set against progress?"

"What I'm set against," Maddie snapped, "is ruining some perfectly lovely countryside with a great big ugly canal."

"It's just a straight river," he ground out.

She shook her head, stubbornness in every line. "We'll just have to agree to disagree on this subject, *my lord*."

The corner of his eye flickered at her mocking use of his title. He took a menacing step closer and a little thrill of excitement—or terror—shot through her veins. He really was an imposing specimen.

The glow of their lanterns and the unfathomable darkness beyond gave the oddest impression that they were the only two people in the universe, floating somewhere out of time and space.

His shirt brushed against her chest and his breath warmed her face as he glared down at her in exasperation. Her stomach contracted as she inhaled his scent.

A muscle twitched on the side of his jaw and his eyes had darkened almost to black. "You are just as vexing as I remember, Miss Montgomery," he growled.

Maddie returned his look stare for stare, refusing to be cowed by his arrogant displeasure, but her heart was beating so hard against her ribs that she was sure it echoed around the still chamber.

"Likewise."

For a split second his angry gaze flicked down to her lips, and she had the strangest thought that he was about to kiss her, even as furious as he was. Her body stilled, tingling with an inexplicable combination of fright and desire.

She half expected him to push her up against the wall and ravish her, but after another uncomfortably tense moment he let out a muffled curse and stepped back. He swiveled around, away from her, and Maddie expelled a shaky breath, unsure whether to be relieved or disappointed.

Dear God, they were enemies! She must be light-headed from the lack of air. These were clearly the first symptoms of asphyxia: lurid fantasies and shameless hallucinations. She was succumbing to madness, like some lust-crazed female hermit.

She squinted over at the far wall, trying to gather her wits, and something odd caught her attention.

"Gryff," she murmured. "Look."

"What?" His tone was nothing short of sullen.

She gestured with her lantern. "Over there. Is that . . . daylight?"

He stomped back to her side and squinted at the area she'd indicated, a corner of the rock where the shadows seemed a paler gray than the rest. And then his brows lifted in reluctant agreement.

"Damn it all, I think you're right."

He set off with unflattering haste, skirting a rocky ledge and leaping over another with athletic ease.

Maddie followed, hampered by her skirts and by her shorter stride, and soon the dim glow she'd detected grew more distinct. They rounded a curve in the rock, and the pale patch revealed itself to be a semicircular hole, about ten feet across, through which a slow trickle of water flowed.

Gryff edged up to it and, keeping a strong grip on a nearby pillar of rock, thrust his head through the aperture. His delighted cry almost made her jump out of her skin.

"We did it! We found a way out."

Maddie rolled her eyes. "You mean *I* did," she muttered. "You were too busy bellowing."

He pulled his head back through. "It was a team effort."

"What's out there?"

"Another cave, but this one opens out onto the sea."

Maddie blinked. "The sea! You mean we've walked all the way to the coast? But that's impossible."

He shot her a grin, his good humor apparently restored with the prospect of soon being rid of her.

"Obviously not. Time just flies when you're having fun. We've probably only walked a few miles, all in, it's just hard to tell when you're underground."

He edged his big shoulders beneath the overhang and climbed through. His face reappeared, uplit by his lantern; it gave him a dangerous, devilish appearance. He seemed quite at home down here, like Hades in his underworld.

A blast of fresh air, laden with the unmistakable scent of seaweed and salt, ruffled his hair, and Maddie tried not to notice how attractive he looked. She was glad they would soon be out of the darkness.

"There's a bit of a drop to the floor on this side," he said. "Twenty feet or so. But we should be able to climb down without getting too wet. Come through."

Twenty feet? Maddie wasn't particularly fond of heights, and she hadn't climbed anything higher than a five-bar gate for years, but she could do this. She wouldn't shame the name of Montgomery by falling at the final hurdle.

"Pass your lantern through to me," he commanded.

She sent him a warning look. "You're not going to leave me here in the dark are you? Remember your promise."

"You have my word. I'll wait to strangle you until we're *out* of the cave," he said drily. "I want decent light to witness your last, gasping breaths."

She sent him an unimpressed glare and relinquished the light, then gathered her skirts and clambered through the gap between the water and the low-hanging ceiling. Her hair snagged on a rock, but she gave it an impatient tug and emerged onto a perilously narrow ledge next to Gryff.

A swift peek downward had her pressing back into the rock face behind her. "That's forty feet, not twenty!" Her voice had risen an octave in panic.

"Breathe," he chuckled. His warm, rough hand slid over hers where she clutched the rock, and he gave it a reassuring squeeze. She sucked in a steadying breath.

The outcrop they were on was barely a foot wide, high up near the domed ceiling of a very large cave. The entrance—with a welcome patch of blue sky and gray sea just visible through it—made Maddie's spirits soar.

Below them—*far* below—the cavern floor was a mixture of sandy ridges and tumbled rocks, some still filled with watery pools. The high-water mark, a band of dark seaweed and clustered black mussels, could be seen about halfway down the walls.

The lower half of the cave clearly filled with water when the tide was in, making it virtually inaccessible from the beach, but where they stood, higher up, the rocky shelves remained dry.

"Good thing the tide is out," Maddie gasped. Her voice still sounded a bit breathy. "Or we'd be trapped. We'd have to wait until the water got low enough to walk out, because I certainly don't fancy a swim."

Gryff turned to face the rock and caught her gaze. "I'll go first. This isn't a difficult climb. There are plenty of places to put your hands and feet."

Maddie shook her head. Her legs felt like water and her fingers were white-tipped from where she clung to the rock as tightly as a shellfish. "I really don't think I can do this."

"Of course you can. You once told me that girls could do everything boys could do. And then you beat Rhys climbing to the top of an apple tree."

"I was thirteen, and wearing breeches. How can I climb now, with these skirts?"

"Feel free to take 'em off."

She gave him a hard stare.

"Oh, come on. It wouldn't be the first time I've ever seen your unmentionables, now, would it?"

The heat of embarrassment crept up her neck. "If you're referring to that time you and Morgan came across Harriet and me panning for gold, it's something I've tried hard to forget."

His amusement was a wicked rumble in his chest. "I haven't laughed that much in years."

"You tackled me, pulled my skirts up over my head so my arms were trapped inside like a sack, and tied the top with string."

"It was a brilliant plan, if I do say so myself. I'll never forget the sight of you rolling around, petticoats flailing." He grinned, utterly unrepentant. "I had no idea well-bred young ladies even *knew* such shocking language."

"It took me ages to get free. I rolled on a thistle."

He snorted. "You got off lightly compared with some of the lads at boarding school. We once staked Hugo Bambury to the chapel lawns using croquet hoops and left him there all night, covered in honey. All you had to contend with was a little mud."

"You were a monster."

"True. But you have to admit, never dull." He took another assessing glance downward. "Now, since we've established that I've already seen your underthings, I'll go first. I'm fairly confident I won't get distracted and fall to my death if I happen to glance up and see your stockings."

Maddie lifted her brows. "Fairly confident?"

The wicked twinkle was back. "If I'm wrong, at least I'll die happy."

She was wearing a chemise, petticoats, stockings, *and* cotton drawers beneath her skirts, but there was still no way she was going to risk him seeing her from below.

"I know what you're doing, Gryffud Davies. You're trying to distract me so I forget to be afraid of the climb. And while the thought of your mangled body is entertaining, I think we should go down together. Side by side."

"All right."

His easy acceptance gave Maddie the distinct impression that climbing down in tandem had been his original intent all along. Irritating man. She decided to test the theory, just to be perverse.

"On the other hand, maybe you *should* go down first. That way, if I fall, you'll provide a soft landing."

She heard a soft snort of laughter at her shoulder. "If there's ever the prospect of your body landing on top of mine, Miss Montgomery, accidentally or otherwise, I sincerely hope I'll be alive enough to enjoy it."

The image that burned into her brain—her sprawled on top of him, her breasts pressed to his broad, muscled chest, her legs entangled with his own—brought a hectic flush to her body, and Maddie cursed herself for her wayward tongue. She really shouldn't cross verbal swords with him. The man had an uncanny ability to turn the most innocuous phrase into one laden with promise.

She turned and lowered her left foot gingerly over the lip, then swung it about until she found a satisfactory toehold. She readjusted her hands and did the same with her right foot.

"That's it," Gryff said encouragingly. "Just think of it as a slightly uneven ladder."

Since the natural light from the cave entrance was sufficient, he extinguished the lamps and replaced them in his satchel, then started to climb down the rocky wall beside her. "Good girl. Almost there."

Maddie bit her lip in concentration. Her heart was pounding and her palms were alarmingly clammy. Every time a rock crumbled beneath her fingers or fell away from under her foot she caught her breath, but she somehow made it to the bottom without mishap. Rather pleased with her own daring, she brushed her still-shaky hands on her skirts. "Right. Let's get out of here."

Gryff, however, had ventured even farther into the cave and was peering up at the curving walls. He paused beneath another rocky overhang. "One moment. I thought I saw something."

He started climbing back *up* the rock face.

"It's probably just some debris, washed up during a storm," Maddie said impatiently. Now that she could see daylight and smell the fresh coastal air, all she wanted was to be back outside.

Gryff pulled himself up over the rocky lip, and she reluctantly admired his effortless strength. What would it be like to have all that—

His soft whistle stopped her wayward thoughts.

"Bloody hell, would you look at that?"

Chapter 10

Maddie braced her hands on her hips and glared up at him. "*Now* what?"

"There's another tunnel, going back into the cliff. And it's being used as a store."

"For what? Lobster pots?"

"Come up and see."

With a huff of annoyance—she'd done enough climbing for a lifetime—Maddie scrambled up to where he stood in the shadowed overhang. She ignored his outstretched hand out of principle, but when she pulled herself over the lip she saw what he was talking about.

At least thirty small, hooped wooden barrels had been stacked along the side of the enclave, along with several crates covered in oilcloth.

Gryff bent over the nearest barrel and sniffed at the cork that was wedged tightly in the top. His brows drew together. "Brandy."

"Good heavens! This must be a smugglers' stash." Maddie

sent a panicked glance toward the cave entrance. "It's low tide. What if they're coming to get it right now?"

"Unlikely. Whoever this belongs to won't risk transporting it in broad daylight. They'll wait for a cloudy, moonless night."

"We need to report this to the authorities immediately."

Gryff nodded. "Agreed. Where's the nearest customhouse?"

Maddie racked her brains. "There isn't one, not locally. The riders sometimes make patrols along this part of the coast, but not on a regular basis. The nearest outposts are either at Bristol or Cardiff. And they might not send men for days, maybe even a week."

"By which time, this could have disappeared, and we'll look like fools who cried wolf," Gryff muttered. He rubbed the flat of his palm along his jaw, and she could practically see his mind working to come up with a plan. This was doubtless how he'd been in the army too, planning the next offensive against the enemy.

"The smugglers probably know there aren't any customs men nearby," he mused aloud.

"Which means they might not be waiting for a dark night, after all. They might be coming back this very evening."

"Who's the local magistrate? He can arrange to have men come and watch."

Maddie gave a silent inner groan. "The nearest justice of the peace is Sir Mostyn Drake."

"That old codger's still alive, is he? My father couldn't stand him. They almost came to blows when father dressed him down for mistreating a horse, years ago. Old Drake never forgot it."

"That sounds like Sir Mostyn," Maddie mumbled. The man was about as appealing as a week-old fish head.

Her tone must have betrayed her dislike, because Gryff lifted his brows, unerringly scenting intrigue. "Oh, dear, what's Sir Mostyn done to incur *your* displeasure, Miss Montgomery?"

Only offered to marry me so he can get an unpaid drudge for the rest of his days.

She bit back the resentful thought. "Nothing in particular," she lied. "I just find him rather unpleasant. And besides, even if he does agree to help, I'm not sure it's a good idea to enlist local men. For all we know, they could be the smugglers. Or know them, and tip them off."

"That's a very good point."

Maddie experienced a tingle of pleasure at his ready agreement. Unlike many men of her acquaintance, he treated her as a reasonable equal, not as some weak-brained inferior without a thought in her head.

How refreshing. How . . . unexpected for a Davies.

"Come on," he said. "I need fresh air to think."

They picked their way down and around the various tidal pools to the entrance to the cave. The stiff breeze that greeted them plastered her skirts against her legs and played havoc with her hair but it was a welcome change from the dank, still air inside the tunnels.

She inhaled deeply. "Oh, that feels good."

Gryff scanned their surroundings. "Where are we?"

There were no buildings visible along the craggy shoreline, nor any obvious landmarks. The cave was tucked into a curved bay, enclosed two rocky headlands, one on each side, that shielded it from all but the sea. Fern-laden hillsides descended steeply to the crescent beach.

She shielded her eyes with her hand. "I'm not sure."

Since the tide was out, they crossed the exposed ridges of sand with ease, avoiding the shallow puddles, then clambered over a low section of rocks and started up the hill.

"This way," Gryff said. "There seems to be a path."

A barely visible trail had been trodden through the

greenery—presumably by the smugglers—and Maddie cursed her damp boots and uncomfortably tight corset as she tried to keep up with Gryff's long-legged strides. Really, men had such an advantage when it came to practical clothing.

The path led them through a small patch of woodland and they finally emerged onto a narrow farm track. A larger vista opened up when they crested the hill, and Maddie squinted toward a large stone building a few miles farther inland, silhouetted against the sky.

"Oh, I know where we are! That's Mathern Palace. I went there once with Harriet for a picnic. Nobody's lived in it for years, it's practically a ruin. The village of Mathern is just over that hill."

Gryff gave a satisfied grunt. "Let's hope someone there will lend us some horses."

Maddie bit her lip as she belatedly realized her predicament. Here she was, several miles from home, with no horse, no carriage, and no chaperone, in the company of a known reprobate. Her hair, despite its ruthless pinning, was a mess, and the bottom six inches of her skirts were wet and filthy. If anyone saw the two of them together, she'd become a social pariah.

She glanced over her shoulder toward the beach. Walking back through the caves, even uphill and in the dark, suddenly seemed a better option than simply walking into Mathern with Gryffud Davies.

He turned to see why she'd stopped.

"We can't be seen together," she blurted out. "I'll hide at the edge of the village while you get us horses."

His lips twitched. "What? You don't want to be seen fraternizing with the enemy?" His sparkling green gaze flicked her head-to-foot in a brief, yet thorough, inspection that had her longing for the darkness again.

"I suppose you're right," he continued drily. "Even if you

weren't looking so charmingly disheveled, our arrival would set the rumor mill flying. A Montgomery and a Davies together? Without deadly weapons? People would think it was the end of the world."

"I'd be ruined," Maddie stated baldly. "And *you'd* be expected to make an honest woman of me. We'd be hounded to the altar quicker than you can say 'social disgrace.' And while I truly believe my father would prefer death and dishonor—including mine—to a forced marriage to a Davies, I still think we'd better err on the side of caution, don't you?"

He composed his features into a solemn expression, but his eyes still twinkled. "Absolutely."

They started off down the lane again shoulder-to-shoulder, or rather shoulder-to-elbow, considering their respective height difference. He shortened his stride to match hers and glanced down at her.

"We need to do something about those smugglers. As joint landowners we have a responsibility to prevent the spread of crime."

"I'm surprised you care," she taunted. "You haven't even been here for the past six months. Are you finally planning to stay at Trellech full-time?"

She held her breath as she waited for his answer, but he shook his head.

"No. I'll be heading back to London soon. My steward can run the estate perfectly well in my absence. But since I *am* here now, there's no reason we can't set an ambush. The problem is, I don't know which of the locals I can trust."

He raked his hand through his hair. It was already messy, but the move managed to make him look even more attractive. What would those strands feel like, beneath her fingers?

"I could enlist some of my old army friends from London," he continued, mercifully unaware of her ogling. "Half of them have already been recalled to fight Bonaparte, but I could round up the rest. With a bit of luck the smugglers won't make a move until they get here."

"What about your brothers? Couldn't they help?"

He made a comical grimace. "Well, Rhys is *theoretically* in London, but he's never where you expect him to be. And Morgan's still at sea, so I can't call on him."

"And if the smugglers come back before your friends arrive?"

"I'll keep watch every night. If they *do* come, I might still hear something useful or recognize one of them."

"You? Keep watch all night? Out in the open?"

He raised his brows in an expression of affront. "Why yes, Miss Montgomery. Does that surprise you?"

"I thought you'd prefer the luxury of a warm bed, after so many years a soldier."

"Rejoining my regiment isn't an option, now that I've inherited the title. If I must remain a civilian, the least I can do is protect these shores." He lifted one shoulder in a careless shrug. "It's nothing I haven't done a hundred times before. A few more nights under the stars won't kill me."

Maddie steeled herself against a wave of reluctant admiration. This wasn't the reckless, irresponsible Gryff Davies she'd known as a youth. This was an older, darker version she found even more compelling.

The angry frustration in his tone when he'd mentioned not being able to rejoin his friends was intriguing. Did he resent his position as the new earl? Would he actually prefer to be heading back across the channel to face Bonaparte and possible death?

She shook her head, irritated with herself. She didn't need to be intrigued by him.

"There's a flaw in your plan, you know," she said. "If the smugglers *are* local, you won't recognize them. You'll just sit there and watch them carry the contraband away. You need someone familiar with the villagers. You need *me*."

"Absolutely not."

"Where's the danger? You're not planning to confront them, are you? You won't be discovered as long as you stay hidden, and I'm perfectly capable of staying quiet when the need arises."

He made a noise that sounded suspiciously like a snort.

"Besides," she continued quickly. "I have every right to take part. This is Montgomery land as much as it is yours. We have joint responsibility. And since you're neither my husband nor my father, you have no jurisdiction over me whatsoever."

Chapter 11

Gryff clenched his jaw. Was there ever a more irritating woman?

"My God, if I *was* your husband I'd make sure you kept your nose out of trouble. I'd—"

"Yes?" she taunted. "You'd what?"

Take you to bed and keep you so exhausted you'd never want to leave. Bloody hell, where had that nonsensical thought come from?

He sent her a frustrated glare. "Never mind. It's too horrible an idea to contemplate."

She lifted her brows in that amused, supercilious way that made him want to grab her and kiss the smug look right off her face. He'd wanted to do it for the past few hours.

Years, actually.

"I think I would make someone a very good wife," she said.

"If by 'good' you mean disobedient, opinionated, meddle-some—"

She sucked in an offended breath. "You have no idea how obedient I am. I'm the most dutiful daughter that ever—"

"You'd actually agree to love, honor, and *obey* your husband? I don't believe it."

She crossed her arms. "Yes, actually, I would. Because the man I marry will love me. Which means he won't ask me to do anything I wouldn't be happy to obey him in doing."

He sent her a pitying look. "That is so naïve."

The combative light faded from her eyes, as if she'd recalled something that upset her, but she rallied and lifted her chin.

"Stop changing the subject. We're not talking about me getting married. We're talking about me meeting you back here to wait for the smugglers."

Gryff ran his hand through his hair. He should never have mentioned the idea to her. The past few hours in the close confines of the cave had been torture, a true test of his gentlemanly willpower. He'd been aware of her proximity every minute they'd been down there, haunted by the tantalizing waft of her perfume whenever she stepped too close.

Not close enough.

He shook his head. There must be something about caves that brought out the most primitive parts of a man's nature. The primal, masculine parts that valued shelter and food, fire and woman. *Especially woman.* The temptation to extinguish the lamps, catch her in his arms, and lose himself in the darkness and in *her* had been almost overwhelming. God, the very last thing he needed was to spend any more time in her company.

Unfortunately, she wasn't the type of woman who could be dissuaded by the *it's not a woman's place* argument. She was as reckless and as unmanageable as his sister, Carys. The only thing that seemed to scare her was the thought of being seen in public with him.

Blasted woman.

Still, the risk to Maddening Miss Montgomery shouldn't be too great if he allowed her to come tonight. The smugglers were doubtless waiting for a dark night and the lowest tide, both of which coincided with the moon at its lowest ebb.

The moon had been full a week ago—it had lingered in the dawn sky on the morning of his ill-fated duel. He remembered wondering if it would be the last time he'd ever see it. He'd wondered whether he cared.

He shook off the memory. A full moon last week meant he probably had another full week to gather his men. It was highly unlikely the smugglers would choose tonight to come back and retrieve their contraband.

"Assuming I do let you come and help keep watch tonight," he said slowly. "How would you explain your absence to your family?"

"Oh, don't worry about that. I'll tell Harriet to say I've gone to bed with a headache and sneak out."

"Fine," he growled. "You can come. But only if you do exactly as I say, when I say it. Agreed?"

"Agreed."

The first cottages of the village had come into view, so he pointed toward a cluster of windblown trees by the roadside. "You wait there. I'll go get a horse."

"Two horses."

"No, one horse. Why would I need two if I'm on my own? You'll just have to ride with me."

She let out a little huff, but plonked herself down on a mossy boulder. "Fine. Off you go then."

With her messy hair and bedraggled skirts she looked like a fairy princess who'd fallen into a bog. Sadly, it didn't make her any less attractive. Gryff gave an inward sigh. What on earth was he tangled up in now?

It cost him six shillings to borrow the village blacksmith's horse, and that was only after he'd convinced the skeptical fellow he was indeed the new Earl of Powys by showing him his signet ring, and promising to send the swaybacked creature back that very night.

"It's a wonder they bother with smuggling around here," he groused as he led the animal back to her hiding place. "Six shillings for the loan of a horse. It's highway robbery."

Her lips twitched, but her amusement faded as he gained the saddle and reached down to her.

"Put your foot on mine, and I'll pull you up."

She looked on the verge of refusing, so he added casually, "Unless you'd prefer to walk?"

She capitulated, grasping his hand and placing her dainty foot on the top of his booted one in the stirrup. With a tug he hauled her up and twisted her so she sat sideways across his lap. His blood surged at her nearness and he tried to ignore the torturous sensation of her sweet derriere nestled snugly between his thighs.

She held herself as stiff as a ramrod, gripping the horse's mane with both hands, as he reached around her waist and readjusted the reins, enclosing her slim body within the circle of his arms. He deliberately tightened his grip and pulled her back against his chest.

She gave a breathy little gasp.

He kicked his heels and they set off down the track, but after a quarter mile he turned the horse north and set off across the fields, in the direction of the wishing well.

"Shouldn't take too long to get back to our horses," he said, mainly to distract himself from the womanly curves playing havoc with his pulse. A few wisps of her hair had escaped her bun; they blew across his cheek and he caught a whiff of warm skin and that faintly floral scent that tightened his gut and sent blood rushing to his groin. He adjusted his position in the saddle. "Did you say your horse was called Galahad?"

"Yes, after one of the knights of King Arthur's Round Table."

"Mine's Paladin—named for one of the twelve knights of Charlemagne."

"English and French," she said, laughter in her tone. "I'd expect nothing less. It stands to reason that we'd choose mounts from opposing courts, even fictional ones."

Gryff could only murmur an agreement. It had always been like this between them: strange coincidences that formed an odd, inexplicable bond. For enemies, they seemed to have a frightening amount in common.

He glanced at the sky, trying to gauge the time. He'd left his pocket watch at home, but he guessed it was around four o'clock.

"So what's the plan for this evening?" she asked. "We'll have to hide before it gets completely dark."

"Stick to the woods and fields. Leave Galahad out of sight in that ruined place we passed, and wear dark clothing, nothing pale or white. Come prepared for a long, cold, boring night."

He felt her little snort of amusement and cocked his head. "What's so funny?"

"I bet that's the first time you've ever said *that* to a woman," she murmured. "'Come prepared for a long, cold, boring night.'"

She stiffened in his arms, as if she'd shocked herself with the outrageous comment, and he bit back a delighted laugh.

Naughty girl.

"Miss Montgomery, you shock me. It seems you've been paying far too much attention to the gossip pages. But in this case, you're correct. As far as I know, a night with me has never been described as either cold or boring. Although the word *long* has been mentioned on several occasions."

There, let the little minx contemplate *that.*

Unfortunately, several stirring images flooded *his* brain too. Of her, naked, spread out on his sheets, all that glorious hair spilling over her body. Of him, kissing his way down her—

Gryff ground his teeth. *Never going to happen.*

Letting her come tonight was a huge mistake. Spending time with her was the mental equivalent of beating himself over the head with a shovel. And yet he craved her company.

It was stupid and inexplicable. He must be a glutton for punishment.

Chapter 12

They parted ways at the wishing well, and Gryff returned to Trellech Court alone.

Having fended for himself in the army it was strange to have a small battalion of servants to assist him again, but the staff who'd served his father for as long as he could remember had been so delighted to have one of the family back in residence that he hadn't had the heart to refuse them.

They were all desperate for him to abandon his bachelor ways, marry, and produce the requisite "heir and a spare" for the sake of the earldom, but he wasn't quite ready for that yet. He was perfectly aware of the responsibilities that accompanied the title—and fully appreciative of his privileged position—but he couldn't deny a certain amount of guilt and resentment toward it too.

Guilt, because as an earl it would be frowned on if he rejoined his regiment as he so longed to do; his friends would have to face Napoleon's hordes without him. And resentment, because the responsibilities of his title were considerable, and he'd rather enjoyed the position of carefree heir while his father was still alive.

Gryff shook his head at his own foolishness. He truly had nothing to complain about. And besides, while Trellech might not have the range of sophisticated pleasures that London offered, it *did* have one far more attractive prospect—the chance of another thorny encounter with his nemesis. Their prickly interactions were the highlight of his days.

Cheered by this thought, he bathed, shaved, and ate a hearty meal, then strode to the stables with a spring in his step.

When he reached Mathern Palace he left Paladin in one of the ramshackle outbuildings and tramped down the hill toward the coast. He found a convenient hollow, a natural indentation beneath a rocky overhang that would keep him dry if it rained and provided a good view of the path and the entrance to the cave.

The place was surrounded by a thick layer of waist-high ferns to further aid concealment. He propped his old army pack into a crevice between the stones and flattened a small semicircle of ferns on which to sit. And then he waited for the termagant to arrive.

He heard her coming from at least a hundred yards away; the swish of her skirts, a muttered, unladylike curse that made his lips curl up in amusement as she obviously stumbled over a tree root or a stone.

Was she even *attempting* to stay quiet? She'd have been shot a dozen times by now, if they'd been at war.

Admittedly his ears, in fact, all of his senses, were particularly attuned to her. He seemed to experience *more* of everything when she was around. Colors seemed brighter, his vision more acute. He noticed the smallest, most insignificant of details, like the sinful length of her eyelashes, the way her top lip dipped invitingly in the center, the precise number of freckles on her nose.

He'd been in a haze since he'd returned from the Continent. His days had been filled with activity, but he'd scarcely felt anything. He hadn't cared whether he'd won or lost at the card tables, or whether he fell out of bed at noon. He'd had a few brief liaisons, but while he'd been present in a physical sense, he'd also felt oddly detached. Physical satisfaction had left him feeling empty.

Madeline Montgomery *filled him*. Not necessarily with pleasant sensations, true, but she filled him, nonetheless. With frustration and hunger, with lust and resentment. He wanted to strangle her and kiss her witless at the same time.

A perverse part of him wanted *her* to feel those heightened emotions too. It was only fair. Her pulse should increase whenever he annoyed her. Her brain should turn to mush and her body to flame when he kissed her. Love and hate just were two sides of a very thin coin, after all. Combining them might prove truly spectacular—

No. Nobody was combining anything.

Tonight's mission had a clear objective: to spy on the smugglers without getting caught. He would treat Maddie as he would any member of his own regiment. As a colleague, nothing more.

She appeared on his left, walking easily down the slope, a dark silhouette in the fading light. Her trim figure was clad in a forest-green wool riding habit; an excellent choice, he had to admit, for the cooler evening ahead. The matching hat, however—an undersized version of a gentleman's top hat, embellished with a scrap of netting and a jaunty ostrich feather plume—was utterly ridiculous.

Bloody woman. She was probably making a point about his earlier jab about never wearing a bonnet.

He waved to get her attention, and she sent him a smile that made his pulse beat just a little faster. Annoyed with himself, he took it out on her.

"Was that your best attempt at keeping quiet? A French cavalry charge makes less noise."

"Good evening to you too," she said primly.

"In case you didn't know, *millinery* is not required on a surveillance mission."

She pushed her way through the ferns. "I didn't want to get freckles."

"It'll be dark in ten minutes," he growled.

"Well, yes, I suppose I'm safe enough now."

She reached up and removed the ridiculous thing, revealing a mass of hair once again twisted into submission. The rays of the setting sun picked out the copper highlights, turning them to a fiery rose-gold, and Gryff clenched his fingers against the desire to release it from its confinement.

He folded himself back into the shadow of the overhanging rock and she sank gracefully beside him in an elegant billow of skirts. The accompanying drift of floral perfume that reached him as she arranged the train of her riding habit over her legs tightened his stomach.

She patted the leather satchel she'd brought with her. "I brought a blanket, in case it gets chilly."

He nodded wordlessly.

"And I'm wearing riding breeches under my skirts. For extra warmth."

God give him strength.

"Where, exactly, did you get a pair of breeches made up around here?" It was an effort to keep his tone mild. *Which tailor had taken her inside leg measurement? The lucky bastard better have kept it professional.*

He imagined his own hands flattening a tape measure over her, from stockinged instep to knee, from knee to garter to creamy thigh. It made him a little light-headed.

"Oh, they're an old pair of Tristan's," she said, blithely

unaware of his turmoil. "From when he was younger. I'd never fit any of his clothes now."

Gryff dragged his thoughts from the gutter. She was still producing things from that infernal satchel.

"Tea, in a flask. And some peppermints."

"God, woman. This isn't a picnic!"

She sent him a reprimanding look. "No mints for you. Didn't you bring anything?"

He patted his coat pocket. "A hip flask of brandy. Which will do a much better job of keeping us warm than your tea."

She huffed and treated him to her delightful profile.

"You're going to be cold and bored in less than an hour, you know," he predicted.

"I will not. I'm exceedingly patient. I've spent hours and hours outside on archaeological digs, in all kinds of weather. You'll see."

She drew her knees up, wrapped her arms around them, and stared out over the sea. The sun finally slipped below the horizon, drowned in the purple waves, and they lapsed into a silence that was almost companionable.

Gryff began counting backward from three hundred. Maddie Montgomery might think she could keep quiet, but he gave it less than three minutes before the urge to talk became too much.

"Did you bring a weapon?" she whispered.

One hundred and twenty-two. He smiled at her delightful predictability.

"Yes." He'd brought both his regimental sword and a loaded pair of pistols.

She turned her head to look at him, her eyes wide. "I thought you said we were just going to observe."

"Only an idiot would come unprepared. Best to expect the worst."

Chapter 13

Maddie turned her gaze back to the sea.

Looking at Gryff this close—their shoulders were almost touching—made her feel even more jittery about the evening. The fading light threw intriguing shadows beneath the sharp angles of his cheekbones and highlighted the sensual curve of his lips.

Why couldn't he be pallid and sickly, with bad skin and greasy hair? All this rugged attractiveness was very irritating.

She could hardly believe she'd come to meet him. Who was this reckless, daring woman she'd become? For the past three years she'd been perfectly content to live a quiet, scholarly existence. But less than twenty-four hours in his company, and all her old restlessness and thirst for excitement had come rushing back.

She shook her head. She'd been so immersed in her own problems that she hadn't paid any attention to what was happening right under her nose. Who would have imagined all this illegal activity, less than ten miles from her own house?

She sincerely hoped she didn't know any of the people

involved. Smuggling was a serious crime, with harsh penalties for the perpetrators. Were those in the surrounding villages aware of what was happening? Did they turn a blind eye and leave their stables unlatched, so the smugglers could borrow their horses in exchange for a parcel of tea or a barrel of brandy left in thanks?

Until six months ago she'd never imagined what life would be like without money, but her own impending bankruptcy was making her consider actions almost as desperate as those of the smugglers. Wasn't marrying someone just for money—whether it was Sir Mostyn or some other wealthy suitor—almost as dishonest as stealing?

Gryff's derisive words from earlier had hit home with the force of a well-aimed arrow. How could she swear to love, honor, and obey someone when she had absolutely no intention of doing any of those things? How could she marry a man who wouldn't care two pins for her opinions or her desires? Who could, legally, force her to do his bidding, however much she disagreed?

Maddie suppressed a shudder that had nothing to do with the cool breeze coming in off the sea. Without love, without complete trust in the other person's integrity, marriage would be a disaster.

Which was precisely why she was here: to investigate all *other* means of salvation.

"Do you think there'll be a reward for catching the smugglers?"

"I don't know." Gryff kept his voice low to match hers. The gravelly growl made her toes curl inside her boots. He sounded like one of the leopards at the Royal Exchange. "The Crown sells any contraband that's seized. We might be given a small percentage of the proceeds. But why do you care? You're a Montgomery, remember? Born with a silver spoon in your mouth."

"Archaeological digs can get very expensive," she said lightly. "I need a new trowel."

"Most women want a new ball dress, or a pair of earrings. Only you would dream of a new trowel. You're a strange woman, Madeline Montgomery."

Her heart sank. Was that how he thought of her? As an unfeminine freak? She quashed the hurt his comment caused. Better that he think of her as an eccentric spendthrift than reveal the truth.

"Well," she said. "I wouldn't say no to a new ball gown either. So if there *is* a reward, we should split the money equally. Agreed?"

He let out a long-suffering sigh, as if he couldn't understand why they were even having this conversation. "Fine. Agreed."

They managed another few moments of silence, but Maddie was supremely conscious of his presence. He hadn't looked away from her, and she was hotly aware of his gaze on the side of her face.

"We should have come up with some clever plan to outwit the smugglers," she said breathlessly. "Did you ever hear of the Ghostly Drummer of Herstmonceux Castle?"

"No."

She lowered her voice to a dramatic murmur, as she often did when she and Harriet shared ghostly tales by candlelight. "Legend says he was nine feet tall, a glowing specter who haunted the battlements, the restless spirit of some poor soul killed at Agincourt."

He snorted at her theatrics. "I take it there's a more prosaic explanation?"

"There is. This spirit only made his dramatic appearances whenever the *other* kind of spirits were involved—before a shipment of brandy arrived in one of the nearby coves. He disappeared when the liquor had been moved. He was really one of the smugglers."

"Why did he glow?"

"They rubbed his clothing in phosphorus. It gives off a greenish light in the dark."

"Interesting. But I fail to see how this information is relevant."

"We could have used the same trick. People around here are very superstitious. I could have dressed up as some ghostly lady, wailing for her lover lost at sea, and scared the smugglers away."

His brows drew together in a forbidding line. "These are hard, cynical men. They're not going to be fooled by some chit in a nightgown, tearing her hair and glowing like a will-o'-the-wisp."

"You're probably right."

Another few minutes of silence went by. "I suppose this is just like being in the army. Did you have to keep watch very often?"

He huffed out an exasperated breath. "Yes. And one of the most important rules of sentry duty was *no chattering.*"

Maddie bit her lip to stop a smile and dutifully looked back out toward the horizon.

Tristan was out there, somewhere, in either Austria or France. She prayed he'd steer clear of Napoleon's rampaging army. An Englishman would hardly be looked on with affection if he was discovered.

Gryff's brother Morgan was somewhere across the waves too. Was he worried about him? She'd always been quite envious of the Davies siblings' tight bond. Tristan had often been busy, or away at school, and Harriet had only been around in the summer months. She'd have loved an extra brother or sister.

A movement caught her attention as Gryff reached into his jacket and withdrew a silver hip flask. He unscrewed the top.

"A toast, to a momentous occasion."

She raised her brows in silent question.

"To the first time in five hundred years that a Montgomery and a Davies have worked together in harmony." He took a healthy swig.

Maddie tried to ignore the strong line of his throat, and the fascinating way his Adam's apple dipped as he swallowed. She had the sudden urge to put her mouth against his skin. She cleared her throat.

"Do you know why our families have always hated each other? I heard it started with a pig."

"Don't be ridiculous. Nobody goes to war over a pig." He held the flask out toward her, and she hesitated. Drinking spirits was a bad idea. Drinking spirits in the company of a Davies was a *very* bad idea.

His expression turned faintly sardonic, as if he guessed her indecision. *Go on*, he seemed to be saying. *I dare you.*

She'd never been able to refuse that look. She took the flask, made a point of wiping the neck clean, and placed it to her lips. His eyes followed the movement, and she took a defiant swallow.

Sweet Lord above! The brandy burned down her throat like molten ore. Her eyes started to water and she pressed her fingers to her lips as it settled in a warm glow in her stomach.

"It wasn't a pig," he said, reclaiming the flask. "It was a woman."

"A woman," she croaked.

"Of course. Women are the root of every conflict, ever. Just look at Helen of Troy. I'll bet you a hundred pounds some Montgomery maiden ran off with a Davies male."

"How do you know it wasn't a Davies damsel and a Montgomery man?"

"Doesn't matter either way. Personally, I'd have stolen the pig. Pigs are simple. Uncomplicated. Women are nothing but trouble."

Maddie rolled her eyes. "That is such a male response, to

blame the female. As if you men are at our mercy, without a will of your own."

"Are we *not* at your mercy?" He lifted his own brows. "We're the ones facing bullets and sabers while you stay safe at home. You tell me who has control."

"Maybe in times of war," she conceded. "But in everyday life, we women are almost helpless. We're passed from one man to the next, from father to husband, little more than chattels to be bartered and sold. The only way to avoid it is to have independent wealth."

He didn't seem to have an answer to that.

"And anyway," she continued. "The Trojan War started because Paris couldn't leave a married woman alone." She sent him a meaningful glance. "A lesson the modern male would do well to heed."

He gave an amused snort. "Digging for information, Miss Montgomery?"

"I am an archaeologist," she said loftily. "Digging is what I do."

"Just ask me about the duel. You're clearly dying to know."

Maddie's curiosity warred with her sense of decorum, and lost. She was desperate to hear it straight from the horse's mouth. "The papers said it was over a married woman."

"Well, that much is true. But I was doing a favor for a friend. I should have remembered that the path to hell is paved with good intentions."

Her mouth dropped open. "You call having an affair with another man's wife a 'good intention'?"

"I do," Gryff said. "There were extenuating circumstances."

Chapter 14

"Extenuating circumstances?" Maddie echoed in disbelief.

"Yes, really. A friend of mine, Ben Turner, was in my regiment. He was killed at Salamanca, and when I got back to London, I went to pay my respects to his sister Sophie, who by that time had married another old school friend, Henry Sommerville. Sophie was desperately unhappy."

"And you consoled her," Maddie finished, trying to sound worldly and cynical even as her stomach twisted in disappointment.

"Not in the way you think. Her parents had arranged the match. Sophie had been in love with Sommerville for years, but he'd only ever treated her with cool reserve. So when he agreed to marry her she was sure it was for her money and not for her person. Her fears were compounded when, two months after the wedding, he still hadn't consummated the marriage.

"Sophie was at her wit's end. She'd tried all sorts of things to goad a reaction out of him; she spent a small fortune on dresses, scandalized the *ton* by racing my own sister, Carys, in a horse race along Rotten Row. But however outrageously she behaved, Sommerville never so much as scolded her. He treated her with the utmost respectability."

"The monster," Maddie said drily.

His lips twitched. "Sometimes a lady doesn't *want* respectability from her own husband. As a final resort, Sophie begged me to flirt with her, to make Sommerville jealous."

"It must have worked. You ended up facing him with pistols at dawn."

"Nobody was more surprised than me when Sommerville challenged me. Turns out he'd been carrying a torch for his own wife for years, but was too shy to tell her. He thought she'd only married *him* for his title." Gryff rolled his eyes. "God, if those two idiots had only talked to each other, I wouldn't have been shot."

"He actually shot you?" Maddie gasped. "I didn't hear that bit. What happened?"

"We met, as agreed, at Chalk's Farm, each with our seconds, and a physician on hand. I tried to explain to Sommerville that I hadn't done anything more than kiss his wife on the cheek, but the idiot had worked himself up into a righteous fury and refused to listen.

"So we took our places. Sommerville badly wanted to put a bullet in me, and I was just debating whether to wing him first, in self-defense, as Rhys suggested, when Sophie and Carys bowled up in a carriage."

His lips quirked at the memory. "I swear, it was like a scene from one of those awful Haymarket melodramas. Sophie screamed 'Stop!' just as Sommerville turned. He flinched at the noise, pulled the trigger, and his bullet grazed my arm." He gestured vaguely toward his left shoulder.

"You could have been killed!"

"Not likely. Sommerville couldn't hit a barn door at thirty paces. He'd have missed me completely if the girls hadn't interrupted."

"So then what happened?"

"Sophie ran to Sommerville and slapped him for being such an idiot. Then she started crying and scolding him for thinking she'd ever take a lover when she only wanted *him*. And *then* she threw herself into his arms and kissed him silly.

"Poor Sommerville didn't know what to do. He finally confessed to loving her the whole time, and kissed her back. Meanwhile, yours truly was bleeding all over his second-best jacket, Rhys was laughing fit to burst, and Carys was arguing with the surgeon about the best way to patch me up."

Maddie smiled at the scene he painted. She'd been so prepared to cast him in the role of shameless seducer, but it wasn't as bad as she'd feared.

Still, he wasn't *completely* blameless. The plan had worked because of his reputation as someone who indulged in flirtatious affaires. He might not have been guilty in the case of Sophie Sommerville, but he had plenty of other scandals to his name.

It wasn't hard to see why an unhappily married woman might be tempted, though. If Maddie was shackled to some whiskery old trout like Sir Mostyn, maybe *she'd* consider taking a lover too. Especially if he was as gorgeous and exciting as Gryff—

She shook her head at her own inconstancy. This was the problem with marrying for duty and not for love: It caused all sorts of moral dilemmas. Her own parents had been lucky enough to have a love match, but they were in the minority. There were scores of unhappily married couples making a mockery of their marriage vows. Half the *ton* had politically expedient marriages designed to keep the wealth of the nation contained to a few hundred elite families. Even the Prince Regent loathed his chosen wife. And Princess Caroline loathed him right back.

She let out a long sigh. "Don't you think it's time we stopped all this feuding nonsense? It takes a lot of effort to maintain such levels of animosity."

Gryff sent her a look of mock horror. "You don't mean that! Having an enemy gives a man purpose. It's *invigorating.* Think of it as a constant battle between the forces of good and evil. With us Davieses being the 'good.'"

She refused to rise to that ludicrous statement. "One of us should give the other a pig. As a symbolic reparation."

"Ah, but who's the injured party?"

"Fine. We could *exchange* pigs."

"It's too late for that. It's bigger than pigs now. There are centuries of insults, on both sides." He sent her a sideways smile and shook his head. "Our histories are too entangled. We'll just have to stay enemies forever."

Maddie didn't know if that sounded like a blessing or a curse.

"Don't worry," he said lightly. "I won't be here to annoy you for much longer. I'll be going back to London soon."

Her spirits sank at the reminder that he would be leaving, but she refused to let him see her disappointment. She cast around for a less contentious topic. "Are you worried about the situation in France? They say Bonaparte's reached Paris."

Gryff's smile faded. "So I heard. He claims to want peace, but there's a battle ahead, I guarantee. I won't be heading back to France, though. We earls are excused from the fighting. We're too important."

This time Maddie couldn't ignore the thread of cynicism in his tone. "Do you feel guilty that your friends will be going without you?"

She didn't really expect him to answer, and was rather surprised by her own boldness in asking such a personal question. Maybe the fact that they weren't looking at each other, but out to sea, made it easier to talk.

"Of course I feel guilty," he growled. "It's just blind luck that I was born the son of an earl and not the son of a chimney sweep. Those other poor bastards have to face that madness all over again."

"What regiment were you in?"

"Twenty-Third Foot, Royal Welsh Fusiliers. It's an infantry regiment, generally an escort to the artillery. Rhys and I were both officers. Morgan, just to be perverse, joined the navy. We saw action at Salamanca and at Nivelle. And then in France; Toulouse in April last year. Napoleon abdicated after that, and suddenly the war was over. We all thought he was finished."

"Do you miss it?"

"I miss the camaraderie. And the clear line of command. But do I miss being shot at? Facing death on a regular basis? God, no."

Maddie sneaked a sideways look at his profile. A muscle twitched in his jaw, and his eyes had a faraway look, as if he were seeing the distant past.

"Do I miss seeing my friends die, or be horribly wounded?" he continued softly. "Definitely not. But I *do* miss fighting for a cause I believe in."

He blinked, and seemed to come back to the present.

"There's no need to feel guilty for staying here, you know," she said quietly. "You've already proved your dedication to your country. And heroism comes in many different forms. You men always think it's great, showy acts, but staying home just requires a different kind of strength. Schools must stay open. Factories and farms still need to run. There's bravery in *carrying on*."

She flushed, suddenly embarrassed by her fervor. Being so opinionated was an unattractive trait—at least according to the *ton*. But Gryff tilted his head and gave her a wry, genuine smile.

"What a wise woman you are, Miss Montgomery. And I do appreciate the privilege of my position. It's just hard to readjust to civilian life after so long in the military, that's all."

Maddie gave a snort and attempted to lighten the mood.

"According to the *Gazette*, you were 'readjusting to civilian life' just fine."

His low chuckle brought an answering curve to her lips. Why did making him smile give her such a sense of achievement?

Chapter 15

Darkness had fallen as they talked; a half-moon lent a silvery cast to the rocks and the sea. Maddie reached into her satchel and rummaged around until she found a bag of paper-wrapped sweets. "Peppermint?"

"Is it poisoned?"

She rolled her eyes, pulled the ends of the paper twist, and popped the sticky lozenge into her own mouth. Her cheek puffed out as she transferred it to one side and began to suck.

Gryff watched, his expression unreadable, and her skin prickled.

"See, completely harmless," she mumbled.

His lips parted as if he was about to say something, but he seemed to think better of it. He took a sweet of his own instead, and she tried not to stare as he placed it between his lips. She heard a crunch, and the muscle on the side of his jaw flexed as he bit down.

"It lasts longer if you suck it," she chided.

He gave a soft snort through his nose, and she had the distinct impression he was choking back a laugh.

"Is that so? I must admit, I've found the opposite to be true. Sucking often *shortens* the experience."

Maddie frowned into the darkness. He was laughing at her, she was sure, but she had no idea what she'd said to amuse him.

"That said," he continued, and there was a distinct smile in his tone, "there's certainly something to be said for savoring. Having it dissolve against one's tongue can be very pleasurable too."

Were they still talking about peppermints?

Maddie tried to ignore the way his gravelly whisper flowed through her veins like the brandy. She felt hot and flustered, as if her skin were too tight.

She swallowed the last sliver of her mint and slid another sideways glance at his profile. He really did have the most inviting lips. He'd taste of peppermint if they—

He turned his head sharply, as if he'd read her scandalous thoughts. Their eyes clashed, and her heart gave a jolt as his intense gaze pinned her to the spot. His eyes dropped to her mouth and she ran her tongue over her lower lip, suddenly self-conscious, convinced she'd left a splinter of peppermint there.

And then he lifted his hand and slid it around her nape.

Maddie couldn't have moved if all four riders of the Apocalypse had chosen that moment to thunder over the hill. Shock held her completely still as he brushed the side of her jaw with his thumb, then leaned forward until they were almost nose-to-nose. He narrowed his eyes.

"Madeline Montgomery."

His low growl sounded more like a threat. Or a curse. His slow exhale filled her lungs, peppermint-sweet, and his expression was the same one he'd worn when he'd offered her the brandy: an invitation to sin.

I dare you.

He was so close she could see the tangle of his dark lashes, feel the warmth of his breath tickling her parted lips. She held his gaze, full of defiant bravado.

Surely he wasn't—?

The press of his lips was soft, questioning—completely different from the kiss he'd given her on the bridge. He paused, as if waiting for her to slap him, or to pull away, but when Maddie did neither of those things he tilted his head and kissed her again.

A soft hum of pleasure rose unbidden in her throat. His tongue slid along the seam of her lips, and when she sucked in a shocked breath he caught her lower lip between his teeth in the gentlest of bites. The faint tug sent tendrils of pleasure spiraling to every part of her body, and when he pulled back a fraction she followed him, desperate to prolong the contact.

No! Don't you dare stop!

He muttered something she didn't quite catch. His tongue slipped inside her mouth, and Maddie met it instinctively with her own, then almost swooned at the taste of him: peppermint spice, hot and cold at the same time.

Gryff Davies was kissing her *properly*!

Amazed, delighted, she closed her eyes and clutched at his shoulder, then slid her hand up over the slope of his neck and tangled her fingers in his hair. His low growl of encouragement made her stomach pitch in jumbled confusion. Goose bumps rose on her skin.

He angled his head and kissed her again, deeper. Light nibbling kisses gave way to slow, wet, decadent swirls of his tongue that made her blood pound in her ears and caused a strange, throbbing heaviness between her thighs.

Let's keep doing this forever—

A rough curse sounded just above them on the trail. They jolted apart as if they'd been drenched in icy water. For one moment they simply stared at each other, eyes wide with shock, both panting hard at the sudden, disorienting interruption.

And then reality set in. Someone was coming down the path.

Maddie sucked in an unsteady breath. Dear God, they'd been moments away from being discovered! If she'd moaned, or made some other noise—

Gryff put his finger over his lips in the universal sign for quiet and pushed her lower in the ferns, ducking down to join her.

Maddie tried to breathe more quietly as the heavy tramp of boots and the rumble of muttered voices came closer. Their hiding place was only a few yards above the trail, and she watched with her heart in her throat as a procession of four men tramped down toward the beach.

They carried no lanterns. She squinted through the ferns, trying to make sense of the dark shapes. One man led the group, while two others appeared to be helping a fourth, who seemed to be injured. His arms were slung over their shoulders and they half carried, half dragged him down the rocky slope.

Why would they bring an injured man here? Perhaps he'd been hurt in some confrontation with the law, and they were planning to hide him in the cave? They might not want to arouse suspicion by taking him to see Doctor Williams, in the village.

She tried to hear what they were saying, but they dropped onto the beach without revealing anything useful.

She sent Gryff a questioning look. He shook his head and indicated that they should wait a little longer. When the men rounded the rocks and entered the cave itself he rose and gestured for her to follow. Staying low, they slipped soundlessly down onto the beach and used the tumbled boulders as cover to sneak closer to the cave entrance.

A light flared as one of the men lit a lantern within, and Maddie heard what sounded like a heavy weight being dropped, then a piteous groan.

"Bind 'im," a deep voice ordered.

The large space amplified the sound of scuffling and

a series of grunts, then a second voice pierced the night. "I won't tell, I swear to God! Let me go."

Maddie crept forward until she could peer inside the cave—then wished she hadn't. Two of the men stood over a third, who was now trussed with rope at ankles and wrists. Her eyes grew wide as she finally understood what was happening: The injured man wasn't one of the smugglers, he was their prisoner!

"I warned 'im what would 'appen to customs boys sniffin' round," the first man growled. "Show 'im."

He nodded at the two standing men, both of whom held ugly-looking cudgels—stout wooden poles like broom handles. They started to beat the prisoner, laying into his legs and ribs as he curled himself into a ball in a vain attempt to protect his head with his bound hands and arms.

"For pity's sake, have mercy!" he screamed.

His pleas fell on deaf ears.

Maddie surged forward without thinking, determined to go to the man's aid, but before she could move more than a few inches Gryff's arm snaked her around the waist. He slapped his hand over her mouth to stop her instinctive shout of denial and tugged them both back against the rocks, her back pressed to his front.

"No," he whispered harshly in her ear.

Maddie sagged against him. He was right, of course. She couldn't just run in there and demand the prisoner's release. She'd likely receive the same treatment. Or worse. She fought a wave of nausea as the sickening cracks and thuds continued. The poor man's piteous shouts turned to groans, and then to an even more ominous silence.

Dear God, had they killed him?

She closed her eyes, grateful for Gryff's reassuringly solid presence behind her. The warmth of him imprinted itself along her back, and a strange weakness enveloped her limbs.

She moved her head. He lifted his hand from her mouth

warily but kept his arm around her waist, and she sucked in a steadying breath. His forearm was like an iron band beneath her breasts, his chest as solid as the rock. The fingers of his right hand curved around her ribs; he must be able to feel her heart pounding beneath her stays.

The leader's voice came again from inside the cave. "Fix 'im to the irons. Let the water 'ave 'im."

The two men reappeared, dragging the limp body of the customs officer between them. They tied his hands to an iron ring that had been hammered into a huge stone near the cave entrance, and Maddie made a horrible deduction: When the tide came in, the man would drown.

"Should we take some o' the barrels, Sadler?" one of the accomplices asked. "Since we're 'ere."

The leader prodded the insensible man with his boot. "Not tonight. The convoy ain't coming till Sunday. Leave 'im till then."

The lantern was extinguished. Maddie shrank back against Gryff as the three men crossed in front of them. She was glad she'd heeded his advice and worn a dark riding habit; they blended into the shadowed rocks.

They waited for what seemed an endless time before the smugglers' footsteps grew indistinct. Maddie belatedly realized that she was standing in the lee of Gryff's parted legs; he'd widened his stance to accommodate her body and her bottom was nestled snugly against his crotch. His chin was tucked unto the crook of her shoulder. It should have felt utterly indecent, standing in such a scandalous embrace, but instead it felt like home.

Flustered by that odd thought, she pulled away, and he released her without a word. She raced across the wet sand and dropped to her knees beside the prone figure. Even in the semi-darkness she could see that his eye was puffed and swelling.

She touched his face gingerly and breathed a relieved sigh when he let out a low groan.

"It's all right," she said softly. "We're here to help."

She tried to untie the rope, but it was knotted too tightly. Gryff nudged her aside and produced a blade from his coat that flashed in the moonlight. He sawed through the ties, and the man's arms dropped lifelessly to the sand.

"Do you recognize him?"

Maddie searched the man's distorted features. He was young, perhaps twenty, and clean-shaven, but he didn't look familiar, although it was hard to tell with all the blood that covered his head. "I don't think so."

A trickle of cold water lapped at her hands and with a gasp of dismay she realized the tide was coming in fast. She staggered to her feet. "We have to hurry."

Gryff bent and pulled the man's arm over his shoulder. Maddie lifted his other arm, and together they managed to drag him almost upright and stagger a short way up the beach, away from the approaching tide. They stopped to rest at the foot of the hill, and Gryff trickled some of the brandy into the unconscious man's mouth.

He came around with a flinch and a groan. "What? No! Get away!"

"We're friends," Maddie murmured. "Let us help you. You've been beaten."

He subsided enough to take several more sips of the brandy, which revived him a little more.

"What's your name, son?" Gryff's tone was curt but not unfriendly; it was the voice of a superior officer quizzing a new recruit, and the younger man responded to the faint air of command. He clutched his head, as if trying to remember.

"Brookes, sir. Gareth Brookes."

"Excellent. Where are you from, Brookes?"

"Cardiff, sir."

"You're a customs man?"

"Aye. A riding officer of the Water Guard. Part of the west coast division."

"Who's your commanding officer?

"Captain Bridges, sir. He sent me up here to investigate rumors of a shipment, come over from France." He groaned and bent over, clutching his sides. "Think me arm's broken, sir."

Gryff nodded. "I wouldn't be at all surprised. You took a bad beating. If you can get to the top of this hill, we'll take you to Doctor Williams in the village."

"Thank you, sir. Me head's poundin', but I'll try."

"Good lad." Gryff put his arm around Brookes's waist and helped him to stand. "Maddie, fetch my satchel and your things from up there." He indicated the overhang where they'd been hiding.

Maddie did as she was asked, and the three of them made slow but steady progress back up the hill. They paused again when they rejoined the lane, and Maddie used her handkerchief to bind an ugly gash on Brookes's temple. Gryff untied the black kerchief knotted around the young man's neck and used it to make a triangular sling for his injured arm.

Maddie marveled at his brisk efficiency. No doubt he'd encountered far worse injuries than a broken arm on the battlefields of France and Spain.

They finally reached the ruined outbuildings of Mathern Palace, and Maddie was relieved to see Galahad and Paladin both still safely concealed. She'd borrowed a hooded cape from her maid, Gwynnie, in case she needed to conceal her face, and now she unrolled it from behind the saddle and draped it over Brookes's shoulders to warm him. Gryff lifted him up onto Paladin's saddle, then went to the horse's head, took the reins, and led them into the darkened lane.

Brookes slumped over the horse's mane.

"How long have you worked for the excise, Brookes?" Gryff

asked, and Maddie suspected it was an attempt to keep him conscious.

"Only eight months or so."

"And you were sent down here on your own?"

Brookes grunted. "Aye. We usually work in teams, three or four of us together, but we're short of men right now. When Captain Bridges got a report of smugglers along this stretch, he sent me down to make inquiries. I've been staying at the King's Head."

"What happened tonight?"

Brookes was silent, trying to gather his thoughts. "A fellow bought me a drink in the taproom. Said he'd heard I worked for the excise and had a tip for me. He told me to meet him in the stables, so we weren't overheard. I went outside, and three of 'em cornered me. They must've knocked me out, because the next thing I know, I'm being dragged down to that beach and thrashed in that bloody cave."

He squinted up at Maddie. "Beggin' your pardon, ma'am."

Maddie shook her head. "Don't worry, Mister Brookes. I've heard worse."

"I'll write to your Captain Bridges tomorrow and let him know what's happened to you," Gryff said. "The smugglers are planning to move their stash on Sunday—I'll ask him to send a detachment of men to help catch them in the act."

Brookes nodded wearily.

"How many men do you think he'll send? And how quickly will they come?"

Brookes groaned. It was clear he was having trouble staying awake. "Couldn't say, sir. Half the lads 'ave gone back to fightin' Old Boney. There's only ten cutters an' thirteen boats to cover the whole west of England, and Wales too. We used to call in the navy ships to help out, but they're all takin' troops back over to France."

Gryff frowned at this unpromising news and plodded on.

Chapter 16

The church clock struck ten as they approached the village and Maddie swallowed a groan. The streets were far from empty, even at this hour. Cheers and shouts emanated from the King's Head public house on the main street, and several dark figures loitered near the stables and staggered along the lanes.

"Could the smugglers still be here?" she whispered.

Gryff shook his head. "I doubt it. They're probably from farther up the coast. But we should avoid being seen, just in case." He glanced up at Brookes, who was swaying in the saddle. "Where does the doctor live?"

"On the east side of town. We can cut around the church-yard." Maddie led the way, but stopped when they entered the orchard at the side of the house. "You'll have to deal with Doctor Williams on your own. If he sees the two of us together he's bound to tell my father."

"Fine. You stay out here with the horses." Gryff guided Brookes gently down from the saddle, supporting him under one arm.

Maddie reclaimed Gwynnie's cloak from Brookes's shoulders and pulled the hood up to shield her face. She stepped back into the shadows near the garden wall as Gryff rapped on the door.

Doctor Williams greeted him with a scowl, ready to berate his unexpected visitors, but his disgruntled expression changed to one of concern when he saw the near-insensible Brookes sagging in Gryff's arms. "Oh dear. What have we here?"

"This lad needs your urgent assistance, sir."

"So I see." The old man clucked his tongue disapprovingly. "Young men these days. Always getting into brawls."

Gryff didn't bother to correct him. "His left arm's broken just above the wrist, and I suspect he has some broken ribs too."

The doctor peered at Gryff through his spectacles, his gray brows raised in faint disapproval. "And who might you be, sir? His doctor?"

Maddie bit back a smile at hearing the Earl of Powys dismissed in such a sarcastic manner.

"Just someone who's seen his fair share of broken limbs, sir," Gryff said, unruffled. "Please, would you examine him?"

Doctor Williams harrumphed his displeasure. He'd obviously been preparing for bed; he was wearing a voluminous red-and-green-striped banyan robe over his nightshirt, and a matching nightcap on his frazzled gray hair. Maddie realized she'd never seen him in anything other than his usual funereal black.

"Well, well, you'd better come in."

He stepped aside, and Gryff half carried the groaning Brookes through the door.

Maddie sank down onto the low stone wall of the garden, her back to the cobbled street. A light came on in the front room and she watched through the window as Gryff was directed to lower Brookes into an armchair.

She winced in sympathy as the doctor peeled back her

blood-soaked handkerchief to inspect the gash on Brookes's forehead and was glad she wasn't any closer. She'd never been particularly squeamish; she'd dealt with her own blistered burns after the lightning strike, after all, but it had been dark when she'd bound the wound, and now she could see an alarming amount of blood.

The doctor disappeared from view, and Gryff's lips moved as he conversed with Brookes. He really did have the most attractive lips—

A noise directly behind her made her jump. She started to turn, but before she could complete the motion she was grabbed from behind. A pair of strong, masculine arms enveloped her in a hug that could have strangled a bear. She let out a startled shriek.

"Got you, m'lovely!"

The rough, slightly slurred voice rumbled in her ear, and a wave of cider-scented breath sloughed over her cheek as her assailant nuzzled his nose against her neck like a pig snuffling for truffles.

Maddie squirmed in dismay, trying to get away, but the man's roving hands slipped up from her waist and gave her breasts a fond squeeze.

She gave a muffled scream of outrage. "Get your hands off me, sir!"

"Now, Gwynnie, don't be like that!" her captor cajoled, with drunken good humor. "Give me a kiss, you naughty girl."

He lifted her from the wall, twirled her around, and thrust his face toward hers, blindly seeking her lips in the darkness. Maddie pushed against his broad chest and turned her head this way and that to avoid his mouth.

"I am *not* your Gwynnie!"

At that very moment the door to the house opened, throwing a shaft of light across the garden and illuminating Maddie and her "swain." The hood of her cloak fell back, revealing her face, and a wave of both relief and dread swamped her.

Her assailant's reaction was instantaneous. He jolted as if he'd been jabbed with a poker.

"What?" he gaped drunkenly. "You ain't Gwynnie!"

Maddie straightened her bodice with as much dignity as she could muster. "No, I am not."

Now there was a little light, she realized she recognized the man: Ned Thomas, the burly hostler from the Red Dragon. Apparently, he was a good "friend" of Gwynn.

The poor man's aghast expression was almost comical, and now that the immediate danger of molestation had passed, she began to see a glimmer of humor in the situation.

"But this *is* Gwynnie's cloak," she said apologetically, "so I can see how the mistake could have occurred. A case of mistaken identity, I'm afraid."

Ned shook his head, like a dog shaking off water after a dip in the stream, and seemed to come out of his alcoholic stupor. He stared at her in growing dismay.

"Miss Montgomery! I didn't know it was you, I swear. I thought you was Gwynnie. I never—"

Maddie cut him off with a shake of the head. "No harm done, Mister Thomas. It was an innocent mistake."

With an air of impending doom, she turned to face Gryff and Doctor Williams, who stood silhouetted in the doorway, both wearing identical expressions of shock. She bit back a curse. So much for remaining incognito.

Gryff's jaw was tight and there was a combative look in his eyes. "Get your hands off her, Thomas."

He said it softly, almost pleasantly, but there was an edge of steel beneath the words that made the other man's eyes widen in alarm. Ned glanced down and belatedly realized he was still clutching her elbow. He dropped his hand as if she were made of burning coals.

"Sorry," he mumbled.

"You may go." Gryff commanded, and poor Ned didn't need telling twice. He tugged his forelock at all three of them, and lumbered off into the night as fast as his staggering steps could carry him.

There was an awkward silence, finally broken by the doctor's shocked tones.

"Miss Montgomery? Is that you? Good heavens! What on earth are you doing here? And at such a late hour?"

Maddie felt her cheeks heat. "Oh, ah, well. I was—"

Gryff interrupted her floundering. "Perhaps I should introduce myself properly, sir. I'm Gryffud Davies, Earl of Powys."

The doctor's bushy eyebrows shot up toward his hairline. He peered a little closer at Gryff's face.

"Powys? Good Lord. Yes, you do have the look of your father about you. Well. Welcome home, my lord. But, forgive me . . . what's a Davies doing with a Montgomery?"

Gryff bent forward in a confidential manner. "It's rather a delicate matter. I trust we can rely on your discretion?"

Doctor Williams's eyes widened at the prospect of an intrigue. "Of course."

Gryff glanced over at her, and for a moment Maddie thought he was going to tell the doctor about the smugglers. And then she saw the wicked twinkle in his eye and her stomach plummeted in dread. She knew that look; he was about to say something utterly outrageous.

"The truth is, Miss Montgomery and I are secretly engaged."

Chapter 17

"What—?" Maddie spluttered.

Gryff's indulgent chuckle overrode her instinctive gasp. He stepped forward and threw his arm around her shoulders, tugging her forcefully into his side.

"No, my love. It's time to come clean. We can trust the good doctor." He glanced at Doctor Williams. "I'm sure you understand, sir, the delicacy of the situation. My father, God rest his soul, forbade the match. But now he's gone, it's my *fervent* hope that Maddie's father can be prevailed upon to accept the union." He shot her a mocking, lovelorn look. "I've waited so long to make her mine."

Maddie's mouth dropped open. Surely Doctor Williams wouldn't believe such poppycock? But the older man's scandalized look had eased into a conspiratorial smile.

"Well, well. Who'd have thought it? Still, you wouldn't be the first to vote across party lines, as it were. Your great-uncle Horace ran off with a Montgomery chit, back in seventy-five. Eloped to Gretna, they did."

Gryff gave a solemn nod. "I'm sure you remember what it's like to be young and in love, sir."

Maddie rolled her eyes at such blatant manipulation. The doctor had been a bachelor for close to fifty years.

"Miss Montgomery's involvement tonight is entirely my fault," Gryff continued smoothly. "I persuaded her to meet me in the churchyard, but when I heard young Brookes being beaten, I went to his aid. And because she's so sweet and good-natured, Maddie ran to help too. So here we are."

He shrugged, palms out, in a hapless gesture—the epitome of a man at the mercy of love.

The doctor nodded knowingly. "You don't want to show your hand until you've had time to soften up her father, eh? Very well, I shan't say a word." He sent them both a stern glare. "But no more shenanigans in churchyards, you hear me? Miss Montgomery's a good woman. She don't need a rogue like you turning her head and then leaving her in an embarrassing condition."

Maddie was sure her cheeks were bright red. Dear God, could this night get any worse?

Gryff nodded. "Of course not, sir. Miss Montgomery has my utmost respect."

"I should hope so. The poor girl's been hurt enough, what with that lightning strike, eh?" Williams turned back to her. "How *is* your arm, Miss Montgomery? I've been reading the most interesting paper by a German named Lichtenberg, on the effects of static and electrical fluids. He studied people who'd survived a lightning strike. In fact, I believe the scarring pattern you have is named after him. A Lichtenberg figure."

Maddie smiled weakly. "How interesting. And the scars are fading, slowly. They're lighter every year."

"Good, good." The doctor patted his pockets and nodded. "Now, if you wouldn't mind, I'd like to see to that head wound of young Brookes. I trust you can escort Miss Montgomery home?"

Gryff nodded. "Yes, sir. Thank you. And good night."

Maddie waited until they were well out of earshot, then swirled to face Gryff and struck him forcefully on the chest. He barely flinched. She might as well have punched a tree; he was just as solid and immovable.

"Are you *mad*? Why on earth did you tell him we were engaged?"

He gave a nonchalant shrug.

She whacked him again. "He'll think I've been sneaking out to meet you for a . . . a—"

"For a tup?" Gryff supplied helpfully. "For a good, hard—"

"For a lovers' tryst!" she blurted out, her cheeks burning.

His eyes crinkled in amusement.

Maddie groaned. "Doctor Williams has been my family's physician for years. He's bound to tell my father."

"You should have considered that spotless reputation of yours before demanding to come adventuring with me." He lifted his brows in that smug *it's your own fault* expression that made her want to punch him again.

"Why didn't you just tell him the truth?"

"About the smugglers? The fewer people who know about them, the better. I told Brookes not to mention it either."

"You can't think the doctor's involved. That's ridiculous. He's a pillar of the community."

"It's unlikely, I admit, but we need to treat everyone as a suspect. I don't want the smugglers tipped off before Sunday. I'll go and see Sir Mostyn in the morning and ask him to either contact the customs officers in Cardiff or provide some trusted men to catch them."

Maddie shook her head. "Fine. But whatever possessed you to say we're secretly *engaged*?"

The white gleam of his smile flashed in the darkness. "It was the first thing that came to mind. And it's brilliant, if you think about it. Everyone knows how disapproving your father would be of a match between us. It explains why we'd be sneaking around, trying to keep it a secret."

"Well, he'd better keep his mouth shut. I can't afford to be the subject of gossip from here to Hyde Park because of your overactive imagination."

For a brief moment she considered what would happen if the doctor *did* tell her father. Father would be cross, certainly, but he wouldn't go around telling people she'd been consorting with a Davies. The shame! He'd probably just swear her to secrecy and pack her off to London with the Aunts.

And even if Doctor Williams told someone else, she doubted a rumored dalliance with Gryff would cause enough of a scandal to make Sir Mostyn withdraw his offer. He seemed distressingly eager to have her as his wife under any circumstances.

She squinted over at the church clock, trying to see the hands. "I have to get home."

They set off toward Newstead Park, and she let out a long, silent exhale into the cool air. What a night! She'd hoped for a little adventure when she'd come out this evening, but she never could have predicted the extremes of emotion she'd experienced—from the sickening violence of the smugglers' attack, to the unexpected assault by Ned, and the shocking heat of Gryff's kiss.

She sneaked a subtle glance sideways and her heart gave a jolt at the sight of him, flecked by moonlight. His tumbled hair gave him a wild look, and she drank in the line of his straight nose and the perfect slant of his cheekbones.

Her gaze flicked to his lips. She still couldn't believe he'd kissed her. Had it been a joke? A way to keep her quiet? Or had he been as intrigued as herself to see what it would be like between them?

God, if they hadn't been interrupted—

Heat rose in her cheeks again and she glanced away, fearful that he'd sense her embarrassment, even in the dark. Now was not the time to be thinking of it.

Perhaps there would *never* be a good time to think of it.

They finally reached the gate that gave entrance to the grounds of Newstead Park and she cleared her throat, suddenly shy.

"I hope you can sneak in without being seen," Gryff said.

"It wouldn't be the first time."

They shared a conspiratorial smile, and a strange glow warmed her chest. At some point in the evening they'd moved past "antagonistic adversaries" and into something more like "partners in crime." Were they becoming *friends*?

Her mind stuttered on the word. She wasn't even sure friendship was possible between a Davies and a Montgomery.

Galahad snorted, and she nodded curtly to hide her disquiet. "Well, good night then."

Gryff sent her his mocking two-fingered salute. "Thank you for your company on a most exciting evening, Miss Montgomery. I bid you good night."

Chapter 18

Maddie woke to the sun shining through the curtains and a tingle of anticipation in her belly. She felt like a child on Christmas morning, excited for the day to come.

It was all Gryff Davies's fault.

Harriet was at the breakfast table, and she sent Maddie a look loaded with speculation. "So what happened last night? Tell me everything!"

Despite Gryff's warning, Maddie didn't even consider withholding the evening's discoveries from her cousin. In a few brief sentences, she described what had happened, although she left out the fact that Gryff had kissed her. That felt too raw, too unbelievable to examine closely in the light of day. She also left out his ridiculous claim that they were engaged, since surely Doctor Williams wouldn't mention it, and she was oddly loath to discuss that too.

"Good Lord!" Harriet exclaimed. "How exciting. I do hope that Brookes is going to be all right."

Maddie took a sip of tea. "Lord Powys said he'd ride over and tell Sir Mostyn about the smugglers this morning."

Harriet made a face at the mention of Sir Mostyn. She disliked the man as much as Maddie did.

"He also said he might write to London for some of his friends. He's worried the customs officer at Cardiff won't be able to send anyone in time."

It felt strange to call Gryff by his title; she'd always thought of his father as the Earl of Powys. And surely, when you'd shared a kiss hot enough to melt glass, using someone's first name was permitted? She'd *tasted* him, for heaven's sake—

"Oh," Harriet said suddenly, "You know how we were looking for books that might be worth something? Well, I've found one. Or, at least, *half* of one."

"What do you mean, half?"

"It's a first version of Doctor Johnson's dictionary—signed by the great man himself. I'm sure it will be of interest to collectors, but the stupid thing is, I can only find the first volume, letters *A* to *M*. I've looked everywhere. Why would someone shelve the two halves in different places?"

"You know what Father's like. Remember that time he spent three weeks looking for his spectacles, and found them in the potting shed? Perhaps he's left the other volume in his study. Or the pantry. What does it look like?"

"I'll show you." Harriet bustled out and returned a moment later with a large, leather-bound tome, which she set on the breakfast table with a thump.

Maddie inspected the handsome cover, then opened it to the first page. The book's full title was *A dictionary of the English Language: in which the words are deduced from their originals, and illustrated in their different significations by examples from the best writers. To which are prefixed, a history of the language, and an English grammar.*

"No wonder it's just known as Johnson's dictionary," she chuckled. "That's quite a mouthful. I'll go and ask Father if he knows where the other half is."

Her father grunted a welcome when she poked her head around the study door.

"Sorry to disturb," Maddie said, hefting the dictionary in her hands. "But I'm looking for the other half of this book. Have you seen it?"

Her father's welcoming expression darkened into a scowl, and she marveled at the abrupt change in his demeanor.

"Seen it?" he said ominously. "Of course I've seen it. That there is one of only ten copies produced in two volumes, for Johnson's wealthiest patrons. Every later version comes in four smaller volumes."

"So it's expensive, then?" Maddie ventured.

"Of course it's expensive. I paid next to nothing for it back at Christie's when they sold off Johnson's library after his death, but it's worth at least a few hundred pounds now. Maybe even a thousand."

"So why haven't we considered selling it?" Maddie asked, perplexed. "We have newer dictionaries. If you can remember where the volume *N* to *Z* is—"

"I know exactly where it is," her father said testily. "And you may as well forget the idea, Maddie, because there's no getting to it."

"Is it lost?"

"Powys!" Her father spat the name of his nemesis like it was a curse. "The other half of that book is in the library at Trellech Court."

Maddie's heart sank. "But why? Did you lend it to the old earl?"

"Ha! I wouldn't have lent him a bucket of water if he was on fire. There was a mix-up at the auction. One half of the book went into a box I bought. The other half went into a box bought by Powys. Of all people." Father's eyebrows twitched in silent fury. "That meddling old bugger had been bidding against me all day. When I realized what had happened,

I offered to buy it from him for a shilling, but he refused." He shook his head, nursing his righteous anger. "He'd only paid sixpence for the whole box!"

"Hmm," Maddie said, trying to think of something soothing and diplomatic, but her father wasn't finished.

"The cheeky blighter's tried to buy *my* half, for a paltry sum, for the last twenty years. He knew as well as I did that one volume on its own is practically worthless. It's only valuable if the two volumes are combined."

Maddie bit her lip. "Well, there's a new earl now. Perhaps he'll be more reasonable than—"

Her father snorted in disbelief.

"Or perhaps," Maddie said with asperity, "you can stop being so unreasonable yourself. If the new earl doesn't want to sell you his half, why not offer an olive branch and ask if he'll work *with* you? You can send it to a book auction in London, and split the proceeds."

Her father's brows rose in surprise at her unexpected chastisement.

"You've spent so many years maintaining this feud," Maddie continued, more gently. "I know it's a matter of pride to you, but what will pride matter if we're turned out of our home and end up penniless on the street?"

"It won't come to that," he huffed. "I'm off to Bristol, to have a word with a couple of moneylenders." He waved away her frown of displeasure. "Just a word. I'm not going to commit to anything. I just want to understand my options. I'll be back tomorrow, in time to take you to the dance. I know how much you and the Harpies enjoy gossiping. Stay out of mischief while I'm gone."

Maddie gave a dutiful nod. "Yes, Father."

Chapter 19

Maddie bit her lip as she mulled over her father's revelation about the missing book.

Surely her newfound truce with Gryff would give her an advantage when it came to negotiating? She'd take care not to reveal how desperately she needed the money, of course.

Harriet had disappeared, but the Aunts were ensconced in the breakfast room, so Maddie deposited the dictionary at the far end of the table and poured herself another cup of tea, adding an extra-large spoonful of sugar.

Aunt Constance took one look at her expression and tilted her head, like an inquisitive bird. "Good morning, Madeline. You look rather grim. Has that awful Sir Mostyn been pestering you again?"

"No, it's not that."

"I'll bet it's a man, though." Constance nodded sagely. "They're always at the root of our problems."

Maddie bit back a smile at how closely that echoed Gryff's sentiments about *women*. Her aunt was right, though: All of her current vexations involved the male of the species, namely her father, Sir Mostyn, and Gryffud Davies. If she counted her perpetual worry about her brother's safety, she could add Tristan to that list too.

"Is that why you never married?" she asked, with sudden insight. "Because men are so much bother?"

Constance swallowed a healthy bite of buttered crumpet. "In a sense. You know how people are always saying you should 'find your other half'? Well, I never did. All the men I ever met would barely have made up a *quarter*. I decided I didn't want to settle for a fraction."

Maddie chuckled. "No, a fraction doesn't sound very appealing."

"But believe me," Constance continued with a wheezy snort, "if I'd ever encountered a man who *was* a real match for me, I'd have pounced on him like Sooty on a hapless sparrow."

She reached down and scratched the black cat who'd positioned himself near her chair in the hope of a dropped piece of kipper. Sooty was just one of the innumerable felines her aunts had living with them at any one time. Maddie's father darkly referred to them as "their familiars."

Aunt Prudence bobbed her head in agreement. "I *did* find my other half, you know, but sadly it wasn't to be."

Maddie lifted her brows in surprise. "I didn't know that. What happened?"

"It was long before your time, my girl. His name was Lord Peregrine Vale and he hadn't a penny to his name. But Lord, what a twinkle in his eye! And the way that man filled a pair of breeches—!" Prudence gave a lusty sigh. "He near swept me off my feet. We were engaged, but then he went off to fight in the colonies and was killed at the Battle of Golden Hill. After that, no other man measured up."

Her face fell, and Maddie's heart clenched in sympathy at this new revelation. She'd always assumed her two aunts had remained unmarried through choice.

"Yes, it was terribly sad, but shall I tell you something shocking?" Prudence's expression brightened and her face took on a naughty look that made her look more like a girl of fifteen than a woman of seventy. "Just because I never married doesn't mean I never had any fun."

Maddie almost choked on her tea. "Aunt Pru! What did you do?"

Her aunt folded her hands in her lap and her eyes twinkled merrily. "Well—"

"Now, Pru, I don't think—" Aunt Connie began.

"Oh, hush, Constance. The girl's twenty-two, not just out of the schoolroom. It's high time she heard some of the more interesting family gossip."

"You should have been named *Im*-Prudence," Aunt Connie muttered. "You always were a hellion."

Maddie smothered a laugh at their bickering.

"As I was saying," Aunt Prudence continued loftily. "We certainly had a little fun. We were engaged, after all. In fact, I found out I was in an 'interesting condition' only a few weeks after Perry left for Boston."

She sighed. "It would have been a great scandal, of course, what with us not being married. My father—your grandfather—shipped me back to the country, so my shame wouldn't become common knowledge, but I came down with scarlet fever only a month later, and lost the babe."

"I'm so sorry," Maddie murmured. "I had no idea."

Prudence waved her hand. "It would have been lovely to have had a child in his image, to remember him by. Still, it was a long time ago. I've made my peace with it. My point is—don't let yourself get bullied into some dreadful marriage of convenience. You're better off unwed, like Connie and me, than shackled to some old fossil who'll only make your life a misery."

"Sir Mostyn offered Father two thousand pounds if I marry him," Maddie said glumly.

"That's because the only way he'll ever get a wife is by bribery." Aunt Pru snorted in disgust. "You don't have to fall on your sword just to save the family name. We'd never ask you to do such a thing."

Both Aunts gave identical firm nods.

"My advice?" Prudence continued briskly. "Get yourself to London. There are scores of rich mill owners on the lookout for a title. See if you can't fall in love with one of them."

"And make sure he's young. And handsome," Aunt Constance chimed in. "Then, even if he turns out to be a scoundrel, at least the bedsport will be fun. You can even take a lover or two, once you've given him a few heirs."

Maddie's scandalized laugh turned into a cough, and Aunt Prudence sent her sister an amused glance.

"Honestly, Connie, this younger generation is terribly uptight. You'd think none of 'em had even *heard* of an amorous liaison."

Maddie wiped her watering eyes. Perhaps her aunts were onto something. Times were changing. New fortunes were being made in trade and industry. Maybe she *should* go and find some textile merchant's son or tin-mining heir?

With an inward sigh, she forced herself to face an uncomfortable truth: Whoever she chose, she doubted she'd find him half as fascinating as Gryffud Davies.

No. That line of thought was far too dangerous. She pointed at the leather-bound book at the end of the table instead. "I don't think I'll have to marry *anyone* if I can get the new Lord Powys to sell us the other half of that book."

The two old women peered over at the item in question. Aunt Constance's brow wrinkled.

"The old earl would rather have poked his own eyes out than sell something to a Montgomery, even for ten times the price."

"Well the new earl isn't as bad as his father," Maddie said

evenly. "I'm hoping I can appeal to his good business sense. If he won't sell it to us, perhaps I can convince him to put the two halves together for auction and split the profits."

"I know *we* need the money," Aunt Constance said uncertainly, "but Powys certainly doesn't. He's as rich as Croesus, what with his coal mines and whatnot. How will you convince him, Maddie?"

"She should seduce him," Aunt Prudence said firmly. "Look at her. She's beautiful enough to make a man agree to anything."

Maddie smiled. "I appreciate the vote of confidence, but you're biased. The earl's refused far prettier girls than me."

"You'll have to outwit him, then," Constance said. "We might be no match for men physically, but we women have been outfoxing 'em in the brains department for millennia."

"The string in the Minotaur's maze was Ariadne's idea," Maddie murmured.

"Precisely! History's full of clever women, getting what they want. And you're just as clever as old Ariadne." Aunt Constance squeezed her hand. "You'll find a way to get us that dictionary, Maddie, I know it."

Chapter 20

Gratified by the Aunts' confidence, Maddie returned to her room and composed a letter to Gryff, asking him to meet her on neutral ground, at the clearing by the well. She waited with barely restrained impatience for a reply, and when it finally came, with Gryff's agreement to meet her at five o'clock that afternoon, she experienced the same excited, butterflies-in-the-stomach feeling she'd felt on waking.

Father would be horrified to know she was negotiating with the enemy, but the possibility of raising upward of five hundred pounds for the family coffers was worth a little fraternization.

Harriet frowned when she heard the plan.

"You're going alone? Would you like me to ride with you?"

"No, it's all right. The days of a Davies dispatching a Montgomery and hiding the body in the woods are long gone."

Harriet sent her a piercing look. "I wasn't talking about mortal danger, Maddie, but Lord Powys's reputation with women is legendary. Aren't you worried he might try to seduce you?"

The memory of their stolen kiss flashed heat across her skin, but Maddie fixed her cousin with a sunny smile. "Of course not. He still thinks of me as the girl he loved to torture back when we were younger. I'll be fine."

Harriet didn't look convinced, but she returned her attention to the map she was illustrating. Maddie went to the stables and saddled Sir Galahad, then set off across the parkland toward the west gate, where Gryff had left her the night before.

In contrast with the dark-green habit she'd worn yesterday, today she'd chosen her most flattering outfit: a formfitting riding jacket and matching skirt in peacock blue, which enhanced the reddish highlights in her hair and made her skin glow. Or perhaps it was the thought of crossing swords with her nemesis again that had brought the color to her cheeks? What was it Gryff had said about having an enemy? Invigorating, he'd called it. She had to agree. Exchanging banter and insults with him was rather addictive.

He was already in the clearing when she arrived, and her skin prickled at the way his gaze traveled over her curves as she dismounted.

"What's all this about?" he asked curtly.

The direct question flustered her, and she noted with a little thrill of alarm that he didn't look particularly welcoming. In fact, he looked rather annoyed to have been summoned. The loose coat he'd worn last night had been replaced with a severely cut dark blue jacket and a pair of buff breeches that disappeared into spotless black leather riding boots. The whiteness of his cravat was a stark contrast to the tanned skin of his jaw.

The strength of his body was apparent in every taut line and broad curve. She swallowed a sudden tightness in her throat.

His gaze lingered on her face for another heart-stopping second, and then he turned his head away, as if he couldn't bear the sight of her, and slapped the end of his riding crop idly against the side of his boot.

"Did you go and see Sir Mostyn?" she asked warily.

His lip curled in contempt. "I did. The man hasn't improved since I last saw him. You'd think he'd be grateful for information about people breaking the law in his district, but he seemed more concerned about the fact that I'd interrupted his breakfast."

Maddie gave a snort of amusement. "What did he say?"

"I told him about the contraband, and that I'd witnessed a man called Sadler and two others beat Brookes and leave him for dead. I also told him of their plan to move the cargo on Sunday."

"You didn't say I was with you, did you?"

He sent her a cynical glance. "Of course not, Miss Montgomery. Your spotless reputation is perfectly safe. Unless the doctor decides to gossip."

Maddie breathed a silent sigh of relief. "Did you tell him you'd be able to recognize the men again, if you saw them?"

"I did. He said he'd deal with it."

"Oh. Well, good."

Gryff paced to the low wall of the well and leaned back on it casually, crossing his booted ankles. "Sir Mostyn did ask if I'd seen you since I'd returned to the area."

Maddie glanced up warily. "What did you tell him?"

To her intense annoyance, a blush rose on her skin. Gryff hadn't just seen her. He'd touched her. Kissed her. *Tasted* her. And, if she was completely honest, she wanted him to do it again.

His hungry gaze lingered on her mouth, and despite his forbidding expression she knew he was thinking about it too.

"I told him we'd had a brief conversation," he said drily.

Oh, please, let's continue that conversation.

Maddie bit back the traitorous words.

"He's looking forward to seeing you at Squire Digby's," Gryff said.

Maddie couldn't contain her groan. She was about to say more when a twig snapped behind her and Gryff's head whipped around. He straightened and scanned the trees that ringed the clearing.

She was about to tease him for his overactive vigilance—presumably a remnant from his soldiering days—when she heard a sharp crack and something whistled past her. A chunk of the stone wall next to Gryff shattered, sending fragments shooting out in a puff of limestone, and she squinted behind her in confusion.

"What was that?"

"Get down!" Gryff growled.

A rider burst from the trees to their left and Maddie gasped as she registered the pistol in his hand. Gryff lunged for her, his hard body slamming into hers as he tackled her to the ground, just as the rider fired again.

The breath left her lungs in a painful wheeze as they landed, but Gryff's weight left her almost immediately as he sprang back to his feet.

She crawled forward, blindly seeking the protection of the wall, and glanced up just as the attacker threw down his spent pistol and raised an ugly-looking cudgel instead—the same kind used to beat Brookes. He spurred his horse and rode straight at Gryff, who stood, legs braced wide, awaiting him in the clearing with a composure Maddie couldn't fathom.

The man swung the club in a wide arc, leaning sideways in the saddle to increase his range, but Gryff sidestepped the charging horse at the very last minute. He ducked and launched himself at the rider, somehow managing to pull him from the saddle, and the two of them fell to the ground in a jumbled blur of limbs.

A crashing sound made Maddie swing around. A second rider had appeared at the far end of the leafy track; he was approaching fast, his attention fixed on Gryff and his assailant.

The horses were both rearing and snorting in alarm. Maddie raced forward, caught Galahad's reins, and pulled herself up into the saddle. She wheeled him around and set him charging down the lane, directly toward the second man.

He pulled his horse to a skidding halt when he saw her and Maddie's heart jolted in terror as he tugged a pistol from his belt. She ducked instinctively, then realized he wasn't aiming at her; his arm was pointed at Gryff, now standing over the inert body of the first man.

"No!" Maddie kicked her feet out of the stirrups and leaned over, making a grab for the weapon. Galahad's shoulder bumped the other horse's withers as she shoved the pistol skyward. The two horses wheeled around in confusion and Maddie fought to keep her seat.

The man's rancid breath bathed her face as they grappled for control.

"Let go, ye bitch!"

The pistol's stock banged painfully against her collarbone as the man threw his full weight against her. Before Maddie could even scream, she was tumbling backward from the saddle, her iron grip on the pistol pulling the man down along with her.

They crashed to the ground. His smothering weight crushed her and she kicked with her legs in instinctive panic, hampered by her skirts. Sheer terror kept her fingers clenched tightly on the gun. The barrel glinted between them and then she heard a deafening explosion and a flash filled her vision.

A searing pain lanced through her shoulder.

The man's weight disappeared. Gryff's fierce face replaced it, haloed by a patch of blue sky, as he caught the man by the back of the coat and threw him sideways onto the grass. He lifted his arm, another shot rang out, and the man fell backward, flopping limply beside Maddie like a rag doll.

The peppery scent of spent gunpowder stung her nose, even as her brain tried to make sense of what had just happened.

Her arm was agony.

Gryff lowered the smoking pistol and glanced down at her, and for a moment he seemed like a stranger. His expression was fierce and cold, utterly terrifying. His chest rose and fell in labored exertion—he must have sprinted along the lane to reach them.

Maddie's own breath was coming in rapid, shallow pants, and the burning sensation in her arm had intensified to an almost unbearable level—it was as if she'd been struck by lightning again. She brought her shaking right hand to her forehead and tried to sit up, but a wave of pain and nausea assailed her and she fell back into the grass with a gasp.

"Don't move." Gryff dropped to his knees beside her, frown lines creasing his forehead. "You've been shot. Let me look."

He began unbuttoning the fastenings at the front of her jacket, but his fingers were too large for the dainty buttons. With a muffled curse he grabbed the lapels and pulled the sides apart, sending buttons flying. She gave a weak cry of protest.

"You can buy another," he growled. He lifted her slightly, caught her left cuff, and tugged it down over her hand. "Pull your arm out of the sleeve."

Maddie groaned in pain. The sleeve was fitted and narrow, but she managed to do as he ordered. Her upper arm felt like it was on fire.

Gryff hastily unbuttoned the top three buttons of her cotton shirt, exposing her chemise and the top of her stays below, and pushed the fabric aside, over her shoulder. Maddie struggled, not wanting him to see the scarring that already marred her skin, but he sent her an impatient glare, misinterpreting the reason for her resistance.

"Stop being missish. We have to see if there's a bullet in you."

Maddie subsided, panting, and glanced down to see the extent of the damage. Thankfully, the dappled light from the trees and the bright blood streaking her skin disguised the worst of her scars. Her blood pounded in her ears.

Gryff's taut expression eased as he let out a harsh exhale. "It's not too bad. It's gouged a furrow, but it's not a through-and-through. It's bleeding quite a bit, though."

He reached into his jacket and withdrew a handkerchief, which he twisted into a band and placed over the wound, grimacing in sympathy as Maddie flinched and hissed in a breath. He tied it off neatly.

Maddie tugged her bloodstained shirt back over her shoulder as he stood.

"Can you stand? We need to get that cleaned and dressed as soon as possible."

She sat up slowly, her head spinning, and glanced over at the man on the ground. There was no sign of movement. "You killed him," she croaked.

Gryff squatted back down next to her so his eyes were level with hers. "Yes, I killed him. And I'd do it again." He shook his head, and a tortured expression flashed over his features. "God, six inches to the left and he'd have shot you in the throat."

She sucked in a breath that was almost a sob. "You saved my life."

"Christ." He slid his hand around the nape of her neck and drew her forward until her nose was crushed against his chest in an awkward sort of hug. "You saved *mine*."

A shudder passed through his body and into hers. Maddie inhaled a steadying lungful of his scent, burrowing into the comfort of his shoulder. They stayed like that for the space of ten heartbeats, until he gently disengaged himself and stood.

Maddie glanced away, her awkwardness returning with the distance. "Where's Sir Galahad?"

"Over there by Paladin. I'll get him."

Maddie rose slowly to her feet, but a wave of nausea threatened as she straightened. Black spots swirled in her vision. She groaned and reached blindly for Gryff, and with a muttered curse he turned back and caught her against him, then swept her up into his arms.

"You're in no state to ride." He tightened his arms around her and hitched her closer to his chest. "We'll have to ride double."

Maddie nodded. Her pulse seemed to be centered in the throbbing wound on her arm, and the world was swirling alarmingly.

Gryff tied Galahad's reins to Paladin's saddle, mounted, then pulled her gently up in front of him, sideways in his lap. She wrapped her arms around his waist. The ground seemed much farther away than on Sir Galahad.

The first attacker lay sprawled on his back by the well, and Maddie tried to see if his chest still rose and fell, but she couldn't discern any signs of life. Had Gryff killed him too? The clearing blurred green and brown as Paladin wheeled around and she closed her eyes, nauseous and exhausted.

"Stay with me, *cariad*," Gryff murmured.

For the first time the word sounded like an endearment and not a mockery. Was that worry in his voice? Maddie felt shivery-cold and yet sweaty at her hairline. Her arm burned like it had been touched by a red-hot poker.

"I can't take you back to Newstead Park like this," Gryff muttered against her hair. "Your father would have me drawn and quartered. We'll go to Trellech Court."

Chapter 21

The ride to Gryff's ancestral home passed in a muddled blur of pain. Maddie was aware of his arms around her, of her head lolling against his shoulder, then tucked beneath his chin as he shielded her from the worst of the horse's jarring gait. She clung to him, her hands fisted in his coat, drinking in his comforting scent: vetiver-scented linen and man.

Despite her injury, a sense of anticipation dawned. She'd only ever seen Trellech from a distance. She and Harriet used to dare each other to ride close enough to spy on its imposing turrets; she'd always longed for a closer look.

They crested the final hill, and she sucked in an awed breath at the sight that spread out before them. Trellech Court was a genuine castle, complete with crenellated ramparts and a profusion of mismatched towers—the kind that fairy tales were made of.

"Is that a drawbridge?"

"It is. There's a portcullis too. But no water in the moat. It was drained years ago, much to my brothers' disgust. Carys keeps some of the menagerie animals down there now, like at the Tower of London."

With immaculate timing, the shrill cry of a peacock echoed across the valley, and Gryff winced. "Bloody Geoffrey," he muttered. "I hate that bird."

They rode closer, skirting the castle walls, and entered the outer keep beneath an enormous stone arch. The main house came into view, and Maddie couldn't hide her gasp of surprise.

The imposing outer ramparts were just one part of the overall structure; the rest was an astonishing cluster of architectural styles that seemed cobbled together as if by some mad, drunken architect. A crumbling medieval tower butted up against an Elizabethan gable—a half-timbered, red-brick section that didn't have a straight line on it anywhere. Another wing, sprouting from the other side, was pure Palladian, all elegant cornices, huge windows, and pillars.

Maddie blinked. Perhaps she was hallucinating from loss of blood? But when she opened her eyes the amazing place was still there.

"Now you know Trellech's secret," Gryff said drily. "Breathtaking isn't it?"

The overall effect was a confusing blend of charming and chaotic, almost too ridiculous to be believed. Tristan—the architectural purist—would have an apoplexy if he ever saw this ramshackle conglomeration. The disorder would hurt his soul.

But Maddie found it so much more interesting than her own home. Newstead Park was, in architectural terms, relatively new, being only a few hundred years old. Her great-great-grandfather had demolished the previous buildings and erased almost all evidence of the past to build the elegant country house that now graced the site.

Here, however, the rich history had been preserved. Maddie could almost hear the stones whispering to her, begging to be investigated, like one of her architectural dig sites.

"What an amazing place!"

Gryff glanced down with a wry smile. "There's no need to be polite. You can say it; it's grotesque. I think every generation of Davies tacked on their own section, just to leave their mark."

"It's *unique*," Maddie corrected firmly. "And wonderful."

Her delight dimmed a little at the realization that the Davies family had obviously been wealthy enough to add to their keep in almost every century. Gryff could probably build his own new wing whenever he fancied.

In stark contrast, *her* family couldn't even afford a new pigeon coop.

Gryff tilted his head at the towering walls. "The south wing's all for show. A medieval fortress is all very well to impress people with, but it's damn drafty to live in. Most of my ancestors wanted a little more comfort."

They entered an imposing U-shaped stable block, and Maddie blushed in sudden embarrassment when a smartly dressed groom came out of the stalls and took Paladin's reins. Gryff, however, acted as if riding in with a disheveled woman in his lap, like some barbaric spoils of war, was a perfectly natural thing to do. Perhaps, for a Davies, it was.

"Think you can stand?" he murmured.

Maddie licked her dry lips. "Yes, I think so. I feel less dizzy now."

He lowered her to the ground, taking care not to jostle her injured arm, then dismounted himself. "Thanks, Huw," he said, nodding at the groom and indicating the two horses. "See they're both rubbed down and given extra mash. They've had an exciting day."

He took Maddie's arm and escorted her through a large door at the back of the house and into a hallway checkered with black and white tiles. An elderly footman accosted them almost immediately, frowning in concern at the bloodstains on Maddie's white shirt.

"Master Gryffud, what mischief is this?" he demanded.

Maddie contained a smile. The old man had all the famil-
iarity of a longtime retainer—and he obviously hadn't yet ac-
customed himself to referring to Gryff as the new earl.

Gryff brushed off his hovering. "Don't look at me like that,
Beddow. I didn't do it. This is Miss Montgomery. We were set
upon by bandits, near Ffynnon Pen Rhys, and she's taken a
scratch to her arm."

The ancient servant peered sharply at Maddie's face, aghast.
"Montgomery, you say!" Maddie half expected him to cross
himself to ward against evil spirits. "Your father would—"

"I have no interest in what my father would or wouldn't have
thought," Gryff interrupted sharply.

The servant frowned. "Yes, sir. Should I send someone to
the village for Doctor Williams?"

"No. I don't think it's too serious. Send Lucas for my medical kit. And tell cook to send up a bowl of hot water and some
clean towels. We'll be in the study."

"Yes, my lord."

The man hobbled away, slightly stoop-shouldered, and Gryff
sent Maddie a rueful, apologetic grimace. "That's Beddow.
He was my father's valet for sixty years. In his mind, I'm still
the twelve-year-old scamp who got caught by his breeches on
the flagpole on the west tower." He shook his head. "He's too
old to be working, really, but he refuses to retire."

Maddie sent him a smile. "I understand. This is his home,
as much as it is yours. You couldn't possibly send him away."

"Exactly."

Gryff ushered her into a handsome, masculine study whose
deep stuffed armchairs and imposing mahogany desk spoke
of centuries of study and stewardship. He gestured to a leather
armchair and she sank into it gratefully.

He crossed to a sideboard, poured some amber liquid from
a decanter into two tumblers, and offered one to her. "Here,

have a sip of this. It's brandy. The same as was in my flask last night."

Maddie accepted the heavy glass and took a cautious sip. The burning sensation was no more enjoyable than it had been the last time, but the warmth that spread in her belly was welcome. The pain in her arm subsided to a dull throb.

A young footman appeared with a rolled cloth bundle, closely followed by a maidservant, who placed linens and a creamware washbowl full of steaming water on a side table as Gryff directed.

When they'd both left, he drained the rest of his brandy and replaced the glass on the side with a brusque click.

"Right then. Let's have a proper look."

Maddie shifted uncomfortably in the chair. The fact that they were alone, unchaperoned, seemed much more obvious here, in the civilized confines of a house. What made her *more* uncomfortable, however, was the fact that the study's tall windows provided excellent light; there was little chance he wouldn't discern the unsightly scarring on her skin this time.

Still, it would be the height of foolishness to try to ride home without having her injury seen to. And for all Doctor Williams's many years practicing medicine, she'd bet the man in front of her had dealt with far more bullet wounds.

She shrugged fully out of her jacket and used her right hand to undo the buttons of her shirt. Baring her shoulder to the elbow, she held her breath as Gryff untied the knotted handkerchief and drew it away. He dipped one of the cloths into the bowl of hot water and wrung it out.

"I'm going to have to clean it. It will hurt, I'm afraid, but it can't be helped."

Maddie sent him a weak smile. "It can't be worse than being hit by lightning."

She tried not to flinch as he dabbed the wound, even though he was far gentler than she expected for a man of his size, and soon the water in the bowl was pink with blood. She lowered her chin to assess the damage, her head dropping close to Gryff's as he bent to see what he was doing.

She forced herself to stay perfectly still as he wiped the smears of blood from her neck, shoulder, and arm, revealing the unsightly scars left over from the lightning strike. Her heart pounded in her throat as she waited for him to make a comment, but he remained silent, assiduously washing every last trace of blood from her skin.

With the area cleaned, it was clear that his initial assessment had been correct. The bullet had nicked the outer edge of her left arm, leaving a bloody furrow perhaps two inches long.

"Well, the good news is, it doesn't need stitching."

He dabbed one last time at the fresh blood that welled from the scratch, then unrolled the cloth bundle the footman had brought to reveal a neatly arranged collection of medical supplies: tweezers and swabs, cotton pads and rolls of gauze— presumably a lightweight, personal medical kit he'd used as a soldier.

"We can't leave any dirt or strands of fabric in there, have to make sure it doesn't get infected. I've seen smaller wounds than that kill a man."

He reached for Maddie's unfinished brandy and thrust the glass toward her. "Another sip. This is going to sting."

She took a fortifying gulp, and when she was done he dipped the corner of a cotton pad into the remaining liquid and pressed it firmly against her arm. She sucked in a breath and he grimaced in sympathy, even as he retained the pressure.

"Sorry. But alcohol helps." He used a clean roll of gauze to neatly bind her arm. "There. All done. Brave girl."

Maddie sagged back in the armchair with a sigh of relief. Whether it was the relaxing effect of the brandy, or simply that it was too late to start worrying about being embarrassed now, she didn't bother trying to re-cover her shoulder.

Gryff replaced the scissors and roll of bandage on the table, then leaned his hips back against the desk, ankles crossed in front of him. From his frowning expression she could tell he was dying to ask about the scarring but too polite to do so, so Maddie decided to take the bull by the horns. What was the point in hiding now? He'd already seen most of the damage. If he hadn't turned away in horrified revulsion by now, then perhaps he never would. That, in itself, made him rather extraordinary.

"I expect you've seen all kinds of injuries, during the war," she said tentatively.

"Too many to count."

She didn't move as his gaze roved over the pale, fernlike patterns that stretched from the side of her neck, over her shoulder, and down to her elbow. His expression was stern, appraising, but she couldn't detect disgust or even pity, for which she was grateful.

"They appeared about an hour after the lightning strike," she said. "At first they were red, then they turned to blisters. They started to fade over following weeks, but as you can see, they never disappeared completely."

Gryff stayed silent, and Maddie's nerves forced her to carry on talking, to fill the silence, like a confession. "They're more visible when the skin is hot or cold, or if it's stretched tight."

She held her breath, awaiting his verdict.

He raked his hand through his hair and finally met her eyes. "It must have hurt a great deal. I'm sorry." His voice had an oddly rough edge. "God, it's a miracle you survived."

"I know." Maddie sent him a smile and tried to lighten the mood. "Believe me, I'm very grateful to still be here—if only so I can be shot at by bandits not ten miles from home."

The corner of his mouth curled up at her dry attempt at humor and she gave a rueful shrug. "It's just another scar, after all."

He shook his head. "It shows what a remarkable life you've led. What a remarkable woman you *are*. I doubt there's another woman in England who could boast of such battle scars. If you were a man you'd be rolling up your sleeve at every opportunity and showing them off."

The expression in his eyes was one of undisguised admiration and Maddie's heart missed a beat. He'd called her remarkable.

"Maddie, I—"

Chapter 22

Whatever Gryff had been about to say was interrupted by the entrance of a stooped, elderly woman, bent almost double under the weight of a rattling tea tray. She was barely five feet tall, with a traditional Welsh shawl draped over her black-striped dress and a pair of sparkling dark eyes in her wizened face.

She sent Maddie a wide grin as she bustled over to the desk and deposited the tray with an audible crash of the teacups and plates. Gryff winced.

"Welcome to Trellech Court, Miss Montgomery. It's been too long since we had a neighborly visit from one of your family."

Gryff snorted. "The last 'neighborly visit' probably included boiling oil and claymores."

The old woman clucked her tongue at his impudence.

"Miss Montgomery, may I introduce you to Nanny Maude." Gryff's voice was warm with affection. "Nanny Maude has been with us almost as long as Beddow. She's administered more spanks to my backside with the back of a hairbrush than I care to count."

The old lady nodded. "You deserved every one, you scamp. You and your brothers. A bunch of wild heathens, the lot of you. And your sister was the wildest of the lot."

Maddie couldn't hide her grin. The thought of Gryff as a naughty little boy was rather delightful.

Nanny Maude gestured to the tray. The knuckles of her hands were gnarled and swollen with age. "I had cook make a batch of Welshcakes, to tide you over until dinner. They're Lady Carys's favorite."

She was watching Maddie expectantly, so Maddie reached across and dutifully took one of the offered treats. Despite the name, they weren't truly cakes, more like flattened English scones studded with raisins, and instead of being cooked in an oven they were heated in a cast-iron pan over the stove, like a thick pancake. Extra spices, like mace and cinnamon, made them wonderfully aromatic.

Maddie bit into hers with a little hum of delight and then smiled around the mouthful as she chewed. She glanced at Gryff, and her skin heated as she found his gaze lingering on her lips. She swallowed carefully, then licked a morsel of sugar with her tongue.

The muscle in the side of his jaw twitched, as if he was grinding his teeth. He glanced up and their gazes clashed. Her stomach did a little somersault.

"You should give Miss Montgomery a tour of the house," Nanny Maude said cheerfully, apparently oblivious to the scorching undercurrents suddenly swirling between Maddie and Gryff. "But not now. The poor girl's had a nasty shock. She needs to eat." She smiled at Maddie. "You'll stay for dinner, of course."

Maddie swallowed the last of her Welshcake and glanced around in search of a clock. What time was it? She'd completely lost track.

"It's almost seven," Gryff supplied, as if reading her mind. "Are you expected back at Newstead Park for dinner?"

She shook her head. "Father's gone to Bristol on business, but Harriet and my aunts will worry if I don't return soon."

"You can send them a note." Nanny Maude beamed.

Gryff snorted again. "A letter from Trellech Court? They'll think it's a ransom demand. Be sure to tell them you haven't been abducted under duress. We don't want them sending in the cavalry."

Maddie ignored his foolery and smiled at the older woman. "Very well, I'll stay. Thank you."

Nanny Maude gave an approving nod. "You'll want to change out of those dirty clothes. I've told one of the maids to find some of Carys's dresses for you. You're much the same size." She beckoned impatiently, effectively silencing Maddie's instinctive refusal. "Come along, child. You'll feel much better cleaned up, I assure you."

Gryff sent her a laughing glance. "There's no point arguing. Nanny Maude always gets her way."

"You make me sound like a tyrant, Gryffud."

"If only we'd had you and your hairbrush at Badajoz," he joked. "We would have sent Napoleon packing in minutes." He stood and gave Maddie an elegant, mocking bow. "I'll see you at dinner, Miss Montgomery."

Maddie watched him leave with a combination of confusion and regret. She turned back to find Nanny Maude watching her with a knowing, indulgent smile. Flushing, she allowed the older woman to bustle her out of the study and up a grand staircase, trying not to stare at all the fascinating family portraits and suits of armor that lined the walls.

They entered a bedroom decorated in frothy, feminine tones of seafoam and palest green. Gilded mirrors and candle

sconces blended with an array of pretty French furniture up-
holstered in floral silks and satins.

A selection of dresses had been laid out on the bed, and
Nanny Maude lifted a claret-colored gown from the pile.

"Lady Carys has the most outrageous taste in clothes," she
chuckled indulgently. "And beautiful red hair—which makes
this particular color a ghastly mistake. I told her so at the
time, but she wouldn't listen. She's only worn it once, to a
masquerade ball, when her hair was powdered. It will look
lovely with your coloring, though."

Maddie eyed the dress with alarm. Gryff's younger sister
was notorious for her exquisite, flamboyant outfits. They'd
rarely crossed paths at *ton* functions, but Maddie had always
been rather awed by the younger girl's effortless charm and
apparent confidence. The daring flourishes she added to her
outfits always set people talking—and had them emulating the
style the very next day.

True to form, the scooped neckline of this dress was cut
daringly low. Maddie swallowed. Carys Davies had men eating out of the palm of her hand. Would some of that devastating feminine allure transfer itself to her?

Then again, did she even *want* Gryffud Davies eating out
of her hand? Hanging on her every word? If it helped get his
half of the dictionary, then yes.

And besides, the thought of having a worldly, sophisticated
man like Gryff see her as something more than a disheveled
country spinster was extremely appealing.

Maddie stripped off her bloodstained clothes and heaved a
sigh of regret for the ruined outfit. The skirt was covered in
grass stains and mud, and the jacket was ripped at the shoulder where the bullet had gone through. Half the buttons were
missing; it was beyond repair. Gryff had told her to replace it,
but she could hardly afford that now, could she?

A sweet, freckled maid helped her into a decadent silk chemise and then the dress itself, which had an ingenious built-in corset. Maddie stared at her reflection, impressed at the way it enhanced her own figure. She'd never worn this deep-red shade before; she looked like an opera singer. Her breasts mounded enticingly above the scalloped neckline, and her waist seemed even smaller than usual, thanks to the exquisite tailoring. The elbow-length sleeves were puffy enough not to aggravate her wound.

The maid brushed her tangled tresses—politely ignoring the dried leaves and twigs that fell out—and pinned it into a flattering half-up, half-down style.

"There, miss." She stepped back with a reassuring smile just as Nanny Maude reappeared in the doorway with a folded square of fabric in her arms.

"I believe this is yours, Miss Montgomery."

Maddie frowned as she took it. It was a cashmere shawl, with a swirling paisley pattern in a gorgeous combination of cream, red, and orange. It looked vaguely familiar. She gasped in sudden suspicion, checked the corner, and turned her astonished gaze on the older woman.

"This *is* mine! There's an ink stain on the fringe. Where on earth—?"

It had been a favorite of hers when she'd been a girl. She'd lost it—she wrinkled her nose as recollection came. "Gryff *stole* this! Years ago. And I couldn't catch him. He rode back here and tied it to the flagpole, right at the top of one of these towers, just to taunt me."

Nanny Maude chuckled. "He did indeed, the naughty boy."

Maddie gave a shocked laugh. "I can't believe he kept it all these years."

The older woman gave a mysterious shrug, but her eyes were sparkling. "He never could bring himself to return it."

Maddie frowned again, intending to ask her what she meant

by that oblique comment, but the older woman gestured to a pretty writing desk in the corner.

"There's paper and ink there, for you to write to your aunts and cousin."

Maddie obediently dashed off a short note saying she'd "accepted an invitation to dinner at Trellech Court" and was "working on the dictionary plan."

When she glanced around for something with which to close the letter, she found a silver-handled seal engraved with the crest of the Earls of Powys. The impression left in the blob of red wax showed a wyvern: a mythological creature with a snake-like body and tail, but the wings and top half of a dragon.

She handed the finished note to the maid, drew the shawl around her shoulders to conceal the low-cut bosom of the dress, and hurried after Nanny Maude.

"Time for dinner," the old woman said merrily.

Maddie took a fortifying breath. She'd never in her life expected to be having dinner *à deux* with Gryffud Davies in the heart of his private domain, but this was an opportunity she couldn't afford to squander. She needed the other half of that dictionary.

It was time to beard the lion in his own den.

Chapter 23

To Maddie's consternation, she was not shown into a grand dining room. Instead, Nanny Maude led her back to the study, where a small round table had been laid for two. Gryff waited, perched on the arm of one of the leather chairs. He stood as she entered and swept her body and face with an appreciative glance.

"I told Beddow we'd eat in here. The main dining table seats twenty-four, but it's stupid to make the servants set it up when there's only the two of us. I often eat my meals in here when I'm alone. I hope you don't mind."

"Not at all."

He suddenly noted her shawl, and his eyes narrowed. "Where did you get that?"

Maddie tightened her grip on it, holding the edges together across her chest. She turned to the older woman, only to find that Nanny Maude had disappeared.

"Nanny Maude gave it to me. Or should I say, *returned* it to me." She fixed him with an accusing glare, and his lips twitched into that half smile she knew so well.

"I remember the day I stole it from you. You promised to bury me alive in quicksand."

"You flew it from the flagpole."

The grin grew wider. "The spoils of war. I knew you'd come close enough to see it. I always hoped you'd pluck up the courage to ride in here and reclaim it, but alas, you never did." He shook his head in mock regret. "Such a disappointing adversary. I had dreams of you scaling the walls and breaking into my bedchamber to demand its return."

His expression was dreamy and wicked, and an image of the scenario he'd described flashed into her brain: of herself standing over him as he lay in bed, chest bare, sheets pooled around his hips. Of his eyes flashing open, his fingers shooting out to catch her wrist and topple her onto the bed. Of her body, trapped beneath his—

She shook her head to dispel the disturbing thoughts. "You would have locked me up in a dungeon and never let me out," she managed, only half joking.

"I would have been tempted," he agreed easily. "Although I'd have made it a very comfortable dungeon." Something dark flashed in his eyes, as if he relished the thought of having her at his mercy, and her body reacted instinctively. She flushed hot and cold. "You might never have wanted to leave."

Flustered, she stepped up to the table and let the shawl drop from her shoulders, then immediately regretted it as his gaze slid over the pale expanse of her chest exposed by the daring neckline of her dress.

His throat constricted above his cravat as he swallowed. "My compliments." His voice was even deeper than usual. "That dress looks a hundred times better on you than it ever did on my sister."

He pulled out a chair and Maddie sat, conscious of his breath fanning her collarbone as he leaned over her to push her back in. He took his place opposite, and the table was so small she could feel the warmth of his knees almost touching hers.

A silver posy vase held a spray of wildflowers, and a triple candelabrum sent a flattering glow across his face and hands. The atmosphere was private, intimate. Seductive.

He'd changed his clothes too. A small gold stickpin twinkled in the folds of his snowy cravat, a sharp contrast with his navy jacket and buff breeches. He looked precisely like the suave London sophisticate she knew him to be, but the effect was ruined by the hint of a bruise that was developing on his jaw, and a cut she hadn't noticed on his temple. He must have received them during his fight with the attackers.

The hint of wildness amid the elegance produced a strange sensation in her belly. He was just like his home: a host of contradictions. By turns elegant and barbaric.

She pursed her lips at her own foolishness. She needed to keep her head, not drool over his handsome face like some dumbstruck country bumpkin.

Two servants appeared with the food, breaking the loaded silence that had fallen, and she nodded her thanks as her wineglass was filled with claret almost as red as her dress. She picked up her silverware, but Gryff sent her a teasing smile.

"Can I propose a toast?"

She paused, caught with knife and fork suspended over her lamb and roast potatoes. *The beast. He just loved discomfiting her.*

He lifted his wineglass. "To friendly enemies."

She set down her cutlery and raised her own glass. "Friendly enemies."

They both drank, and her pulse fluttered as he watched her from over the rim of his glass. She cast about for a safe topic of conversation.

"I'd love to see Tristan's reaction to this place," she said.

"His hair would probably turn white. He likes order. Precision."

Gryff chuckled and began to eat. "Well, he won't find it here. There isn't a straight wall or a right angle in the whole place. He'd probably say we should tear it down and start again."

"Don't," Maddie said impulsively. "I like it."

He paused, as if she'd startled him, then carried on eating. "I live to please you, Miss Montgomery." His tone was gently mocking, but she wasn't sure if it was directed at her or himself.

They ate in silence for a few moments, and then he said, "Both you and your brother have interests that begin with *arch*. Architecture for him, archaeology for you."

"Hmm. I've never thought about that before," Maddie admitted with surprise. "But they're not really related. *Archaeology* comes from the Greek words *arkhaios*, meaning ancient, archaic. *Architecture* is from *archos*, which means chief, or king. Like *archbishop*."

"And *archenemy*," Gryff smiled. "The very *best* of enemies." He took another sip of wine. "You're a regular walking dictionary."

She flinched at his subtle mockery. She knew very well she was regarded as an overeducated bluestocking. But the fact that he'd brought up dictionaries was so perfect that she couldn't let it pass. She took another fortifying sip of wine.

"Speaking of dictionaries," she said, as casually as she could, "my father told me about a volume of Samuel Johnson's version he'd been trying to buy from your father for years."

"Really? My father never mentioned it."

"Apparently he had one half, and my father has the other."

"And he refused to sell, like the dog in the manger? That sounds like my father. He was a belligerent old bugger."

Maddie reminded herself of the power of the dress she was wearing. She was fascinating, a woman who could make a man agree to anything. She leaned forward, shamelessly offering a better view of her cleavage, and sent him a long, slow smile.

"I was rather hoping I could persuade you to part with it." She glanced at him from under her lashes in what she hoped was a provocative manner. "It's Father's birthday soon, you see. And I would love to surprise him with the second volume. He'd be thrilled to see the two halves reunited."

Gryff's attention, as she'd hoped, slid to the mounds of her breasts. But as it lingered, she realized *she* was the one affected. Her chest rose and fell faster as she suddenly found it hard to breathe. His gaze was like a physical touch: Her nipples tightened within the bodice, and heat bloomed over her skin.

She gave a delicate cough, and his gaze snapped back to hers. His eyes were almost black in the candlelight, and the stark hunger in his expression made her stomach swirl.

He calmly replaced his silverware on the table and she echoed the movement, never taking her eyes from his.

"Perhaps your father kept it in the library?" she suggested breathlessly. "Do you think we could look?"

The scraping sound as he pushed back his chair was deafening in the quiet room. He stood, looming over her, and she leaned back, suddenly convinced he was going to bend down and grab her. Or kiss her.

But he simply held out his hand. "The library it is, Miss Montgomery."

Chapter 24

Maddie followed Gryff as he strode purposefully across the checkered hall—almost as if he was trying to get away from her—and entered an immense, two-tiered library. There was no sign of any servants; they seemed to have melted into the shadows.

The candelabrum he'd lifted from the dining table barely illuminated the vast space, but she caught a brief, flickering impression of the ceiling: a painted sky filled with clouds and figures, and a railed balcony running around the upper floor.

A burst of scholarly envy seized her. This was at least twice the size of the library at Newstead Park. What treasures did it hold? She could spend *years* in here.

Her conscience, which had started to nibble at her for manipulating Gryff so outrageously, quieted. With so many books, he certainly wouldn't miss one half of one, would he? Whereas for the Montgomerys, that same volume could mean the difference between bankruptcy and salvation.

He placed the candles on a gilded side table and turned to

her within the narrow circle of light. "What are we looking for, again?"

Maddie smoothed her hands down her skirts. "The second volume of Samuel Johnson's dictionary, letters *N* through *Z*. First edition. It's a large book, about this tall." She held up her hands to indicate the size. "The binding's brown leather, with gilt."

Gryff pushed at a wooden sliding ladder, forcing it sideways along the wall. The little wheels at the top squeaked as they ran along the metal track. "The reference section's along here. Bring the light."

Maddie tried not to stare as he ascended a few rungs, giving her a tantalizing view of his long legs encased in his breeches. The soft fabric molded faithfully over taut, muscular calves and strong thighs. When he reached overhead, the tails of his jacket lifted and provided a mouthwatering glimpse of tight buttocks and slim hips.

She clenched the stem of the candelabrum, resisting the urge to reach out and smooth her hand up the back of his legs. What was *wrong* with her? She'd never felt the urge to explore another body before. But he was like one of those spotted cats in the Royal Exchange: all lazy power and grace. Her fingers had itched to touch their fur and stroke their sleek length, regardless of the danger. Or perhaps because of it. To have something so dangerous purring under her touch.

"Hold the candle still," Gryff scolded from above. He tugged a volume from the shelf and held it up. "Is this it?"

Maddie was sure her cheeks were a guilty pink from her ogling, but she managed to turn her gaze toward the book in his hands. It looked identical to the one Harriet had found at home. Excitement rose in her chest.

"Yes, I think it is."

He handed it down and descended the ladder as she crossed to a gilded desk and opened the book to the title page. He moved to stand next to her, his shoulder brushing hers as they both glanced down, and the scent of him teased her nose.

"This is the one," she said, trying to hide her eagerness.

His long fingers turned the page. "I remember this book. My brothers and I looked through it once, when we were younger. It was *very* disappointing."

"Disappointing? Why?"

"Because Johnson was such a prude, he left out all the rudest words. Or most of them, anyway."

A scandalized laugh escaped her. "You looked?"

"Of course we looked. That's what thirteen-year-old boys do. We took great delight in discovering what he'd omitted. Obviously, because your family had the first half, we could only look for profanities in the second half." He turned to her, laughing. "We found *piss* and *turd*."

Maddie rolled her eyes. "I'm sure Tristan did exactly the same."

"Then he would know that Johnson left in *arse* and *fart*, but missed out some of the finest words in the English language."

"Which ones?"

He pursed his lips in mock disapproval. "You've already had one shock tonight. I'm not sure you can take any more."

She sent him an exasperated look. "I'm made of sterner stuff, my lord. Go on."

"Well, most of the words for the male reproductive member were ignored. *Penis* definitely isn't in there. And human procreation is hardly mentioned at all."

"I can see how that would have been frustrating for a young man trying to educate himself," she said drily.

Maddie knew her cheeks were pink with embarrassment. This conversation was totally unsuitable to be having with *anyone*, let alone a scoundrel like Gryff Davies, but she couldn't deny that she was enjoying herself. He was treating her as an equal, as one of the boys, and the idea that they might discuss any topic at all without her having to worry about being thought unladylike or outrageously forward was incredibly liberating.

Still, enough was enough. She closed the cover of the dictionary with an audible thump. "Well, incomplete or not, I would still like to buy your half."

"How much are you offering?"

She thought quickly and tried to sound offhand. To show too much interest would be fatal. "Well, neither half is worth very much on its own. So how about . . . ten pounds?"

She had no idea where she'd get the money from, of course, but if she could just get him to agree to selling, she'd worry about the details later.

His mouth curved at the corner as he gazed down at her. "Do you know, I think you're trying to swindle me, Miss Montgomery. The two halves might not be worth much separately, but I bet once they're back together they'll be worth more than the sum of their parts." He glanced down at the book. "This is a fancy binding. An unusual size. *And* a first edition. I bet there are plenty of collectors who'd be eager to get their hands on it when it's complete."

Maddie cursed his perspicacity. Gryff Davies was no idiot.

He paused and she held her breath, despite knowing he was doing it on purpose, to torture her.

"I'll accept a hundred pounds."

A disappointed whoosh of air escaped her. There was no way she could come up with that kind of money. Still, she feigned indifference with a little shrug.

"That's far too high. Forget I asked. I'll get Father something else. A new snuffbox maybe."

His eyes twinkled and she had the infuriating suspicion that he knew exactly how desperate she was for that damn book, and was just playing with her. Could he somehow sense her eagerness?

He rocked back on his heels. "I tell you what, I'll play you for it."

She stilled. "What do you mean?"

"All or nothing. We'll play a game, and if you win, I'll give you this half of the book."

Maddie narrowed her eyes, instantly suspicious. "And if *you* win, I have to give you the Montgomery half? No. I won't do that."

"No. If I win—" His eyes flicked down to her mouth and her blood heated at the speculative look on his face. "If I win, I get . . . a kiss."

Her heart started to pound as she tried to sort through all the ramifications of his offer. Games of chance were notoriously risky, but she'd have a 50 percent chance of success. If she beat him, she'd get the book. And if she lost, she'd be in no worse position than now: still without the book, but having kissed Gryff Llewellyn Davies again.

Which was exactly what she'd dreamed of doing ever since their interrupted moment at the beach.

"All right, then." Her voice was firm but breathy. "What shall we play? I don't know many card games, so if that's what you're suggesting, you'll have the advantage of me."

He'd gambled at the finest gaming houses in London. If he chose cards, she wouldn't stand a chance.

He sent her a lazy grin. "You're right. A card game would be unfair. I don't want you saying I won because I cheated."

She scowled at his arrogant confidence that he would be the victor.

"And games of chance are boring," he continued. "There's no skill involved." He tilted his head and eyed her speculatively. "I have it! A game of wits. And in keeping with the spirit of the prize, how about a word game?"

"Go on."

"How about a game using words from the dictionary? Does that sound fair?"

"I suppose so," she said slowly. It sounded innocent enough, but she didn't trust the look on his face. It was too full of amusement, of self-satisfied humor. Gryff Davies was up to something.

He gestured toward a pair of wing chairs grouped in one of the window embrasures, and Maddie accepted the offer to sit. She sank into the deep-red velvet upholstery and spread her skirts as Gryff took the chair opposite her and leaned back, casually crossing one booted foot over his knee.

"All right. The rules. For this game you're only allowed to give answers that start with letters found in your half of the alphabet, letters *A* through *M*."

"How do we play?"

"It's a matching game." His sly, *cat got the cream* smile had her instantly on her guard. It was the same smile he'd always had before he pulled some dastardly trick on her as a youth. Like when he'd tied her to a tree, or stolen her shoes while she waded in the stream.

"There are multiple words for saying the same thing, correct? So I'll say a word, and all you have to do is match it with one that means the same thing from your half of the alphabet."

"That doesn't sound too difficult." Maddie tried to imagine the catch. He probably meant to come out with all sorts of complicated, Latinate words to confuse her. Or soldiering terms.

"One point for each word you can match. If you reach ten points, you win the dictionary."

"And if I can't think of an equivalent?"

"Then you lose, and it's a kiss."

Maddie feigned indifference, even as her heart beat faster. "I should warn you, my vocabulary is excellent."

"A bluestocking like you? I should hope so. But I'm still going to win."

Chapter 25

"Wait," Maddie said abruptly. "What's to stop you making up spurious words? I'll never know the difference."

He looked comically offended. "You have my word of honor as a gentleman."

She pursed her lips and tried not to laugh. He really was fun to tease. "Fine. I suppose I'll just have to trust you."

"Good. All right, we'll start with something easy." His gaze dropped to her lips, and they tingled as if she could actually feel the touch. "For one point, give me another word for . . . *mouth.* Answers starting *A* to *M*, remember."

"*Lips.*"

"Hmm. Not an exact synonym, but I'll take it." His gaze slid over her chin, and downward. "Number two: a word for *throat.*"

Maddie swallowed, well aware that he watched the muscles contract as she did so. Heat rose on her skin. "*Neck?*"

"Wrong half of the alphabet."

Damn. "Ummm. *Gullet?*"

His lips twitched. "Rather unromantic, but it'll do."

His gaze trailed lower, to the expanse of skin revealed by the neckline of her dress, lingering on the shadowy valley between her breasts. She became hotly aware of her ribs expanding against the constriction of the whalebone ribbing, of the way her breasts spilled upward with every breath.

"Now a word for . . . *breasts*."

Her nipples tightened; she just *knew* he was thinking about them. Oh, he was a devil. He wasn't even touching her, and he was still making her squirm with nothing but words.

She tried to order her scrambled thoughts. There were lots of names for breasts, weren't there? *Tits.* No, that was in the second half of the alphabet. *Jugs? Bubbies? Bust?* The thought of saying any of those aloud was excruciating. She settled on the least embarrassing synonym she could think of. "*Bosom.*"

He nodded, and she prayed he wouldn't say *nipple* next. She couldn't think of a single alternative, except for *teat*, and that came after *N*.

"All right. Number four." His gaze slid over her arms, leaving goose bumps in its wake. "I think we'll have . . . *kiss*."

His voice was a little lower, a little hoarser than before. She cast around for an alternative.

"*Peck?*"

He gave a disapproving little tsk. "Wrong half again. And a peck sounds like something you'd get from a chicken."

She let out a long-suffering sigh. "Fine . . . *buss*, then."

"Neither of those words really convey *passion*."

That was true. The kiss they'd shared at the beach could never have been called a peck.

He propped his elbows on the chair arms and steepled his fingers in front of his mouth. "Considering the numerous ways one can kiss, I'm surprised there aren't more words for it, to be honest. A kiss on the cheek between friends, for example, is very different from the passionate kiss one might get from a lover."

The gravel in his voice brought a heaviness to her limbs. He'd used his tongue to kiss her. Would he do it again, if she lost?

He shifted slightly in his chair. "All right. Number five. *Taste*."

"*Taste* as in *style*?" she said quickly. "Or *taste* as in *eat*?"

His eyes glittered. "*Taste* as in *consume*."

Oh, goodness. The way he said it made her stomach flip.

"Uhm. *Sample*?"

"Wrong half."

"*Lick*?" she managed weakly.

His smile widened. "Ah now, *lick* is an *excellent* word. And this is clearly too easy. I'm going to have to raise the stakes for number six. Let's move on to words that would have shocked Samuel Johnson." He uncrossed his legs and placed his feet flat on the floor. "Give me another word for . . . *testicles*."

Maddie suddenly understood his devious plan. He was going to make her say every naughty word she knew. He probably thought she'd cry off in mortification—or fail due to her own sheltered innocence. Well, she had a few tricks of her own. She'd heard the curses bandied about by the stable hands. She'd listened to the teasing and muttering of the men she hired to help on her dig sites.

She met his gaze head on. "*Balls*. And for a bonus point, I'll give you *bollocks* as well."

This time he couldn't contain his amusement. "Excellent! I'll give you the points. Which means you're on seven now. Only three to go."

His smile grew wider, more wicked. "For eight, give me a synonym for the male appendage. My half of the dictionary has plenty, even if old Johnson did leave out *penis*. I have *prick. Shaft. Rod*."

Maddie couldn't help it; her gaze dipped to his lap. He dropped his hands, obscuring her view of the front of his breeches. Oh, this was a dangerous game. But it was also wickedly fun. There was nothing she enjoyed more than their verbal sparring.

"*John Thomas.*"

He shook his head. His eyes seemed darker, almost completely black. "That's two words. Try again."

She summoned all her bravado. "All right. *Cock.* How's that?"

"I commend your clear enunciation." He was definitely laughing at her, the beast. "Now for point number nine, another word for . . . *pleasure.*"

The way he drew it out was positively indecent. His lips pouted to make the *P*, and his tongue licked the underside of his top teeth to make the *L*. Her face felt flushed, her blood slow and sluggish in her veins.

"*Enjoyment,*" she breathed.

He made a face. "Such an insipid word. I would have said *ecstasy.* Or *climax.*" His gaze roved her face, and his wicked, gleeful expression told her he'd saved the best for last. "Oh, dear. I only have one more chance to win."

"Get on with it, then."

"For ten points, and my half of the dictionary, give me another word for . . ."

He was going to say something dreadful. Like *shit.* Or *bugger.* Or—

"*Tongue.*"

Maddie's mind went completely blank. *Tongue?* What was another word for *tongue*?

She tried to think of a scientific term, and failed. What was it in French? *Langue,* that was it. Like the English word *languid.* And *language.* But in English there wasn't—

Gryff's gleeful chuckle was a wicked thing in the still room. "You might as well accept defeat. There really is no substitute for tongue. Trust me."

His wicked intonation suggested he was making a joke. Presumably some double entendre she was too inexperienced to understand. Of course, she couldn't help thinking about *his* tongue. The way it had slid against her own in a delicious, lazy glide. What if he were to use it on other parts of her body? The thought gave her a funny gnawing sensation in her belly.

"Do you have an alternative word?"

She shook her head.

"You admit defeat?"

"Yes." She let out a thoroughly irritated sigh. "You win, Davies."

"It delights me to hear you say it." His gaze was back on her mouth. "That means I get my kiss."

He stood abruptly, so she did the same, her pulse beating in alarm. How had she not noticed how tall he was? How broad. His shoulders seemed to fill her vision.

Not wanting to show how flustered he'd made her, she stepped closer and lifted her face in preparation. Her lips were already tingling. She closed her eyes.

He leaned in, so close she could smell him, could feel the heat radiating from his chest. His warm breath tickled her mouth, but he paused a hairbreadth away from her lips.

"I never said *where* I would kiss you."

Her eyes snapped open.

Oh, bloody hell.

He turned his head and his lips skated across her cheekbone to her ear. It was the lightest of touches, like gossamer, and it caused every nerve in her body to come alive. Her skin fizzled in awareness.

His long fingers slid beneath her hair as he cupped her nape, and when his thumb rubbed the sensitive patch of skin behind her ear she shivered.

Oh, he was a master at this, this *beguiling*. And she was in a whole world of trouble.

She swayed toward him, utterly bewitched, but he ducked his head and trailed his lips down the side of her neck, then along her collarbone.

He paused at the dip at the bottom of her throat. "Here?" he murmured absently.

The word was a humming vibration against her skin.

"No, I don't think so," he said, answering his own question. He trailed lower, over the top curve of a breast that was exposed like half a peach by the scandalous bodice of the dress.

Maddie could scarcely catch a breath. The scrape of the slight stubble on his cheek against her skin was like the rasp of fine sandpaper. It caused a heavy, throbbing fullness between her legs. She fisted her hands at her sides, clutching her skirts, fighting the impulse to grab his hair and pull him even closer.

He made a low sound of pleasure as his chin slid into the valley between her breasts. She sucked in a scandalized breath, but all that did was to push them up even further, like an offering.

"Here, maybe?" His voice was dreamy, low. "Would you like that, Maddie?"

Speech was beyond her. Her blood was pounding—her injured arm throbbed, but even that was no more than a vague irritation, scarcely worth thinking about. Her entire focus was on him. His wicked words. His wicked touch.

"I've dreamed of tasting you."

Her knees almost gave out. She gave a little squeak of surprise as his tongue flicked against her skin.

"That's not a kiss," she gasped. "That's a lick."

"Semantics."

He straightened and caught her in his arms. His hands smoothed down her back and ventured lower, over the rounded curves of her bottom, molding and pressing the fabric of her dress into the cleft.

Maddie gazed up at him in shock. No one had ever touched her so intimately. Even through the layers of dress and chemise, she could feel the warmth of his fingers. She was loose-limbed and coiled tight, all at once.

"Perhaps I should kiss you here?" he said, and his voice reverberated through her with thrilling intensity. "Between your legs. Did you know that people do that?"

She gave the tiniest of whimpers. She was so hot, she was going to faint.

His eyes lost a little of their intensity, and a sparkle of amusement appeared. "No, I don't think you're quite ready for that. I'd better kiss that wicked mouth of yours, then."

He bent down and drew her into a kiss that was a hundred times more passionate than the one they'd shared at the beach. His lips caught hers and his tongue demanded entry, and Maddie didn't even consider pulling away. With a moan of delight, almost *relief*, she brought her hands up to his shoulders and kissed him back.

He growled low in his throat and framed her head in his hands, angling her jaw to his liking then sweeping inside with his tongue.

This was no slow stoking of the fire. This was an immediate conflagration: heat and desperate urgency. Ten years of teasing and flirting—yes, that's what it had been, she could admit it now—had always been coming to this. This bonfire.

Chapter 26

He didn't stop at one kiss, and Maddie would have killed him if he had. He took her mouth again and again, teasing and coaxing, fanning the flames.

Maddie tangled her fingers in his hair and lifted herself up on tiptoe, pressing into him, desperate to get even closer. She wanted to crawl inside him and never leave. She wanted the taste of him imprinted on her soul.

When he finally wrenched his mouth from hers they both gasped for air.

"Christ," he panted raggedly.

Maddie suppressed the bizarre urge to laugh. He looked as ravished as she felt. A lock of his hair had fallen over his brow, and a pink flush colored his cheekbones. Her whole body felt light, weightless, as if her heart were singing. And in that moment everything became clear.

She wanted to do more than just kiss Gryff Davies. She wanted everything from him. Everything he'd teased her with: his tongue on her breasts, his hand between her legs.

Everything.

A jolt of desperation seized her. This might be her only chance. He would be going back to London soon. And if Father couldn't find the money he needed, they'd have to sell Newstead Park and live in genteel poverty somewhere. Gryff wouldn't be her neighbor. She'd never have the thrill of wondering if she might run into him in the village, or stumble upon him on her morning ride.

As of this moment they were still equals, both in social standing and—as far as he knew—in fortune. The coming weeks might force her to accept a pragmatic, passionless match, even if it wasn't with someone quite as bad as Sir Mostyn, but there was only a slim chance that she'd grow to love the man she chose. How likely was it that she'd find the same scorching passion she experienced with Gryff?

Almost impossible. It was the depth of their shared history that added the spark to every interaction. Each kiss was a delicious revenge for some previous slight. An adult remedy for a childish tease. No one else in whole world would kiss her the way Gryff kissed her, nor elicit such a passionate response.

The thought was both depressing and oddly empowering, and Maddie gazed up at him in wonder. He was her shadow, her blight, and her curse. But she couldn't imagine a life without him in it, even only as a memory. She was grimly certain she'd never desire anyone more.

If there was one thing being struck by lightning had taught her, it was to seize the moment, to live while she still had the chance. That didn't mean being reckless or taking stupid risks, but she'd vowed to stop being so timid, to stop being so afraid of failing that she didn't achieve anything at all.

She tightened her fingers in his hair and pulled him back down toward her.

"More."

He caught her firmly around the waist and lifted her up, up, until her face was level with his. "You don't know what you're saying."

She narrowed her eyes.

"You've had a shock," he said, as if he was explaining something simple to a stupid child. "This is a natural reaction to a close call. I've seen it after battle: The survivors want to reassure themselves they're still alive in the most basic way."

"That's not what's happening here."

He shook his head, even as he tightened his grip. "This is madness."

She slid her arms around his neck. "Of course it's madness. You're a Davies. I'm a Montgomery. The world will probably implode if we keep going. I *don't care*. I want you to kiss me. Now."

For a moment his dark gaze glittered down at her, and she knew a moment's panic that he would refuse. And then he kissed her.

Heat and darkness enveloped her. Spirals of excitement corkscrewed through her body. He staggered back and sat heavily in the wing chair, tugging her down with him, and she straddled him, bending her knees, settling on his lap in a billow of scarlet skirts.

His hands began a devastating exploration. He shaped her ribs, then cupped her bottom again and she groaned deep into his mouth in encouragement.

Yes!

He hooked his fingers into the top edge of her bodice and pushed it down, baring her breasts to his hungry gaze. She gasped, but didn't have time to feel embarrassed before his mouth descended to her skin.

Sweet heaven!

"Madness," he repeated thickly.

He palmed one breast and caught the nipple of the other in his mouth, and Maddie almost swooned at the wet rasp of his tongue against the stiffened peak. She lifted herself up on her knees, lost to sensation, arching her back to give him even better access.

"More."

"So demanding," he chuckled.

The pad of his thumb flicked over her crest and she let out a low groan. There seemed to be an invisible line from her breasts to between her legs; every flick produced a corresponding throb of need. She clutched at his head, scarcely able to catch her breath as he showered kisses over her, squeezing and fondling until she thought she might die of pleasure.

When he finally reclaimed her mouth she was almost glad of the reprieve, but he had even worse torments in store. His hands stroked down to her ankles and slid under her skirts. She shivered in delight as he reversed the motion, fingers gliding up over her stockinged calves and higher, to the ribbons of her garter.

The jolt of skin on skin as he slipped beneath the silk of her chemise was like a tiny bolt of lightning. The thrill of his work-roughened palms smoothing the back of her thighs made her pant.

She wasn't wearing drawers, and she whimpered with a combination of nervousness and desire as he cupped her bare bottom, gently squeezing the soft mounds in a wicked counterpoint to the slide of his tongue in her mouth. She pushed her hips forward, following her instincts, grinding against him with abandon. She could feel the hard length of him pushing against her belly, through her skirts.

He let out a tortured groan. At least she affected him too.

His fingers curved around her inner thighs, stroking upward, and Maddie held her breath, desperate to feel him there, where she ached and throbbed. She needed . . . *something*, with a desperation that made her want to scream.

"HALOOOO!"

A door banged and an earsplitting shout echoed down the hallway, quavering with the singsong cadence of someone deep in his cups. "Gryff, you lazy dog, where are you?"

Gryff froze, his hand so agonizingly close to where she'd wanted him to be that Maddie almost screamed in frustration.

And then he moved faster than she'd ever thought possible. He plucked his hands from beneath her skirts, caught her by the waist, and practically threw her off him like a sack of coal. She toppled back into her own armchair just as he shot to his feet and sent her a look that could have stopped a charging bull in its tracks.

"Rhys," he whispered hoarsely.

Maddie's stomach plummeted in dismay. Gryff's brother? What on earth was he doing here? He was supposed to be in London.

"Surpriiiise!" A second voice reverberated through the library door. Whoever it was sounded equally inebriated. There was a crash as someone walked into one of the suits of armor. "We're hooome! Blast it all, where *is* everybody? Beddow? Nanny Maude? It's not even nine o'clock. They can't all be asleep, surely?"

Gryff's eyebrows lifted in almost comical shock. "*Morgan?*"

Some boisterous singing began, a rude mariner's song to do with cockles and Sally in the alley. Pounding footsteps came ever closer, and Maddie shot Gryff a horrified glance.

She tugged up her bodice and leapt to her feet, smoothing her hair with frantic movements. She must look an absolute fright; her lips felt swollen from kissing, and her body was a pulsing jangle of nerves. Anyone with eyes would instantly know what they'd been doing.

What they'd been about to do.

Embarrassed heat flushed her face. Dear God. She'd been

seconds away from letting Gryff Davies make love to her in an *armchair*!

Gryff was already striding for the door, raking his hair to put it in some semblance of order. He shot her a stern, almost desperate look over his shoulder.

"Stay here. I'll get rid of them."

Without another backward glance he slipped out into the hall, closing the door firmly behind him.

Maddie listened, her heart pounding, as his brothers greeted him.

"Ah there you are!" Rhys bellowed. "Look who I've found, back from the seas! Hope we weren't interrupting anything?"

Gryff's response was inaudible. Maddie prayed he would remember the table set for two in the study and steer his brothers away from that telling little tableau. Drunk or not, they'd immediately realize they'd interrupted a dinner *à deux* and demand to know where he'd hidden the lucky wench of the evening.

Maddie slumped back in her chair, every emotion she'd ever felt swirling around inside her. She felt energized and wrung out at the same time. An incredulous snort escaped her, and she slapped her hand over her mouth to stifle the sound.

What *horrible* timing! Gryff's brothers couldn't have chosen a worse moment to interrupt. What would have happened if they'd arrived ten minutes later? Would Gryff have made love to her in that armchair? Would he have debauched her on the floor, or taken her upstairs to his bedchamber?

Or would he have come to his senses and pulled away?

Maddie let out a slow, shaky exhale. She'd been *so close* to finding out.

She glanced over at the closed door. Maybe she should be glad? Maybe fate had meant to intervene—and since she could hardly be struck by a blast of lightning indoors, the powers that be had sent the next best thing: two boisterous, drunken brothers to interrupt an event that might have had cataclysmic consequences.

Still, her heart gave a little thud of frustration.

She couldn't stay here. Despite what Gryff had said, he wouldn't be able to escape from his brothers for a good long while, and she needed to get home.

Perhaps the cool evening air would bring her to her senses.

She stood, cursing the fact that she'd left her shawl in the study. Gryff's half of the dictionary still lay on the desk and she stared down at it for a long moment. A long scratch marred the front cover and she ran her finger along it, filled with indecision.

Just take it.

It would be so easy. Gryff would realize she'd stolen it, of course, but she had the feeling he wouldn't accuse her publicly of theft. Still, however desperately she wanted to ease her family's money troubles, her conscience wouldn't let her do it. She'd wagered and lost; she needed to accept the consequences with honor.

With one last, regretful glance at the book, she crossed to the window and opened the sash. The casement looked out onto some sort of formal garden; she straddled the sill and climbed out, then walked briskly around the side of the building until she came to the quadrangle that housed the stable block.

The stablemaster who'd greeted them was busy in the stalls, settling two handsome horses that must belong to Gryff's brothers. He exhibited slight surprise at seeing her suddenly appear.

"Evening, my lady. Can I help you?"

"Yes, please. Could you saddle up my mount and escort me back to Newstead Park? Lord Powys is busy welcoming his brothers."

The man nodded respectfully. "Of course, ma'am. Beggin'

pardon, but that dress might be little . . . chilly for ridin'. There's some coats on that peg you might use."

Maddie flushed and accepted the offer. She chose a heavy, caped greatcoat from the hooks on the wall, and the scent of it immediately told her it was Gryff's. She buried her nose in the folds with a little quiver of triumph. He'd stolen her shawl. It was only fair that she should steal his coat.

She waited impatiently for the stablemaster to finish his preparations, half expecting Gryff to stride out of the back door and order her back inside, but there was no sign of him. A few minutes later they were clattering out of the yard and she let out a sigh that released the tension she'd been holding.

What an extraordinary evening.

How on earth was she expected to act when she next saw Gryff? Would he attend Squire Digby's dance tomorrow? Would he consider what they'd done a horrible mistake? Should she pretend that nothing had happened at all?

Maddie shook her head. She didn't have any of those answers.

Chapter 27

Gryff rolled over and groaned into his pillow as the shrill cry of a peacock roused him from sleep. His head was pounding, and he cursed his brothers' inhuman talent for consuming spirits. Rhys and Morgan had always been able to drink him under the table.

When he'd first seen the two of them in the hallway his brain had been so muddled by the intoxicating things he'd been doing with Maddie that he'd simply stared at them in shock, scarcely able to believe that they were standing right in front of him.

He'd seen Rhys only last week in London—laughing when Sommerville accidentally put a bullet in him—but the younger of the two, black-haired Morgan, had been away at sea for the better part of two years.

Gryff had gaped at him, cataloging his tanned skin and the addition of a few more lines around his eyes. He was still the same good-looking scamp who'd had the women sighing over him since he was barely old enough to walk, but there was a new maturity in his gaze, a hint of worldly cynicism in his smile.

He'd been about to drag the two of them into the study—far away from Maddie in the library—when he'd remembered the table set for two. He definitely wasn't prepared to explain *that*, so he'd steered them into the formal parlor instead. Luckily they'd both been too tipsy to notice.

Beddow had materialized with a tray of brandies, and the three of them had celebrated Morgan's safe return into the early hours. They'd finally staggered up to bed somewhere near two.

Gryff had managed to return to the library, briefly, while Nanny Maude tearfully welcomed Morgan home, only to find that Maddie had gone. One of the footmen said she'd ordered Huw the stablemaster to escort her home.

He threw his forearm across his eyes to shut out the shaft of light stabbing through the curtains. *Bloody hell*. He'd rushed out into the hall as if all the hounds of hell were after him. Had Maddie taken offense? Surely she'd recognize that he'd been trying to protect her reputation, not escape.

A wave of guilt and frustration flashed through him. He should have been the one to see her safely home. He hadn't even had the chance to say goodbye.

If Rhys and Morgan hadn't barged in, maybe she wouldn't have said goodbye at all.

His chest tightened at the thought. Would he even now be waking up with her naked and rosy in his bed? His cock throbbed in enthusiastic approval. God, he'd never be able to look at that damn wing chair again without seeing an image of her, lips pink and swollen from his kisses, perfect breasts exposed for his mouth. The scent of her still coiled in his head.

What had he been thinking? He'd only started that word game as a light flirtation. And the winning kiss was meant to be a silly tease. But the moment he'd taken her lips his brain had ceased to function. She'd kissed him back so sweetly, so ardently, that he'd been powerless to stop. And when she'd demanded more, he'd been unable to deny her.

Gryff ground his teeth. How far would she have let him go? He'd been seconds away from sliding his fingers into the honey-eyed wetness he knew he'd find between her legs. It would have been the work of a moment to tease her to a climax. And then he would have undone his breeches, positioned her over his throbbing cock, and shown her the meaning of another word Johnson had undoubtedly left out of his precious diction-ary: *fucking*.

Madness.

She couldn't have meant for things to go that far. Her choked cries of surprise when he'd touched her suggested a woman of limited experience. She probably thought lovemaking only happened in a bed, with the candles out. She'd have been shocked to the core if he'd taken her in an armchair in his li-brary.

Or maybe she'd have loved it.

Gryff pressed his face into his pillow. *No.* Making love to Madeline Montgomery would have been a monumental mistake. She was probably a virgin, saving herself for the man she would eventually marry.

He was definitely *not* that man, however much attraction blazed between them. Even ignoring the fact that their fami-lies had been sworn enemies for hundreds of years, and that her father would probably geld him if Gryff so much as hinted that he lusted after his daughter, he wasn't remotely ready to settle down. He'd only just become the earl, for God's sake. He'd been popular with women before, but now—with the title—he'd have his pick of the most beautiful and talented partners in London.

Unfortunately, his body didn't seem to understand that per-tinent fact. His stupid body wanted Madeline Montgomery with a painful desperation. The practiced accomplishments of other women didn't appeal half as much as the aggravation he experienced every time he was in her presence.

He'd hoped intoxication would help him sleep soundly, but she'd even invaded his dreams. He'd conjured all manner of sinful scenarios, most of them involving the two of them and very few articles of clothing.

He needed to clear his head.

Thirty minutes later, freshly shaved and dressed, he strode around the side of the house and headed toward the infamous Davies menagerie. The motley collection of animals had been started by some quixotic Davies in the sixteen hundreds, and had grown with each subsequent generation to the small zoo it was today.

A few of the animals, like the peacocks and the incongruous flamingos, roamed freely around the grounds, but most were contained in their own vast, open-air enclosures. Gryff's father had had a soft spot for rescuing animals, especially those who had been forced to work in circuses and street shows, and Carys had inherited the same softhearted approach. The place was now a rogues' gallery of animal misfits from almost every continent, including a spotted African cat with only three legs, a trio of mischievous otters, and a sloth named Hugo, who moved slower than treacle but always looked like he was smiling.

Gryff paused next to the large cage that housed his sister's favorite animal of all: an ex-dancing bear, whom Carys had christened Buttercup.

She'd seen the poor creature a decade ago on a London side street, a tiny cub chained and forced to dance on its hind legs to the tinny sound of his owner's hand organ. When Carys had seen the man whip the little bear, she'd lost her infamous temper. Despite being only eight years old, she'd grabbed the whip from the man's hand and started hitting *him* with it. Only the presence of all three of her brothers had been enough to prevent a riot.

Gryff had grabbed her to stop her assaulting the man further. Rhys had given him ten pounds for the bear—and to keep his mouth shut—and Morgan had taken the beast's chain and coaxed it to follow them home to the house on Grosvenor Square. Buttercup had been with them ever since.

Despite the vendor's claim that the bear hailed from Russia, subsequent research had shown that it was, in fact, a spectacled bear from Peru. And much to Carys' disappointment, Buttercup was male.

Carys had lavished years of love on the animal, and her patience had been rewarded with absolute, undying affection. Buttercup was now too used to humans to ever be released back into the wild, but he enjoyed a large and luxurious enclosure at Trellech and the love of everyone there.

Since the animal still liked music, Gryff picked up the hand organ left near the door of his cage and turned the handle. The cheerful, tinkling noise brought the bear lumbering up to greet him, and Gryff patted the beast on the head and scratched it behind the ears.

"Morning, Buttercup."

"Morning to you too, sweetheart."

Gryff turned to see a laughing Morgan and Rhys, both of them looking disgustingly healthy in the morning light. Morgan's teeth flashed white against his tanned skin.

An earsplitting squawk from one of the peacocks, balanced on the ramparts, interrupted his reply. All three of them glared up at the bird with loathing.

"Geoffrey!" Morgan growled. "I certainly didn't miss *him* while I was away. *I hoped you'd be dead by now!*" he shouted up at the bird. "Did you hear him, screaming the place down at some ungodly hour this morning? We should bake him in a pie."

Gryff smiled. "I'm afraid we have more pressing matters to deal with. You'll be happy to hear that the two of you have arrived just in time to be useful."

"We have?"

"You have."

Morgan frowned. "I've spent the last two years making my-self useful to His Majesty's Royal Navy. I was rather hoping to do absolutely nothing for several weeks."

"It's dangerous. And probably involves fighting."

"Oh, well in that case, count me in."

Rhys nodded eagerly. "Me too. London was so dull. Not a bit of excitement since Sommerville shot you. I nearly died of boredom. What's afoot?"

As succinctly as he could, Gryff told them about the events leading up to the attack in the woods. He didn't mention Mad-die's presence in the caves or at the doctor's house, but did say that she'd been at the clearing, entirely coincidentally, when he'd been set upon by the two men. He indicated that she'd rid-den straight home after the attack.

"I sent two footmen to the clearing with a cart, with orders to collect the bodies, but they said there was only one—the man I'd shot in the chest. The first man must have only been insensible, and escaped after I left."

"You were clearly the target," Rhys frowned. "Are you cer-tain the smugglers didn't see you that night at the beach?"

"Completely certain."

"And you don't think this Brookes would have said any-thing to the doctor about it?"

"Not unless he became delirious and blurted it out."

"That only leaves one solution, then," Morgan said. "The justice, Drake, must be in league with the smugglers. You told him you'd be able to identify them, and he must have told *them* to put an end to you."

Gryff nodded grimly. "That's what I think. They must have been lying in wait for me, and followed me to the well. I bet they hoped to finish me off there and hide my body in the woods."

"Bloody hell," Rhys said.

"I know it sounds far-fetched, but what other explanation is there?"

Rhys shrugged.

"So what do you want to do?" Morgan asked. "Confront Sir Mostyn? Accuse him?"

"We can't. We don't have any hard evidence that he's involved. I want to set up an ambush, catch the smugglers, and make them confess. Hopefully one of them will implicate him." Gryff pulled a letter from his pocket. "I wrote to Brookes's superior officer myself, asking for help. He says he'll come with four extra men to capture the smugglers on Sunday night, when they plan to move their cargo."

Rhys wrinkled his nose. "That's not many men."

"He can't spare any more at such short notice. Only three smugglers beat Brookes, but I expect at least triple that number to move those barrels from the cave."

"So we'll be outnumbered? And up against a bunch of desperate cutthroats?" Rhys grinned suddenly. "Sounds like my kind of adventure."

"Mine too. But that's not until tomorrow." Morgan said. "What shall we do tonight? I've a mind to go into Trellech and find those two charming barmaids at the Red Dragon. Are they still there? Bess and Tess?"

"They are indeed. But you're not going," Gryff said.

"Why not?"

"You're coming with me to Squire Digby's dance."

Rhys and Morgan groaned in unison. "What? No! Digby never has any good wine!"

"And the gaming will be limited to a shilling a bet."

"And all the women will be *respectable*."

"Drake will be there," Gryff said, unmoved. "We might get him to say something incriminating."

Neither brother looked impressed. Gryff sent Morgan a sly, sideways smile. "There will be Montgomerys to tease."

Rhys brightened. "Montgomerys? Which ones? Please say Tristan's back from the Continent. He's always so much fun to annoy. It's a shame Carys isn't here. She's wonderful at it."

"I'm afraid not. But the baron still dislikes anything that resembles a Davies, and he's been spoiling for a fight ever since Father passed away." Gryff chuckled, remembering Maddie's anger at the mention of a canal crossing the valley. "Tell him I'm thinking of digging that canal Father mapped out."

Morgan squinted into the sunlight. "I don't suppose that ridiculous cousin is staying with them? What's her name? Hattie? Horry?"

Gryff and Rhys sent him identical amused looks at his pathetic attempt to pretend that he'd forgotten. Morgan had been obsessed with Harriet Montgomery ever since they were children—almost as obsessed as Gryff had been with Maddie.

"Harriet," Rhys said drily. "I believe her name is Harriet."

"And yes, she'll be there too," Gryff added.

"Fine. I'll go," Morgan said grumpily. "When do we leave?"

Chapter 28

Harriet had been waiting up for Maddie's return, but she curbed her questions until they were safely ensconced in Maddie's bedroom. She gasped when Maddie threw off her borrowed greatcoat to reveal the scandalous red dress.

"Where did you get that? What happened to your riding habit?"

Maddie gave her an abridged version of her adventures. Harry sat back on her heels on the bed, her mouth open in amazement. "Ambushed, shot, and then taken back to Trellech Court for dinner?"

"I honestly don't know which was the most traumatic," Maddie joked weakly. "Being shot, or realizing Gryffud Davies wasn't the one to do it."

"And then *both* of his brothers arrived? You're certain it was both? Did you see them?"

"Well, no, I didn't actually see them myself, but Gryff recognized their voices. He said it was Rhys and Morgan."

Harriet's skin turned pink, and then white. "Do you think they'll attend the squire's dance tomorrow?"

Maddie shrugged, then winced as the bandage scraped against her wound. "I have no idea. It would be as good a place as any to announce their return to the neighborhood."

"I can't believe you finally got to see inside the castle! Think of all the times we spied on them. What was it like?"

Maddie furnished her with the details and confirmed that she'd seen the Davies half of the dictionary with her own eyes. "It's definitely the right one."

"But he rejected your offer to buy it?"

"Yes. Although there might be a chance of further negotiation."

Maddie fought the telltale blush that rose to her cheeks. *Further negotiation?* She wasn't certain she'd survive any further negotiation. She'd expire of heatstroke.

After Harriet had left, Maddie undressed and got into bed. She was physically exhausted, but her mind couldn't settle. She kept recalling the insanely pleasurable sensations Gryff had coaxed from her body.

She lay awake for a long time.

Her father returned from Bristol late the following morning, looking rather disheartened. Maddie cornered him in the study, and to her great relief he informed her that he hadn't taken out a loan from one of the notorious moneylenders.

"They're nothing but scoundrels and thieves," he groused. "Do you know the interest they charge? Ten percent! Ten! That's double the legal amount!"

He sank into his chair with a sigh and rubbed his forehead. "And I've heard enough tales of the unpleasant ways they ensure their payments are met to be wary. No, Maddie, I was not tempted to take their money, no matter how desperate we may be." He sent her a wan smile. "I'll have another word with our more pressing creditors. It's not that we won't have the money *in time*. It's just that most of my investments take longer to make a return. The consols—government-backed

securities—pay out at three percent, but they aren't easy to
cash in. I won't have the money for a year."

Maddie bent and kissed the top of his frizzy head. "We'll
think of something. Even if I can't stomach marrying Sir
Mostyn, I promise to seriously consider all the other single
gentlemen of our acquaintance."

Father patted her hand. "Thank you. And you can start this
very night, at Squire Digby's. I'm selling him that matched set
of bays I bought at Tattersalls last year, so we have to go."

Maddie dressed for the evening with unusual care. She'd
hidden the red dress at the back of her wardrobe and chosen
another gown that was slightly more demure, but nevertheless
very flattering. The sage-green sarcenet had a pretty ruched
bodice, and matching embroidery along the bottom hem. It
complemented the reddish highlights in her hair.

She was a bundle of nerves at the thought of seeing Gryff
again as they bounced along in the carriage. The Aunts were
both in high spirits at the prospect of company, but Harriet
seemed to be in an equal state of agitation as herself. Maddie
was sure it was the possibility of encountering Morgan Davies
that had her so on edge.

They'd barely entered the crowded ballroom when Maddie's
father stiffened at her side.

"Good God. Do my eyes deceive me? Is that all *three* of
those dreadful Davies boys? The youngest back from the
tropics?"

"I believe so, Father."

"Harrumph. One Davies is bad enough. Two is a pestilence.
Three in the same county ought to be classified as a plague."

Aunt Connie rolled her eyes behind his back. "Oh, go
have a drink, William. And find Sir Arthur. I hear he's looking for a partner at whist."

It was the perfect diversion. Father grumbled but stomped
off in the direction of the cardroom.

Aunt Connie caught Maddie's eye and smiled devilishly. "I know. Crisis averted. It was masterfully done."

Maddie laughed at her complete lack of modesty.

Harriet, who had been exerting a tight grip on Maddie's arm, leaned in. "I need some air. I'm going out on the terrace."

Maddie's arch look accused her of running away, but Harriet just shrugged and muttered, "Discretion is the better part of valor," then melted into the crowd.

Aunt Connie cast her eye across the room and fanned herself vigorously. "All three Davies boys, eh? Do you know, I'd quite forgotten the impact of them all together. They *are* a handsome bunch of devils, aren't they?"

"They're the enemy," Aunt Prudence hissed.

"Pffft. Nothing wrong with admitting they're easy on the eye."

"It was ever thus," Prudence muttered. "Davieses on one side of the ballroom, Montgomerys on the other. Separated by an unbridgeable divide."

Aunt Connie cackled behind her fan. "Oh, it's been *bridged*, Prudence. Any number of times. Why, I myself once spent a very pleasant half hour bridging it in Sir Thomas Tresham's yew maze with a distant Davies cousin."

Aunt Prudence gasped.

"We pointed out each other's numerous failings. Among other things." Connie wiggled her eyebrows, and there was no missing the wicked twinkle in her eye. "In the end, I was forced to admit that even Davies men aren't bad at *everything*."

The Aunts soon drifted off to talk to their friends, and Maddie turned to find Doctor Williams at her side.

"Good evening, Doctor! How is Mister Brookes?"

"Healing nicely, I'm happy to report. I left him reading by the fire."

The doctor shot an unsubtle glance across the ballroom at Gryff and his brothers and Maddie followed his gaze, suppressing the urge to let out a tiny appreciative sigh.

Aunt Connie was right. They really were an abnormally good-looking family. All three of them had been blessed with dark hair and handsome features. The family resemblance was striking, but each had his own subtle differences, like the same piece of music played on three different instruments. Only their sister Carys had broken the mold and inherited the flaming-red hair of some earlier generation.

"I see Powys is here tonight." The doctor slowly closed one eye, and Maddie realized with astonishment that the old man was *winking* at her. "Fear not, Miss Montgomery. Your secret's safe with me."

Maddie didn't know whether to laugh or be completely horrified. The doctor, it seemed, was enchanted by the idea that she and Gryff were young lovers, separated by the cruel hand of fate.

"It's just like Shakespeare's Romeo and Juliet," he sighed. "*Two households, both alike in dignity, In fair Verona, where we lay our scene, From ancient grudge break to new mutiny, Where civil blood makes civil hands unclean.* If there's anything I can do to help the two of you, Miss Montgomery, please do not hesitate to ask. Perhaps I could tell your father about Powys's heroic rescue of Brookes?"

"Oh, no, please don't," Maddie said quickly, grabbing his arm. "Don't say anything. Father gets extremely irritated whenever a Davies is mentioned."

The doctor sighed and nodded. "That is true. But holding such a lengthy grudge isn't good for the digestion. It's a wonder he's not more choleric. Ah! I see your aunt Prudence is beckoning me over. Handsome woman, your aunt."

Maddie bit back a laugh as the doctor unconsciously

tugged down the points of his waistcoat and straightened his cravat.

"Excuse me, Miss Montgomery."

She shook her head in bemusement. The doctor and her aunt? It wouldn't be the worst match in the world . . .

Chapter 29

Gryff shook hands with his host, the jovial, rotund Squire Digby. "I hope you don't mind us turning up without an invitation, sir?"

The squire let out a booming laugh. "Nonsense, Powys. You're always welcome, just as your father was. We don't stand upon ceremony here. And welcome home, Morgan. Back from your adventures overseas? I bet you've some tales to tell."

"I do indeed, sir—including how I was imprisoned on the island of Mauritius thanks to a misprint on a map."

Gryff, Rhys, and the Squire all lifted their brows.

"You didn't tell us about *that* last night," Gryff muttered.

Morgan shot them a lazy grin. "It's too long a tale to get into now. But I'll tell you about it soon, I promise." His eyes raked the assembled crowd. "For now, however, I'm going to ask one of these lovely young ladies to dance. I've been without female company for far too long."

The squire chuckled indulgently. "Please do. I've had a whole host of 'em clamoring for an introduction, you lucky scamp."

Morgan's expression turned wicked. "I thought maybe one of the Montgomery girls?"

"If you're trying to ruffle their father's feathers, you're out of luck," Gryff said. "He's already in the cardroom."

"I'm sure word will get back to him if I dance with his niece."

"What, Harriet? Haven't seen her," Squire Digby muttered, scanning the dancers. "Think she went outside."

Morgan shrugged easily. "His daughter, then." He sent an admiring glance over at Maddie, who was talking to Doctor Williams.

"If anyone's dancing with Madeline, it'll be me," Gryff said, and then could have bitten his tongue as the three of them swiveled toward him in surprise. He cleared his throat. "I mean, I *am* the senior Davies. It'll annoy her father even more if she dances with the Earl of Powys."

Rhys shot him a knowing smile but forbore to comment.

"I suppose you've heard the rumors?" Squire Digby murmured. "Half the county's expecting her to accept Sir Mostyn."

Every muscle in Gryff's body tensed in instinctive recoil. "What?"

The squire nodded, a disapproving frown forming between his eyebrows. "He's been after a replacement ever since his wife died. Seems he's fixed his sights on Miss Montgomery. He's made his preference very clear these past few months."

"But he's old enough to be her father. Surely he can't think that she'll accept him?"

The squire shrugged. "Who knows? It wouldn't be the first match between a young woman and an older man."

Gryff frowned. "Is he here?"

"Drake? Yes, over by the door."

Gryff schooled his featured into an uninterested expression as he sought out the justice of the peace. The man was close to sixty, slim as a reed, with sallow skin and a smile that

never quite reached his eyes. He'd been brusque and coldly unimpressed when Gryff had reported the smuggling cache to
him the previous day.

Surely the squire was mistaken? Maddie couldn't possibly
be considering a marriage to *that*.

It was easy enough to see why Drake would be tempted, of
course. Maddie wasn't just gorgeous to look at, she was witty
and clever as well. What man *wouldn't* want such a woman
in his life?

In his bed.

The very thought of Maddie and Drake together in that way
was enough to turn Gryff's stomach. He suppressed a shudder and took a long swig of brandy from his glass.

Such a rumor made no sense. Maddie was both beautiful
and intelligent. If she *was* on the hunt for a husband—and she'd
made no indication that she was—then surely she could do
better than Sir Mostyn? She might be a little overeducated for
some, but there were plenty who'd overlook that "fault" to get
their hands on that glorious figure of hers.

The only reason bright young things married crusty old
crows like Drake was for money or power. What did Sir
Mostyn have that Maddie—or her father—wanted? Land?
Connections? It couldn't be social position; the Montgomerys
were already higher up the aristocratic food chain.

Was it money? Maddie hadn't said anything to suggest that
her family was in trouble financially, but a Davies would be
the *last* person she'd confide in.

Still, the idea that she might actually consider marrying
for money was as ludicrous as it was distasteful. She had one
of the strongest moral compasses of any woman he'd encountered. Just look at how she'd resisted the temptation to steal
that damn half of the dictionary from him when she'd had the
chance. He'd left it right there on the table in the library. She
could have swiped it if she'd wanted to.

Gryff took another long sip of his drink, ignoring the flow of masculine conversation around him.

Maddie shouldn't be going anywhere near Drake. If the man was responsible for yesterday's attack, then he obviously wasn't above sanctioning murder to keep his involvement in the smuggling operation quiet. And while those men couldn't have known that Maddie would be in the clearing too, she could have been killed in the crossfire, or even executed, as a witness to the crime.

A wave of anger heated his blood at the thought of her being hurt, closely followed by a blood-chilling realization. Maddie might not have recognized the attacker by the well as one of the smugglers who'd hurt Brookes. She'd have no reason to suspect that Drake was involved or know he wasn't to be trusted. What if she told him she'd also seen the smugglers? Gryff doubted the man's lust would be greater than his need to silence her.

Drake was staring intently at something across the room, his expression both possessive and calculating. Gryff followed his gaze, and his heart began to pound as he realized he was watching Maddie. She was laughing at something, unaware of Drake's scrutiny.

As Gryff watched, she took her leave of her companion and headed toward the open doors that led out on to the terrace.

Drake peeled away from the wall and started after her.

Gryff tossed back the remainder of his brandy, muttered an excuse to his brothers, and strode after them.

Chapter 30

The terrace was deserted when Maddie slipped outside in search of Harriet. The evening had grown cool; the other guests had retreated inside to take part in the dancing, but she rubbed her gloved hands over her bare arms and started forward.

"Harry? Are you out here?" she whispered.

A shallow set of steps descended to a lower parterre and she hastened down them, searching the shadows for a secluded bench where Harriet might have taken refuge from the crowd.

A series of neatly tended paths led off into the gardens, and the gravel crunched underfoot as she started toward a small copse of trees and a half-hidden rose arch. The gravel bit painfully through the thin soles of her satin dancing slippers.

The sound of a lively reel and the clapping of the assembly increased as someone else opened the French doors, but Maddie paid no attention. The light spilling from the house was enough for her to see that Harriet wasn't behind the rose arch or in the arbor, and she doubted her cousin would have ventured farther into the unlit section of the gardens on her own. She must have slipped back into the house.

With a sigh of defeat Maddie turned, then reared back in alarm as a dark, thin figure stepped into her path.

"Good heavens, Sir Mostyn!" She clapped her hand over her rapidly beating heart, even as her spirits sank. Of all the people at tonight's dance, Sir Mostyn was the last person she'd have chosen to meet in the moonlight.

Since his back was to the house she could barely make out his features, and as usual he was dressed in unrelenting black, a specter at the feast. Maddie squinted against the light, uncomfortably aware that her own features were doubtless illuminated well enough for him to leer over the snug fit of her bodice.

Sir Mostyn bowed stiffly, and she caught a nauseating whiff of the waxy, floral pomade he used on his hair.

"Good evening, my dear. I was hoping to catch you alone."

She subdued an instinctive grimace.

"I assume your father told you about my offer?"

"He has, sir. I must decline."

Drake stilled, as if the answer had caught him off guard. "Decline?" he said finally, and Maddie's stomach plummeted as she heard the distinct rumble of amusement in his tone. "My dear girl, you can't decline."

Maddie crossed her arms over her chest. "I most certainly can. And I do. I'm not interested in marrying anyone at present, and I do not think wc would suit. Good evening, sir."

She took a step to her left and tried to walk past him but he sidestepped, blocking her escape.

"The choice isn't yours to make, I'm afraid." He didn't sound remotely apologetic, and Maddie cursed inwardly. His unctuous confidence was stomach-churning.

"I have friends in London," he said softly. "In banking. They tell me your father's up to his ears in debt. You can't *afford* to refuse me, my dear."

Maddie stilled. *Oh, hell and damnation.*

He turned, and the light from the house spilled across his sharp features. His gaze roamed over her body like a fly deciding where to land on a freshly baked pie. He licked his bloodless lips, and Maddie quelled a surge of nausea.

When Gryff looked at her like that, she wanted to burn up in flames. Sir Mostyn's ogling made her feel like she needed to bathe.

She opened her mouth, but before she could say anything he caught her arm in a painful grip, just below her wound. She let out an involuntary yelp and tried to twist away, but his wiry strength was surprising.

"It matters not what you want, or don't want, Miss Montgomery," he hissed. "We will be wed, or I'll tell everyone from here to Grosvenor Square about your father's money troubles. He's hidden it well until now, but one word from me and his ruin will be common knowledge. His creditors will beat a path to your door. And when he can't pay, he'll be thrown into debtors' prison, and your disgrace will be complete. You don't want that, do you?"

Maddie's blood was pounding in her ears as fright and fury jostled for supremacy. "That's blackmail!" she panted. "How could you? Let go of me!"

She tried to twist away again, but his grip on her arm was unbreakable.

"Come, let's not argue." He leaned closer, and she came to the awful realization that he was intending to kiss her. She turned her face away, rearing back in disgust.

"I hope I'm not interrupting?"

Gryff's sarcastic tones floated out of the darkness and Maddie let out an audible gasp of relief. Sir Mostyn straightened with a muffled curse and dropped her arm.

Gryff's broad-shouldered silhouette disengaged from the shadows as Sir Mostyn's lips curled in the parody of a smile.

"Not at all, Lord Powys. Miss Montgomery and I were just having a little discussion."

He shot her a warning glance, daring her to dispute his claim, but retreated with a bow: a hyena backing away from a kill in deference to a more dangerous predator. "We can continue our conversation another time."

Maddie shuddered. She watched him stalk back to the house, then tuned to find Gryff looming beside her.

Her stomach flipped. *Dear God, how long had he been listening in the darkness?* Had he overheard what Sir Mostyn had said? Pride and humiliation burned two hot flags on her cheeks and she glanced up at him warily, braced for his scorn.

Tension crackled around him like before a summer lightning storm.

"What are you doing out here alone?"

Maddie stiffened at his scolding tone, even as her heart turned over in relief. If he'd heard Sir Mostyn's blackmail, it would have been the first thing out of his mouth. Which meant he didn't know of her imminent disgrace. *Thank God.*

"I was looking for Harriet."

"And found Drake. Unlucky."

His tone was dry, and she couldn't tell if he was amused at having found her in an embarrassing position, or angry at her for venturing into the gardens unchaperoned.

A spurt of irritation sparked to life within her. He might have arrived at the perfect time to save her from Sir Mostyn, but he wasn't her father to be bossing her about or scolding her.

"Or maybe you were looking for him too?" Gryff said silkily. "Squire Digby seems to think you're considering an engagement?"

Maddie bit the inside of her cheek. He'd heard the gossip, then. Damn.

Chapter 31

"It's true that Sir Mostyn has proposed," Maddie said carefully.

"You can't seriously be considering it."

Maddie frowned. If Gryff wasn't aware of her financial problems, then why would he think she'd accept a man like Sir Mostyn? Did he truly think her so lacking in prospects? His insultingly low opinion of her stung. She might not be the best catch on the marriage mart, but she certainly wasn't the *worst*.

"If I am, it's no concern of yours."

There was enough light that she could see him frown. His lips curled in disgust. "How could you marry a man like that? He's a repulsive old letch."

The sentiment was so close to her own feelings that it was hard to keep her countenance bland, but her pride kicked in and she lifted her nose in the air. "Who I choose is my own affair."

He made a derisive sound and stepped closer. "Will you let him kiss you? Will you let him put his hands on your skin?" His voice dropped to a low growl that brought goose bumps to her arms. "Will you let him touch you the way I touched you, Maddie?"

His gaze dropped to her mouth. Tension arced between them, but before she could answer, his expression turned feral.

"Will you let him bed you? Let him spend himself inside you, shuddering and slobbering?"

Her stomach rebelled against the vile image, and the look he gave her, as if he suddenly loathed her, cut her to the quick.

"If you do, then you're no better than the whores in Covent Garden, selling yourself for a handful of coins."

He ran a hand through his hair, fury evident in every line of his taut frame. "And at least those whores get some pleasure out of the transaction. What would *you* get, Maddie? Money for dresses, and hats? Finance for your archaeological digs? What?"

His scathing assessment had her close to tears, but she held herself tall. "I am under no obligation to explain myself to you."

He made a harsh sound. "I thought you had more self-respect. What about children? Will he give them to you? He already has three of his own, full grown. And you're, what? Twenty-two to his sixty. He's in his dotage and you're in your prime." He stared at her as if seeing her for the first time. "Do you think he'll make you a rich widow soon? Is that it?"

Maddie's heart squeezed in her chest. She'd thought they were friends; *he* thought she was a mercenary, heartless bitch. "You don't know anything about me or my motives," she managed shakily. "It's none of your affair."

"You can't mean to be faithful," he murmured, almost to himself. "Will you take a lover, like half the married women of the *ton*?" His tone was tinged with bitterness. "You'd better hope he's not a jealous husband. I've just faced one those on the dueling field. Damn unpleasant for everyone."

Maddie tossed her head, goaded into replying. "And what if I *do* take a lover? It would have to be someone like you. Someone who wants no commitment, no permanence, just a few nights' pleasure before he moves on."

She'd meant to wound and saw him flinch.

Good. He deserved it.

"Someone like *me*?" He stopped pacing and lowered his face to hers. The air vibrated between them, some terrible combination of frustration and desire, and Maddie had the fierce urge to hurt him as she was hurting. In the same breath she wanted him to take her in his arms and hold her tight.

Impossible. She had to make him leave before she broke down and confessed everything. Her father's debts, her own pathetic longings, *everything*.

Gryff's brows drew together. "Is that why you wanted me last night? As a *stud*? One last hurrah before you're locked away with an old man?"

It was her turn to flinch. He raked her body with a scathing glare that nevertheless managed to increase her pulse, then caught her elbow just above her glove in the same way Sir Mostyn had done.

"Are you pregnant? Looking for a father for your bastard? Is that it?"

Her patience snapped. How could he think such things of her? She'd thought he understood her. *Respected* her. Instead, he was accusing her of being a cold-blooded fortune hunter.

"What if I said yes?" she hissed. "What would you do? Offer for me instead?"

His silence was damning.

She managed a creditable sneer of her own, even as her innermost dreams crumbled into dust. "Your face says it all, Lord Powys. But don't worry. I'm not with child. Both you and Sir Mostyn are safe from my nefarious clutches."

He sent her a look of mystified fury. "Then why? Does he have some hold over you? Are you being forced?"

The sudden switch from anger to solicitude almost broke her. How could she answer that without betraying her father? Herself? The awful truth was, he was right. She *was* little better than a whore. Oh, she might not be selling herself to Sir Mostyn, but wasn't she mentally preparing to sell herself to *someone*, soon, in return for their fortune?

Her face flamed in mortification and at that moment she hated Gryff for forcing her to confront the stark array of options open to her.

He released her with a derisive shake of his head. "Well, I hate to be the one to spoil your plans, but I strongly suspect Sir Mostyn is a criminal."

"What?"

"That was no random attack in the woods. The man who came for me was one of the ones who beat Brookes. Who else but Drake could have sent him after me?"

Maddie's pulse pounded in her ears as she absorbed his words. Was it true? She'd barely caught a glimpse of the first rider before she'd been distracted by the second. And she'd been in too much pain from her wound to look at him when they'd returned to the well.

"But—"

"Drake's hand-in-glove with the smugglers, I'm sure of it," Gryff growled. "But I won't have proof until we catch them in the act. Until then, you need to stay as far away from him as possible. He can't know that you're a witness too."

Maddie caught his sleeve. "What are you going to do?"

"My brothers and I will set up an ambush at the caves tomorrow night. Brookes's superior officer is bringing men to help."

"I want to come. It's—"

"Absolutely not. It's too dangerous, and you'll just get in the way."

Maddie scowled up at him but didn't bother arguing. Gryff's set jaw and mulish expression were ample evidence that he wouldn't change his mind.

She smoothed her hands down the front of her skirts and sent him a polite nod, summoning every ounce of icy poise she possessed. "Very well. In that case, I'll wish you good luck. I can make my own way back to the ballroom."

To her immense relief, he moved aside to let her pass, and she forced herself not to run as she returned to the house.

The gaiety within was at odds with the bleak misery in her heart. She felt empty, burned out, like a tree that had been struck by lightning—hollow and charred inside.

She wasn't *dead*, though. And people didn't die of a broken heart, except in Harriet's gothic novels. She would survive this, just as she had survived everything else.

Chapter 32

The next day dragged by. The Aunts had accepted an invitation to tea with Doctor Williams, and her father was buried in his study beneath a mound of paperwork.

Maddie hated the thought of staying behind while the Davies men took part in the ambush, but she understood why she wouldn't be welcome. Gryff had probably set up countless traps like this in his time in the fusiliers. The last thing he'd want was some untried amateur getting in the way.

Still, the feeling of exclusion stung. She had just as much right to watch the smugglers get their comeuppance as he did. It wasn't fair that she should miss all the excitement.

In an attempt not to think about all the dreadful things she and Gryff had said the previous night, she picked up a copy of *Gulliver's Travels*, hoping the satirical work would satisfy her craving for adventure. But the unflattering parallels between the two warring factions in the tale and her own situation just depressed her. The rift between Swift's Big-Endians and Little-Endians, who were constantly at odds over the "right" way to chop the top off a boiled egg, seemed just as ridiculous as the petty squabbling between the Davieses and Montgomerys.

And yet she could see no end in sight.

"Oh, miss, there you are." Gwynn the housemaid hovered in the doorway, wringing her hands in a nervous, agitated way. "I've been looking for you all over."

Maddie frowned. The last time she'd seen the girl, she'd related her late-night run-in with Ned, and the two of them had had a good chuckle about it. But there was no amusement on Gwynn's face now.

"Whatever's wrong?"

"Oh, miss, I don't know who to tell. It's about your Sir Mostyn, you see."

"He's not *my* Sir Mostyn," Maddie corrected.

"No, miss, and I'm right glad of that. I never heard a good thing about him, and now I got proof that he's a bad'n."

Maddie put down her book. "What do you mean?"

"He's mixed up in some plot against the customs men, miss."

"How do you know this?"

"My Ned, from the Red Dragon. Some strangers were talkin' in the snug. He heard the name Drake, so 'e started to listen."

"What did they say?"

"One of the men said Drake had warned someone named Sadler that the customs boys were trying to catch them in the act. They all laughed and said how Sadler would 'ave a surprise of 'is own."

A wave of dread slid down Maddie's spine. "You mean the smugglers are *expecting* some kind of ambush?"

Gwynn nodded miserably. "Yes, miss. One of 'em mentioned Guy Fawkes."

Maddie pressed her fingers to her lips. Guy Fawkes had set barrels of gunpowder beneath the Houses of Parliament in London two centuries ago, in a failed attempt to kill King James. Did the smugglers plan a similar trick? Did they mean to lure Gryff and the customs men inside the cave, and then . . . blow them up?

She leapt to her feet. "Thank you for coming to me. I'll see that something is done." She squeezed Gwynn's arm in gratitude.

The maid bobbed a curtsy. "Thank you, miss. I don't want nobody to get hurt. Those smugglers are a blight. They give honest people a bad name, they do."

Maddie ran down the hall, her thoughts in turmoil. She had to warn Gryff that he was walking into a trap. But how? He'd probably already left Trellech Court, so sending a note there was out of the question. And he'd undoubtedly arranged to meet the customs men somewhere away from town for secrecy—it was unlikely she'd just stumble across them if she went galloping around the countryside.

Should she ride directly to the caves? She might find Gryff, but she could just as easily run into the smugglers. It was too risky.

The best option would be to go back through the tunnels, retracing the route she and Gryff had taken. If she arrived before the smugglers, she could wait until they set their trap and withdrew. Then she could either disable the gunpowder herself, or be in a position to warn Gryff when he and his men entered the cave.

But the thought of navigating the tunnels alone was very unappealing. Even following the chalk arrows, she could still lose her way or injure herself. It would be the height of foolishness to go alone.

She turned and pounded on Harriet's door. She hated the thought of putting her cousin in danger, but Harry was an excellent navigator and always kept a level head in a crisis.

"Harry, I need your help!"

Harriet listened with wide eyes as Maddie revealed the plan, but her answer was unequivocal. "Of course I'll come. Let's go."

They dressed quickly, in warm woolen skirts, jackets, and shawls, in case they had to wait for some time for the smugglers to arrive. Maddie packed her satchel with an array of potentially useful items, including extra candles and a tinderbox.

They saddled up Sir Galahad and a shy mare named Guinevere, rode swiftly to the clearing, and tied them to a tree near the Virtuous Well.

Harriet was as enthralled and delighted by the tunnel system as Maddie had been. They slid down the rocky embankment, and together they began following the chalk arrows. Harriet made a rudimentary map as they hurried along, noting the major distinctive features they passed.

It seemed to take less time to arrive at the tunnel's end than before. Maddie extinguished their lanterns and crept forward to peer through the hole, just in case a guard had been set in the cave, but after a few minutes of silent observation it became clear that nobody was there. Only the soft suck and slap of the outgoing tide sounded in the space.

"Where's all the contraband?" Harriet asked, poking her head through the opening next to Maddie and peering down into the cave.

Maddie pointed to the second cave, below them and to their left. The smugglers' stash was still there; the dark lumps of oilcloth-shrouded barrels could just be seen, stacked near the entrance.

"The tunnel's like this one—it leads back into the rock."

"We should stay up here," Harriet said softly. "It's unlikely anyone will look up this high and see us." She wrinkled her nose and squinted at some object across the cave. "What on earth is that?"

Maddie followed her gaze. A pale shape was lodged at the high-tide mark, just below the smugglers' cache. Her stomach plummeted in sudden recognition.

"It's my bonnet!" she gasped. "It blew off when I met Lord Powys at the bridge, and floated down the river."

"Well, it must have gone all the way to the sea and washed in here on the tide. Or maybe the river connects to these caves?"

Maddie groaned. "The smugglers will see it. What if they think someone's here, and start looking? We have to get rid of it. Stay here, I'll climb over and get it."

"Be quick, then."

Maddie clambered through the hole in the rock and balanced on the rocky ledge, just as she'd done with Gryff. Unlike the last time she'd been in the cave, the tide was still partially in; the floor was submerged beneath several feet of water. She'd have to clamber sideways, across the rocks, to reach the sodden hat if she didn't want to get wet.

Summoning her courage, she tucked the hem of her skirts up unto her waistband and made her way across the rocky expanse. Harriet called out helpful instructions from her perch, telling her where to put her hands or feet.

"There!" She snatched the mangled bonnet from the rocks and waved it triumphantly in the air, then hauled herself up into the mouth of the tunnel to catch her breath. She was about to start the return trip when Harriet hissed a warning and started gesticulating wildly toward the entrance.

"Someone's coming!"

Sure enough, the sound of deep masculine voices and splashing water was coming closer.

Maddie made a swift calculation of the distance between herself and Harriet.

"There's no time for me to climb back over there to you," she whispered. "I'll hide back here." She pointed into the cave behind her. "Hopefully it's Gryff and his men."

Harriet's pale face bobbed a nod in the darkness.

With a hurried swirl of skirts, Maddie groped her way to the very back of the smugglers' cache. The deeper she went into the cave the darker it got, and she cursed the fact that she couldn't light a candle for fear of exposing her position.

Thankfully, the tunnel extended much farther than she'd dared to hope: The barrels and contraband had been stacked in neat rows near the entrance. She squeezed past them and concealed herself behind a huge wall of stalagmites that rose from the floor like the teeth of some enormous beast.

Several men entered the cave. Flames flickered across the inner walls as lanterns were lit. She strained her ears, praying to hear Gryff's commanding tones.

"Right boys, get up there and start hauling barrels. I want this place empty by sundown."

Her blood froze. She recognized that voice, and it certainly didn't belong to Gryff. It was the man named Sadler, who'd ordered the murder of Brookes. She crouched lower, hardly daring to breathe as several men clambered up to the entrance of her cave and began ripping off the oilcloth coverings and passing the tubs of brandy down to their colleagues below. Their lanterns sent monstrous shadows, like hunchbacked giants, curving up the rock walls.

They were frighteningly efficient. In hardly any time at all the barrels had been removed, along with several huge wooden tea chests and bundles of other goods she couldn't identify. The plaintive braying of a donkey from outside indicated they were using at least one of the beasts to carry the barrels up the steep hillside.

Chapter 33

When the last man climbed down, taking his lantern with him, Maddie risked a peek around her rock. Sadler and a huddle of other men were standing near the cave entrance, but the odd acoustics of the space brought their conversation clearly to her ears.

"Can't believe that customs rat escaped," one of the men groused. He kicked at the rock set with the iron ring to which Brookes had been tied.

Sadler shrugged. "Don't matter. We'll finish off even more o' the bastards now."

A chorus of jeers and laughter accompanied this pronouncement.

Sadler slapped the man nearest to him on the shoulder. "We're too sharp for 'em, eh, lads? It's *them* who'll be gettin' the surprise! Davy, set the barrels. And Turner? Careful with that lantern. We don't want to start without the guests of honor, do we?"

Maddie ducked down as a slim man climbed back up toward her and placed two small barrels on either side of the tunnel mouth. He uncorked one and poured a mound of black powder onto the rocky floor, then ran a line of it right across the entrance. He propped the second barrel on its side with the open mouth nestled close to the heap.

"All set," he shouted down with a macabre cheerfulness. "One spark, and the 'ole lot'll blow."

He climbed down, and the smugglers filed out, leaving behind two lanterns—presumably to fool Gryff into thinking they were still inside.

Maddie waited until the sound of voices faded away, then slithered out from her hiding place.

Harriet's dry tones filtered down from above. "Now what?"

Maddie righted both barrels of gunpowder and considered her options. The water level had dropped since the men had first arrived; only a few inches remained. If she pushed the barrels over the edge, not only would the smugglers hear the crash if they were still close by, but the barrels might simply float, instead of fill with water.

If she tried to climb down with them, she'd probably drop them, or slip on the rocks. And she couldn't just tip the powder into the water; there were too many rocks in the way. She'd have to climb down, fill her brass tinderbox with water, then climb back up and pour the water into the—

A cacophony of shouts erupted outside. Maddie threw herself back into the shadows and pressed against the wall, scanning the sliver of beach visible through the cave entrance as curses and howls rang out from all sides. A succession of gunshots and the bright sound of metal on metal pierced the air.

Four of the smugglers raced into the cave, closely pursued by Gryff, Morgan, and a blue-coated man who must be one of the customs officers Gryff had contacted.

Maddie bit back a gasp as Gryff caught the nearest smuggler by his coat and wheeled him around, knocking him down with a single punch. The man sprawled against the rocks, almost upsetting one of the lanterns that had been left there.

Morgan tackled a second man around the waist and they both tumbled to the wet sand, fists flying as they rolled, each trying to gain the upper hand. Curses and grunts echoed around the chamber as they pummeled each other without mercy.

The two remaining smugglers backed up toward Maddie's hiding place as the customs man drew his sword. Gryff joined the slow advance.

"Put up your hands!" the officer shouted.

Both men ignored him. One pulled a pistol from his coat; the other produced a wicked-looking knife.

Gryff and the customs man both dived for cover. A shot rang out, and the customs man screamed in agony as the smuggler's bullet caught him in the thigh. The two men leapt forward to finish him off, but Gryff pounced on the knife-wielding man, catching his wrist and forcing his arm upward. He dealt him a punishing blow to his kidneys with his free hand.

The shooter grabbed Gryff around the waist from behind, trying to pull him off his friend. Gryff slammed his head back into the man's nose, breaking it with a sickening crunch, and kicked out at the man in front of him. The knife went clattering among the rocks as the man folded over and gasped for breath like a fish out of water.

The man holding Gryff released him with a foul curse and clapped his hands to his nose. Blood dripped between his fingers. Gryff caught him by the collar and dragged him, stumbling and swearing, back to the mouth of the cave. He propelled him outside with a swift kick to the backside.

Morgan was still wrestling with his man among the rock pools, but in one quick move he straddled his opponent and punched him across the jaw. The man slumped back on the sand, unconscious.

The wounded officer was clutching his thigh and groaning piteously. Gryff ran to him and knelt by his side to assess the wound. He unbuckled the man's belt and tightened it around his leg as a temporary tourniquet, so intent on his task that he failed to notice the winded man, who'd silently retrieved his knife.

The blade glinted evilly as he advanced, clearly intending to plunge it between Gryff's shoulder blades.

Maddie lurched forward. "Gryff!"

She kicked a barrel of gunpowder off the ledge. It bounced down the rocks, directly at the knifeman, who leapt out of its path with a surprised yell.

Gryff turned at the noise and swept his leg in a wide arc, knocking the attacker off his feet.

Morgan ran over to help, and within moments the two of them had subdued the man. Morgan marched him to the entrance, but Gryff's attention was firmly fixed on Maddie.

The look he sent her was so ferocious she almost turned around and scurried back into the cave to hide.

"What the *bloody hell*?" he rasped, his chest heaving with exertion.

Maddie sent him a placating smile, the kind she'd give a tiger as she backed out of its cage. "I can explain."

He strode forward, his expression thunderous, and she retreated automatically. Her heel hit the second barrel of gunpowder.

"You might try saying thank you," she said quickly, the words tumbling out as he started up the rock face toward her, clearly intent on shaking some sense into her. "I probably just saved your life. That man was about to stab you."

He pulled himself over the lip with just the strength of his arms and a strange mixture of alarm and excitement rippled through her. Perhaps it was the result of witnessing such a dramatic, violent fight, but she felt both shaky and . . . elated?

The sounds of battle outside had faded. Beyond Gryff's shoulder Morgan was helping the wounded officer, but when Gryff straightened to his full height all her attention snapped back to him.

Her stomach flipped as their eyes met. He looked wild. His pupils were huge, almost black in the semi-darkness, and his chest rose and fell in savage gusts as he caught his breath. The urge to throw herself into his arms was alarmingly strong, but she ignored it.

"Explain," he growled. "Because I distinctly recall telling you to stay away."

Maddie lifted her chin. "Well, it's a good thing I didn't listen, because those smugglers meant to blow you and your friends to kingdom come." She pointed to the barrel at her feet. "That's full of gunpowder."

Gryff glanced down. The line of powder snaked between them, a black demarcation in the sand like a challenge, a line that should not be crossed.

He raised his hands as if he meant to grab her shoulders and shake some sense into her. Maddie braced herself, but before he could touch her a pistol shot rang out. A chunk of rock exploded to her left, and Gryff thrust her backward into the wall, instinctively shielding her with his body.

"Bastards!"

The smuggler named Sadler raced toward them, his face a mask of fury. He caught up one of the lanterns and swung it high over his head with a howl of triumph.

"You'll get what's coming to you!"

The lantern flew through the air and smashed near Gryff's feet. A wall of flame leapt up as the oil ignited and Maddie staggered back, shielding her head with her arms. Gryff cursed. She dropped her hands to see that the loose powder had caught alight; Gryff was desperately trying to stamp out the fizzing ball of sparks. When that didn't work, he grabbed the remaining powder barrel and hurled it down toward Sadler.

"Go!" He shoved her backward, deeper into the cave. "Go!"

She went, blundering into the darkness with his big body right behind her. When she stumbled he wrapped his arm around her waist and lifted her off her feet, crushing her to his chest as if she weighed no more than a rag doll. He propelled them forward in a confused blur of motion.

A blinding flash illuminated the rocks in front of her, followed by the loudest noise she'd ever heard, a roar that made her eardrums vibrate and her internal organs quiver in her chest. It was everywhere, all around her, *inside* her, like a living thing. She had a brief sensation of weightlessness, of falling, and then the most profound darkness.

Chapter 34

Maddie swam inside her own head. Had she been hit by lightning? Her body was floating in the same strange, painless way. A booming sound still echoed in her ears.

Was she dead?

No. She couldn't be dead if she could hear. The skittering sounds of settling rocks were all around her, a light soprano to the deep groaning bass of the earth, protesting the new configuration of its bones.

Not lightning. Gunpowder.

Awareness of the rest of her body returned. She was face-down, her arms flung wide, her eyelids screwed up tight. She opened them, then wondered if she had done so; there was only pitch darkness. She blinked. Was she blind? Her lids were definitely open.

Her lungs hurt; a heavy weight lay on top of her. Dear God, was she pinned beneath a rock? She gasped for air, feeling her ribs expand and protest, and tasted dust on her lips, like chalk.

The weight shifted. And groaned.

Gryff! It was Gryff on top of her, half crushing her. His

chest was plastered against her back, his arms wrapped protectively around her head. One of his legs rested between hers.

"Gryff," she croaked.

He groaned again, and she experienced a relief so profound it shook her to her core. He wasn't dead. He was here, with her.

She wriggled out from beneath him, cautiously feeling around for the limits of their prison in the dark. There was space to move; they hadn't been crushed entirely beneath a mountain of rocks.

Her ears were still ringing. She groped around, relieved when she located the matted thickness of his hair with her fingers. With shaking hands she traced his forehead and temple, then his stubbled cheek and jaw. He murmured something incoherent.

"What?" she croaked, pushing herself to her knees beside him. "Are you hurt?"

"Always imagined being on top of you," he muttered hoarsely. "But not like this. Fewer clothes."

Her heart gave an irregular thump at his weak attempt at a joke, but his words were worryingly slurred. He sounded as if he were drunk. She reached out and squeezed his shoulder. The muscles bunched under her palm as he tried to roll over; then he let out a string of expletives and rolled back to his previous position.

"What is it?"

"Leg," he hissed. She heard a scraping noise and a grunt of pain. The sound of rocks rolling to the side.

"We need light." She felt at her hip, relieved beyond measure when she found the familiar lump of her leather satchel. "I have a candle."

"Good girl."

"What about damps?"

"Least of our problems." He coughed. "Might as well risk it."

She lifted the leather flap and scrabbled around inside,

discarding the familiar lumps of paper-wrapped mints and a broken stick of chalk. Her hands were shaking so much it took several attempts to light the candle from the tinderbox. With each spark she braced herself for another explosion, but none came, and eventually she held the lit candle aloft.

The comforting glow was extremely welcome after the sensory deprivation of the darkness.

Gryff rolled over and raised himself to a seated position, hissing as he straightened his leg out in front of him. He was covered in dust from head to toe: even his hair, as if he wore a powdered wig like the gentlemen of the last century. He looked like some ancient, ghostly Davies ancestor.

Maddie glanced down and realized she'd fared no better. Her clothes were caked with gray dust.

He bent his knee and inspected the back of his calf, rolling the fabric of his breeches up to assess the damage. The bottom half of his left leg, from knee to ankle, was dark with blood.

"You're bleeding!" Maddie whispered.

He sent her a lopsided smile. "Nothing broken. I've had worse. No need to call the sawbones just yet. Are you all right?"

She nodded. "I can't believe we're still alive."

She lifted the candle higher and tried to make sense of where they were. The jagged row of stalagmites they'd fallen behind had protected them from the full force of the explosion—and from the avalanche of rocks that had fallen all around. The walls of the tunnel were—incredibly—still intact, but the mouth of the cave was no longer where it had been. An enormous mound of boulders filled the space, blocking the route out from floor to ceiling.

"Oh, God, the others!" Maddie gasped in sudden horror. "Harriet was with me. Up in the higher cave. And what about your brother?"

Gryff threaded both hands into his hair and ruffled it violently, dislodging much of the powder and small rocks. The dark brown of his natural color reappeared. He rose stiffly to his feet, groaning like an old man, and hobbled past her, picking his way to the foot of the rock pile.

He cupped his hands around his mouth and shouted at the top of his lungs: "Morgaaaan!"

Maddie flinched, half expecting him to start another rockfall, but as the echoes died away they both strained their ears, listening for a reply.

Please, God, let them have survived.

There was a terrible moment of silence, and then her heart swelled in elation as the faint, muffled sound of an answering shout came from far away.

It was impossible to tell who it was, but at least *someone* had survived out there.

Gryff placed his hands on his hips and surveyed the wall of rock in front of him as though it were a personal affront. "There's no way we can dig our way out. Not with bare hands. But at least someone knows we're alive. They'll get a group together and start moving rock as soon as they can."

Maddie lifted the candle higher. Gryff was a big man, but seeing him standing in front of the blockage was enough to make her spirits plummet once again. Her archaeological work had given her plenty of experience in estimating the time and effort needed to move large quantities of earth; they were looking at *tons* of rock.

"There's too much there," she said wearily. "Even without knowing how far this rockfall extends, just this bit will take a team of men weeks to move. This isn't loose soil. It's boulders, most of which are heavier than you."

She didn't bother voicing the obvious—that they would starve to death or die of dehydration before rescue came. Still, even withering away in Stygian darkness didn't seem quite so bad if Gryff was by her side. Of all the people she could have been trapped with, he certainly wasn't the worst. She didn't want to consider that he might actually be the best.

To his credit, he didn't argue with her assessment. "You're probably right. That is a lot of rock."

A crushing sense of defeat swamped her. Her limbs felt shaky and she was on the verge of tears, but she forced herself to keep the candle steady as he turned and hobbled back toward her. She held her breath as he approached, silently praying that he would he take her in his arms and offer some belated comfort. She was desperate to feel the solidity of his chest beneath her cheek, his strong arms enfolding her.

He didn't touch her, though. Instead he limped past, picking his way over the rock-strewn floor toward the far recesses of the tunnel.

"Come on, boots. If there's no hope of imminent rescue that way for a while, we might as well see how far we can get along this tunnel. Who knows? Maybe it joins up with the ones we've already explored?"

Not wanting to be left alone in the dark, Maddie started after him. The cave continued for some distance, but eventually they came to a dead end: another pile of rocks. "Ha!" she said, with grim satisfaction. "Trapped."

Gryff's smile flashed in the candlelight. "It doesn't go all the way up to the top. If I clear a space we can clamber over. Hold this."

He shrugged out of his jacket and handed it to her, rolled up his shirtsleeves, and started to transfer rocks from the top of the pile.

Maddie held the candle aloft and tried to ignore the way his tanned, sinewy forearms flexed as he worked. What was wrong with her? Here she was, facing a tragic, untimely demise. She shouldn't be wasting her final hours ogling the way his breeches molded so wonderfully to his backside, or the way his shoulders flexed beneath his shirt.

On the other hand, perhaps there *wasn't* a better way to use the last hours of candlelight than enjoying the sybaritic pleasure of his fabulous physique. Maybe she should just ask him to strip naked and let her look her fill. At least she'd die happy. And a great deal better educated; she'd never seen a completely naked man.

Maddie shook her head at her own nonsense. The lack of fresh air was obviously starting to affect her brain.

She wedged the candle between two rocks, bent down, and started to help move rock. Gryff made no comment, and soon they'd made a three-foot hole at the top of the pile of rubble.

He stood back, hands on his slim hips. "Ladies first."

Chapter 35

Maddie had no idea how long they spent exploring the multitude of tunnels. Time lost all meaning. They'd clambered over the first obstacle only to discover the cave branched off into a dizzying network of smaller caves and crevices.

This, she reminded herself, was a good thing. Until they'd explored every avenue, there was still a slim chance of finding a way out.

They ventured down the first gap, with Maddie marking the route with chalk, but were forced to backtrack almost immediately when they came to a dead end. They repeated this process countless times, methodically exploring every nook and cranny. Retracing their steps was dispiriting, but it was better than accepting defeat.

The candle had burned down almost to the halfway point when the monotonous gray of the rocks was suddenly split by a seam of pitch-black material, almost a foot wide, that snaked along the wall. Gryff reached out and stroked it, then turned his palm to show her. His hand was as black as soot.

"Look at that! A coal seam!"

He gave the black stripe a fond slap, just as if it were the rump of his favorite horse. "It's probably part of the same vein that runs across my land. It must extend all the way down to the sea. Interesting."

Maddie rolled her eyes. "I fail to see what's interesting about it. What good is coal to us right now? You want to light a fire and smoke us to death?"

He shot her a chiding glance. "Welsh coal is some of the richest in the world. It burns for longer, so it commands the highest price. My father thought we were coming to the end of our seam. It's good to know there's more down here. This is black gold."

"Well, as soon as we get out of here, perhaps we can set up a joint mining operation and make our fortunes," Maddie said sarcastically.

He snorted. "A joint Davies-Montgomery enterprise? You mean like building a canal? That sort of thing?"

His tone was equally sarcastic. He rubbed his finger along the coal face, adding even more grime, then turned and selected a relatively flat piece of rock on the opposite wall. He wiped his finger in a semicircular shape, depositing a black smear on the pale rock.

"What are you doing?"

"Adding our initials."

He applied more coal dust to his finger and completed the letters *GLD* for his own name. "Gryff Llewellyn Davies," he explained. He drew an *M* for her.

"What's your middle name?"

"Charlotte."

He completed her initials next to his, then added a plus sign between the two. *GLD + MCM*.

Maddie stepped back, assuming he'd finished, but he reached for more coal dust and drew an enormous heart around the outside, the kind that lovers carved into the bark of a tree.

"What are you doing?" she shrieked. "That's going to be there forever!"

He grinned, and she knew he'd done it just to annoy her, the beast. "Who's going to see it down here?"

He had a point. She doubted anyone else would venture down here for centuries. Still, she wasn't sure she liked the fact that he'd linked their names in such a permanent way. Even if they escaped these blasted caves, that graffiti would be down here, a silent, *untrue* testament to them being together romantically. One evening of kisses in his library did not a relationship make.

Still, what did it matter? They were unlikely to escape these caves alive.

"When they finally identify our bodies," Maddie said peevishly, "in a thousand years' time, people will think we were lovers."

He sent her one of his ridiculously provocative glances. "We should make it true. If we're doomed to spend our last hours on earth together, we might as well enjoy them."

Heat rose up her neck at his teasing—especially since it echoed her own earlier thoughts—but she sent him a disapproving glance. "I don't believe we've exhausted all avenues of escape."

He chuckled. "Something to consider, though." He started forward again, following the vein of coal deeper into the rock. "If we *do* have to die down here, I always thought it would be funny to be buried in an odd position."

"What do you mean?"

"You're the archaeologist—I bet every burial you've come across is the same: someone lying flat on their back, straight as a stick."

"That's true."

"Just think of how confused future archaeologists will be if they find a couple of skeletons arranged in a different way, like pointing, or holding hands, or kissing. They'll ascribe all manner of ridiculous interpretations to it."

"You'd be messing with history!" Maddie spluttered, appalled. "You'd ruin scientific understanding for years."

The corners of his eyes crinkled as he fought not to laugh. "What a legacy, eh? Admit it, if *you* found an unusual burial, you'd be delighted. It would make your career. You'd spend years trying to explain it."

Maddie fought a smile, amused despite herself by his macabre humor.

"I can see it now," he continued, sweeping his arm in a wide arc in front of him as if reading the words on a circus poster. "The tragic lovers of Trellech. We'd be immortalized for eternity. Scholars would puzzle over our demise. You'd have to make sure you died in my arms, of course. Or I in yours."

Not such a bad place to spend eternity, really.

Maddie cursed her own idiocy. "We should be strangling each other. That would be the perfect testament to our feud."

"So unromantic, *cariad.*"

Maddie was about to take him to task for calling her darling, but he stopped abruptly, his face turned toward a crack between two huge slabs of rock. He thrust his hand back toward her.

"Quick! Hand me the candle. Do you feel that?" His incredulous laugh boomed around the cave. "It's a *breeze*!"

Sure enough, the tiny flame began to flicker as he held it in front of the narrow opening.

"If there's wind, there's a good chance it leads to the outside!"

Maddie's heart began to pound, but she hardly dared to hope that he was right. A breeze might come from a crack an inch wide.

"Come on." Gryff turned sideways and started to wriggle between the two sheets of rock. The back of his breeches scraped along the coal seam. He disappeared, taking the candle with him, but after a tense moment he she heard his long, low whistle.

"Come through. There's something here you need to see."

Maddie sidestepped until the crack widened out. She emerged next to Gryff and her mouth dropped open in wonder. The candle revealed they stood at the edge of a vast underground lake.

"This is incredible!"

It was impossible to say how far the lake extended; the light didn't penetrate far enough into the darkness. A waterfall trickled nearby, descending a wall that resembled molten candle wax: layer upon layer of yellowish stone dripping down toward the water, which was as black as ink. Dark ripples lapped at the rocks that rose around the sides, and great columns of stone stretched from floor to ceiling like the pillars of a great church. More pointed spires rose from the surface of the water, while others descended from the ceiling like enormous icicles.

Gryff handed her the candle and cupped his hands around his mouth. "Helloooo!"

Hello! Hello! Hellooooo!

The call bounced off the walls and water, a cacophony of male voices echoing back at them like some infernal, discordant choir.

He nodded at the water. "Think there's a dragon under there? Like at Dinas Emrys?"

"If there is, you'll have woken it up with all your shouting. It'll come and gobble us up."

He flashed a grin. "*I'll* be all right. It's you who'll get eaten."

"Why me?"

"Because everyone knows dragons like virgins. Those pure of body and heart. That rules me out." He sent her one of his wicked looks. "Maybe you should lose that virginal state of yours, just to be safe?"

Her skin heated, but she managed to keep her tone cool. "Are you offering to help?"

"It's a sacrifice I'd be willing to make," he said loftily, but his eyes twinkled. "Your safety is my highest priority."

"That's very noble," she said dryly. "But I don't believe in mythical creatures."

"What, virgins?"

"No, dragons."

"Pity," he chuckled.

Chapter 36

Despite her words, Maddie eyed the surface of the water with deep misgiving, half expecting to see a stream of bubbles and a scaly head emerge from the black depths. Gryff started skirting the edge of the lake, leaping with irritatingly good balance from rock to rock. "This must be an underground tributary of the River Wye. Or the Usk. One of the two."

"So?"

"The Wye is tidal. If the water levels rise and fall with the tides, we could drown when it comes in."

"How lovely."

It was his turn to ignore her sarcasm. "The level in here seems constant, though. That means there must be an outlet."

Maddie started picking her way between the rocks. "It's probably below the surface of the water. Or too small for a person to fit through."

Something low on the wall flashed in the candlelight, and she stopped, squinting at it. "Wait. What's that? There's something . . . sparkling."

Gryff barely turned his head. "Probably fool's gold. Iron pyrite. You find it next to coal seams all the time."

"And near *real* gold," Maddie insisted. "Because they're formed under the same geological conditions." She crossed over to the shining, reflective area. "Please bring the candle."

He turned, his expression impatient. "You know, we Welsh have a saying. *Nid aur yw popeth melyn.*"

"Which means?"

"Not everything yellow is gold." He stomped back and brought the candle closer as she bent to examine the rock.

"It's not as yellow as fool's gold. Look, it's almost . . . pink." A few currant-sized, butter-colored lumps tumbled into her palm.

Gryff squatted down next to her and nudged at them with his fingertip. "It's fool's gold, I tell you. Real gold is soft. You'd be able to see my teeth marks when I bite into it. Look."

He brought a lump to his mouth and bit down, as if eating a carrot. And then his eyebrows shot up to his hairline as he saw the distinct indentations his teeth had left on the surface. They both looked down at them in silence.

"Bloody hell!" He rocked back on his heels and let out a deafening yell. "It's gold! It's bloody *gold*!"

Maddie toppled backward onto her bottom, clutching the handful of nuggets. "You're teasing me."

"I swear I'm not. Maddie Montgomery, you're a genius!"

They both stared down at her hand, then back at the wall. The gold formed a narrow seam, just like the coal. It was at least an inch thick, and extended in a glittering line for more than twenty feet into the darkness.

Maddie tried to calm her pounding heart. "How . . . how much is this worth?"

"Hard to say, without weighing it, but this lump is about the same as a musket ball. That's almost an ounce." He glanced down at her hand. "And you have a whole handful of 'em!"

"How much is an ounce of gold?"

"Five pounds, maybe?" He glanced along the wall, obviously doing some rapid mental calculation. "You're holding at least a few hundred pounds' worth." He swept his arm to indicate the seam set into the rock. "And all that must be worth thousands."

Maddie let out a shaky, incredulous laugh. "Dear God! We're saved!" She could barely speak for excitement; she felt almost delirious.

Gryff sent her an odd look. "What do you mean, 'saved'?"

She bit her lip. She hadn't meant to say that out loud, but what was the point in keeping the secret now? She fixed him with a hard stare. "First of all, I want your word that we'll split this equally. We're on shared land. We each get half of whatever gold's recovered."

He nodded, as if amazed that he would even question it. "Of course. Half each. Agreed."

"In that case, I should probably tell you that until this very moment, my family has been on the verge of bankruptcy."

"What?"

"Father lost almost all of his investments last year. During the great stock exchange scandal."

Gryff frowned. "I didn't hear much about that—I was off fighting in Spain."

"It was an elaborate hoax. A group of men deliberately spread the false rumor that Napoleon had been defeated, possibly killed, by a group of Russian Cossacks. The news made the price of government stocks surge. Father's man of business bought consols on his behalf when the prices were at their peak—convinced they would continue to rise when the rumor was confirmed, and make Father a tidy profit—but when it proved to be false, the value of them plummeted. Father lost over six thousand pounds."

"Good God," Gryff muttered.

"We've been staving off creditors for months," Maddie admitted. "I only found out how bad it was a few weeks ago. Father's been looking at selling the London house, and even Newstead Park."

"Is *that* why you've had Drake dangling after you?"

Maddie glanced away, too ashamed to meet his eyes. "Well, yes. He heard about our troubles and offered Father two thousand pounds if I would marry him." A glow of happiness warmed the center of her chest, replacing the embarrassment. "But now I won't have to marry *anyone*!"

Her spontaneous shout echoed over the water, but she quickly sobered, glancing up at him uncertainly. "Could you possibly consider *not* selling your half right away? If we both sell it'll flood the market and drive the price of gold down."

Gryff still looked rather dazed. "Agreed."

She let out a heartfelt sigh and placed her hand on his arm. "*Thank you*. You really are a decent man, Gryff Davies. No matter what my father says."

He glanced down at her fingers. His muscles tensed, then he shook his head and stood, brushing the dirt from his thighs. "You know, all this bargaining is purely theoretical unless we can find a way out of here."

He turned and gazed out over the dark water, and the absurd reality of their situation hit Maddie like a physical blow. Her previous elation vanished like smoke. He was right. Why on earth was she celebrating? What was the use of finding a fortune if they were stuck down here?

The irony of it had her stifling a half-hysterical laugh. This was just her luck. The lightning strike hadn't finished her off, but this surely would.

Utterly dispirited, she leaned back against the wall, drew her knees up to her chest, and dropped her forehead onto them. "We're never getting out of here, are we? We're going to starve, surrounded by gold, the richest prisoners in history."

Above her, she heard Gryff sigh. He nudged her foot with his own. She ignored him.

A disturbance in the air told her he'd crouched back down beside her. "Come on, *cariad*. You're not one to accept defeat."

She snorted into her skirts. He was wrong. Even Little Miss Optimism couldn't ignore reality when it was staring her in the face.

"When all this is over we'll celebrate by getting roaring drunk. You'll see."

"I don't like spirits."

"We'll find some other way, then. I'm sure I can think of something fun."

He lowered himself so he was sitting next to her; his shoulder brushed her own.

"Do you know," he said conversationally, as if they were sitting side by side at some genteel tea party, "my father once told me that he and your father used to hide each other's court robes whenever they were in Parliament."

Despite her misery, Maddie couldn't resist a snort. "That is incredibly childish."

"Incredibly. But also, I imagine, quite fun. For the record, if we *are* doomed to die down here, I'd like you to know that I couldn't have wished for a better co-captive than you."

Her heart squeezed tight. "Well, thank you. And . . . like-wise."

They sat in companionable silence for a moment.

"You were equally childish, you know," she muttered into her knees. "All that teasing when we were younger."

He snorted. "You must have known why I did it."

"Because you were a monster?"

"I thought it was obvious. Boys always tease girls they like." He nudged her shoulder with his own. "They steal their shawls and tie them up in their own skirts."

She lifted her head and stared at him. "You did it because you *liked* me? Rubbish. You just liked tormenting me."

His lopsided smile made her heart skip a beat.

"I'll admit, I did try to get a reaction. Because anger was better than indifference. Even hatred was better, because it meant you were still thinking about me. I loved seeing if I could rouse your temper." His smile widened even more. "Of course, *then* I'd think of ways to redirect all that passion. I spent far too much time thinking about kissing you."

Maddie shook her head. "I always thought you hated me."

The look he sent her was amused and a little pitying. He leaned over and caught her chin, exerting gentle pressure with his fingers until she turned to face him. His gaze was so intense, so burning, she felt it right down to her toes.

"Maddie." His voice was so deep it was almost a growl, and her body reacted on the most primitive level. Her heart began to pound and an answering pulse throbbed between her legs.

He spread his fingers along her jaw. His thumb stroked her chin, then slid across her lower lip to the indent at the corner of her mouth, and everything inside her stilled.

"*This* is how much I hate you."

Chapter 37

Maddie sucked in a breath an instant before his lips met hers in a kiss that went from soft to scorching in a heartbeat. She threw her arms around his neck and leaned into him, opening her mouth greedily, snaking her tongue out to tangle with his own.

His arm came around her waist, and she almost moaned in gratitude. Here was the comfort she'd been craving from the moment they'd been trapped. Here was the human contact, the bodily warmth, the proof that she was still alive.

He kissed her with a thoroughness that left her breathless. His wicked tongue licked and swirled as though she were an ice cream at Gunter's. She rose up on her knees, heedless of the rocks pressing through her skirts, and tangled her fingers in his hair, urging him to continue with a hum of pleasure.

He tightened his arms and pulled her even closer. She wanted to clamber on top of him as she had in his library. She wanted his hands all over her, the feel of his skin beneath her palms. Her seeking fingers found their way under his shirt and she stroked his back, savoring the sleek warmth and bunched muscles that flexed beneath her palms.

He groaned against her lips. Emboldened, she stroked her hands around his ribs, then over the intriguing ridges of his abdomen and up, over the swells of his chest. He was so warm. Her fingers slid over the rough circles of his nipples.

He pulled back with a muffled curse. "God, Maddie. We have to stop."

They were both panting hard. His lashes were a dark tangle in the candlelight, and a faint flush heated the jut of his cheekbones. His lips were wet, glistening from the kiss, and she leaned in to capture them again, desperate for another taste, but he caught her arm, keeping her away.

He lifted his eyes to the ceiling as if praying for strength, then with a half groan, half laugh he rested his forehead against hers.

"I never thought to hear myself say this, but we can't do this. Not here, at any rate." He leaned back and stared at her, his fingers tightening at her nape as if to impress on her the sincerity of his words. "Believe me, there is nothing, *absolutely nothing*, I'd rather be doing than making love with you, but we can't do it here, on the rocky floor of some bloody cave. Your first time shouldn't be like this."

A wave of recklessness seized her. The chances of them getting out of here were minimal. And if she *was* going to die, she bloody well wasn't going to die a *virgin*.

She caught a fistful of his hair in her fingers and tugged. Gryff was so chivalrous—at least where she was concerned—he'd probably refuse her even this one, last, scandalous request. Still, what did she have to lose?

"You're right. My first time *shouldn't* be like this. But it might be the only chance we get." She leaned closer. "It's not the location that's important. It's the person." She traced the seam of his lips with her tongue. "I need you to save me from the dragons."

"What?" His confusion was clear in his tone.

"You said dragons only liked virgins. So make me safe."

His entire body stilled as he grasped her meaning. "What?" he repeated stupidly.

"You heard me."

He let out a sharp bark of disbelief. "You must be joking."

"I assure you I'm not."

Suddenly bold, she straddled him, and she couldn't fail to miss the bulge of his arousal pressing against her belly. He was hard, ready for her. *Her*, Maddie Montgomery! Not one of the sophisticated London matrons. Not some highly skilled courtesan. *Her*.

It was a miracle as impossible to believe as her lightning strike, but she wasn't going to question it. She wanted him too.

He kissed her again, hard, but disappointment swamped her as he gently moved her aside. She was about to protest, to *beg*, until she caught sight of his face.

"You realize this is the worst possible location?" he growled. "A man can't be expected to do his best work under such circumstances."

She bit her lip, torn between apologizing and laughter. "I know it's not ideal, but I was hoping a man of your . . . experience . . . might be able to overcome the difficulties."

She'd take his *worst* efforts over anyone else's best.

His brows drew together in an exasperated frown. "Damn it all, Maddie. Couldn't you have asked me somewhere less . . . dank? A bedroom. Or a library. God, we could have done this *so well* in my library."

The sensual promise in his tone made her pulse flutter. "Well, yes. I realize that now. But still . . . this seems to be where we are."

"You really want to do this?"

"Positive."

His hungry gaze roved her face, and she saw the exact moment he gave in. Her stomach somersaulted in excitement.

"Well then. Far be it from me to deny a damsel in distress." In a sudden flurry of movement, he shrugged out of his jacket and spread it flat on the ground, then caught the hem of his shirt and pulled it up over his head.

Maddie sucked in a gasp of delight as he exposed his muscled chest. Oh, he was beautiful, all shadows and ridges in the candlelight.

Seized with the same urgency, she slipped the satchel off her shoulder and wriggled out of her own jacket, then stilled as Gryff reached out and tugged the bottom of her shirt from her waistband. He unbuttoned it with agonizing slowness, holding her gaze captive, his eyes filled with heat and teasing challenge. The slide and pop as each button slipped from its buttonhole seemed unnaturally loud in the still air.

Dear God, they really were going to do this!

When he pushed the material from her shoulders, revealing the bandage tied around her upper arm, she sucked in a breath.

He bent and kissed the side of her neck. "Now, this is the kind of archaeology *I* like. Removing the layers to find the treasure beneath."

His fingers found the ribbons of her stays, and she smiled when they resisted his attempts to untie them. She pushed his hands away and undid the knots herself, and when the constriction fell away she was left in just her thin lawn chemise and her skirts.

There was no time to feel exposed. Gryff's lips found hers again and she closed her eyes and slid her fingers into his hair, sinking into glorious sensation. She lay back and he followed her down, stretching out beside her, and she ran her hands over the muscles in his arms and chest, greedy for the feel of him.

When he pushed her chemise down to her waist and cupped

her breast she shivered in delight. It was hard to see his face clearly in shadows, but there was no mistaking the reverence in his tone as he rose up on one elbow and looked at her.

"God, Maddie, you're perfect."

He brushed her nipple with his thumb, then dipped his head and caught it in his mouth, and her limbs turned to water. Heat raced through her veins. The rasp of his tongue brought her out in goose bumps and she arched her back, shamelessly offering more.

He transferred his attention to the other breast.

"Beautiful," he sighed.

Chapter 38

Gryff groped around for logic. For honor. For some reason why they shouldn't do this. But Maddie's floral scent was clouding his brain and making it hard to think. The desire he'd been tamping down for so long roared back to life with a vengeance. His blood was pounding in his veins. All he could feel was her.

He took her mouth like a man dying of thirst, as if the taste of her could slake the need inside him. She was nectar. Ambrosia. He couldn't get enough. He gave her lower lip a gentle tug with his teeth and then delved inside, stroking his tongue against hers, drinking her in. Her fingers tightened in his hair and she wriggled against him, fanning the flames with her innocent ardor.

His heart felt like it was being crushed in his chest. That day, when he'd ridden over the hill and seen her waiting for him on the bridge, when he'd kissed her that first time and it had felt so bloody right. Why the hell hadn't he just swept her up onto Paladin, ridden back to Trellech Court, and taken her to bed for a week?

He was a bloody simpleton, that's why.

There were so many things he wanted to teach her. So many things they'd never have the chance to do. All those dreams he'd had of making love to her in his bed, in a cornfield, under the stars. A hundred thousand places. None of them would happen now. There was only this. This moment. This woman.

But if this was all they had, he'd take it.

He'd take anything from her.

He sucked in a breath, trying to control himself. Maddie lay beneath him like some pagan goddess, her hair a dark cloud around her face. Shadows painted flickering crescents beneath the curve of her breasts and danced over the smooth lines of her throat.

God, he'd dreamed of this a thousand times.

Each time he'd been about to ride into battle, each time he'd thought he couldn't walk another step, he'd allowed himself this fantasy. It had sustained him for years and he'd sworn that one day, if he could just survive, he'd make it back to England and make love to Maddie Montgomery until they both saw stars.

He wasn't sure if he'd truly believed it. It had been an impossible dream, something to keep him going in his darkest moments. But now it was actually happening, and reality was a thousand times better than his paltry imagination.

He watched, almost in a daze, as his sun-browned hand stroked down the center of her chest and covered her breast, dark against light. She watched him out of half-closed eyes, her chest rising and falling rapidly, wary and yet so trusting.

Her skin was soft, so soft.

In his fantasies he'd seduced her with the silver-tongued words of the Welsh poets. But the poetry of his ancestors had deserted him. He could only think in monosyllables.

Mine. More. Now.

He leaned down and kissed her, drowning as she filled

every one of his senses. He stroked her ribs, her hips, loving the way she writhed beneath his touch, then moved lower, bunching up her petticoats and sliding his palm up her stockinged leg. She tensed when he passed her garter and stroked the top of her thigh, and her fingers tightened in his hair as he slid inward and found the slit in her drawers.

He skimmed the springy mound of hair at the apex of her thighs, then slid one finger through her feminine folds, exactly as he'd dreamed of doing in his library. She moaned against his mouth.

God, she was slippery and wet. So ready for him. Her back bowed and her fingernails dug into his biceps, and when he stroked her she almost jolted out of his arms.

"Oh!"

The base of his throat felt hot and tight. He circled the entrance to her body, loving the way she squirmed against him. His blood pounded heavy through his veins, hot with anticipation.

"Oh, that is . . . unghh . . . don't stop," she breathed.

He pushed his finger into her, barely an inch, catching her little gasp of shock with his lips, loving the way the heat of her welcomed him. Her arms tightened around his neck as she tried to move upward, away from his hand, not knowing what she wanted.

He showed her. He pushed deeper, mimicking what he wanted to do with his body, and her inner muscles clenched around him as he started a slow, rocking rhythm he knew would drive her to distraction.

"Gryff!" Her voice held a brittle, demanding edge as she squirmed to get closer, to end the torment.

He swirled his thumb, and with a hoarse cry of pleasure she convulsed in his arms. She melted against him, utterly boneless as he gently withdrew his hand and hugged her tight to his chest.

"Oh, my God," she breathed against his neck. "I had no idea."

His smile widened at the sheer wonder in her tone. "There's more. Let me show you."

He kissed his way down her body until his broad shoulders were between her legs, then he leaned in and tasted her. She bucked so hard she almost dislodged him, but he curved his arm around her thigh and bent her knee to give him better access.

"Let me. You'll like it. I swear."

She subsided with a shuddery sigh.

He licked the entire length of her, softly, and the taste of her made his head spin. He found the little pearl and flicked it with his tongue, then added his fingers, savoring every hitch in her breathing, every fevered moan. Her grip on his hair tightened to the point of pain, but he relished the sting.

"Gryff Davies!"

His name on her lips was the sweetest thing he'd ever heard. Her limbs stiffened, and her inner muscles contracted around him. A deep masculine satisfaction filled him, but his blood was still pounding in his veins, a steady insistent drumbeat that centered in the head of his aching cock.

With a fumbling hand he unbuttoned his breeches and palmed his own length, stretching out over her. She was still panting, her gaze unfocused, but she reached up and pulled him down for a kiss. He propped himself up on his forearms, careful not to crush her, aware of how small she was, how fragile. *How precious.*

The thought checked him for a moment. Christ, he needed to slow down. This was her first time; she was a virgin, for God's sake. What was he doing, tupping her on the hard ground like some common trollop at Vauxhall?

"Don't stop," she breathed, as if she sensed his sudden indecision. "Not now."

The pleading in her voice was his undoing. With a groan, he moved against her. The blunt end of his cock slid along the seam between her legs, nudging at her entrance. He angled his hips and pushed into her, his muscles quivering with the effort to go slow, when what he really wanted was to pound into her and never stop. *Never stop.*

Her eyes widened at the intrusion and he kissed her, hard. He slid in another blissful inch and almost blacked out with pleasure as she softened and relaxed, accepting him. She wriggled her hips and he slid in even more, then held himself still within her as he waited for her reaction.

She let out a shaky exhale, and he braced for a complaint, for her to tell him to withdraw, but she just wrapped her arms around his shoulders.

"So *that's* how much you hate me," she breathed.

Her voice was a mixture of wonder and wicked laughter, and he let out a surprised snort. The cheeky minx.

"Hate me some more."

Power and elation washed over him. He rocked his hips to punish her for her insolence, and enjoyed the way her eyes widened in shock.

Oh, the things he was going to show her.

Chapter 39

Maddie's body wasn't her own. She moved, driven by instinct, lifting her hips to try to recapture the glorious sensations Gryff had shown her with his hands and mouth. The feel of him inside her was a strange sensation, and yet it felt so right. So *good*. Each rock of his hips sent shivers of pleasure coursing along her limbs.

She wanted that elusive peak he'd shown her with a desperation that made her hold her breath, half agony, half bliss. She dug her nails into his shoulders, silently urging him on, but before she could get there he stopped moving and dropped his head to her collarbone.

"Why are you stopping?" she gasped.

Was that *it*? *Was he finished?* Surely not—he was still rock-hard inside her.

He let out a groan like a man being tortured on a rack. "Bloody hell. I don't have any French letters."

She frowned into the shadows. "What?"

"To prevent a child."

Ohh. Disappointment made her belly swoop. "So we have to . . . stop?"

He raised his head. The change in position slid him even deeper, and the delicious friction made them both gasp. He rested his forehead on hers and she could feel the tremors in his arms as he fought for control.

"We don't have to. I can pull out before I finish," he said. "Do you trust me?"

Maddie didn't fully understand what he meant, but she definitely didn't want him to stop.

Perhaps their close brush with death was responsible for this primal need, but she suspected it was more than that. She'd wanted this for longer than she could remember, before she'd even known what she craved. And she did trust him. Not just with her body, but with her life.

She pushed a lock of his hair back from his forehead. "Don't stop."

He let out a shaky sigh, and she saw a flash of humor as he smiled. "As the lady commands."

He moved, the smallest, most insidious of slides, and his smile grew knowing as a shiver of pleasure ran through her.

Oh, he was a tease. A shocking, shameless rogue.

And she loved it.

He reached down and pulled her leg up, over his hip, and the new angle sent the promise of ecstasy skimming through her limbs. He filled her with slow, lazy strokes, perfectly relentless. Each push wound her tighter, tighter, like the coiled spring in a pocket watch.

Maddie closed her eyes, lost in carnal sensation. She pulled him down and kissed him, loving his taste. He slid his hand between them and another climax rushed up to claim her. Stars exploded behind her eyelids and her body pulsed with pleasure, beat after beat of soul-burning joy.

Every muscle in her body went lax, and she was vaguely aware of Gryff, pressing his face to the hollow of her throat with a muffled, impassioned groan. He thrust again, all power and urgency, then withdrew with a harsh groan. The hardness of him pressed against her belly and he shuddered convulsively. With a sigh that seemed to come from the very depths of his soul, he collapsed on top of her, utterly boneless.

Despite his crushing weight, Maddie smiled at his helplessness; it was such a contrast with his normal, invulnerable state. She loved the fact that she'd reduced this man to such a helpless case. The feeling mellowed into a deep rush of affection, a sense of repletion she'd never experienced before.

She tangled her fingers in the hair at the back of his head and stroked him lightly, like a child. Her heart was full, her senses reeling with the wonder of what they'd just done.

After a few moments he seemed to come back to himself. He rolled off her with a groan, and the cool caress of the air immediately had her wishing for the warmth of his skin. She cast about for something to say, but her brain was a barren wasteland.

"Bloody hell," he panted.

That seemed as good a phrase as any. She let out a soft, incredulous chuckle. "Bloody hell."

Her body was still shaking with aftershocks. What Gryff had done to her was beyond anything she'd ever expected, anything she'd ever imagined. It was like fireworks going off in her blood, the exhilaration of leaping off a bridge and crashing into icy water. His scent was in her nose, his beautiful body next to hers, and she realized she'd never felt this safe, this sated in her life.

So . . . happy.

Which was ridiculous, because they were still stuck in a cave.

But at least she was safe from dragons.

She tried to summon regret, and failed. She might be "soiled goods" now, according to the strictures of the *ton*, but she couldn't really care. She appreciated that those rules existed for her own protection, but they paled into insignificance when faced with matters of life or death.

Gryff turned his head and sent her a wry, regretful smile. "We can't stay here, much as I'd like to. We'll catch our deaths. Come on."

He sat up and began searching around for his shirt, and she watched him, too exhausted to move. The candlelight glanced off the muscles of his shoulders, the sleek lines of his arms and chest, and a lump rose in her throat as she studied him with unashamed admiration. He really was beautiful, honed to masculine perfection by the rigors of war.

He found a handkerchief in his jacket pocket and used it to clean his wetness from her skirts, and she sat up too. The realization that she was naked on her top half rushed in, as if she was waking from a dream, and she became aware of the hard stone beneath her, the distant trickle of running water.

As Gryff refastened his breeches, she tugged up her shift and pushed down her skirts.

How did sophisticated ladies deal with these things? How should she act?

A flash of jealousy stabbed her as she realized *he'd* probably been in this situation many times, while she was in uncharted territory.

She pulled on the rest of her clothes and stood. She tried to move away, to gather herself, but Gryff caught her chin so she looked him in the face.

"Don't get shy on me, Maddie. People do this all the time, every minute of the day and night. There's nothing to be ashamed of."

"I'm not ashamed. Just . . . thinking."

His lips quirked. "That's even worse." He straightened the dusty lapels of her jacket, like an officer inspecting his troops, and gave a brief satisfied nod, then bent and pressed a soft kiss to her lips. "There, boots. Ready for anything."

Her heart was still hammering in her chest but she managed a slight, dazed nod. Perhaps he was right. After surviving such a cataclysmic event as making love with Gryff Davies, was there anything she couldn't do?

Chapter 40

Gryff stepped back and turned his attention to the strip of gold in the wall. "Right. Let's see if we can pry some of this loose. Might as well take a few chunks with us."

They set about gouging at the rocks and managed to extract a fistful of nuggets ranging in size from a pea to a child's marble. Maddie placed them securely inside her brass tinderbox and glanced over at Gryff in question.

He dipped the toe of his boot in the inky water, watching the ripples radiate out across the dark expanse. "Have you a scrap of paper? Or a ribbon? Something that will float?"

She handed him a wrapper from one of the mints. He tossed it onto the surface of the water, and the two of them watched as it drifted about aimlessly. She was about to turn away when the little white scrap picked up speed and started moving to the left.

Gryff let out a grunt of satisfaction. "Ha! I knew it—there's a current. Which means this water is flowing from somewhere, to somewhere."

"It could be going deeper underground," she cautioned,

even as he set off, following the progress of the paper. "We'll end up in Hades," she muttered.

"Already there," he called back over his shoulder. "I'm fairly certain my personal hell is having a gorgeous woman and a pile of gold, both within arm's reach, and not being able to do what I want with either of 'em."

The scrap of paper neared the edge of the cave and began to rotate in an ever-decreasing circle. As they watched, it disappeared, sucked beneath the surface of the water by some unseen force.

Gryff held out his hand. "Another scrap?"

The second wrapper followed the same route as the first.

"Well, that's obviously one way out," he said. "There must be a tunnel under the water. I don't fancy going that way, do you?"

"Absolutely not."

He turned and retraced their steps, past the crack where they'd entered the cave, which Maddie marked with a big chalk X, and around the opposite side of the lake. They rounded a rocky outcrop.

"It's getting shallower," Gryff said excitedly. "And look there." Regardless of his boots, he stepped into the ankle-deep water and started splashing toward a large arched tunnel that appeared to be the incoming source for the lake.

"Let's head upstream. It's not deep, and the current isn't strong." He beckoned her.

Maddie glanced at the candle. "All right. But only for a short distance. We'll have to return to the rockfall soon or we'll run out of light."

"Fair enough."

She twisted her skirts and tucked them up at her waist.

"Leave your boots on. The rocks are too sharp for bare feet."

The frigid water immediately seeped into her ankle boots. They started down the tunnel, which was wide and smooth-bottomed, as if the underground river had scoured its way along it for thousands of years. The sharp fangs of stalagmites disappeared, but the farther they went, the deeper the water became.

By the time it reached her knees Maddie was finding it increasingly difficult to push forward against the current. She muttered in frustration and Gryff reached back and caught her hand. His strong fingers enclosed hers, steadying her and lending strength and confidence.

The water was so cold. When it reached her thighs—which was still only up to Gryff's knees, curse him—she tugged on his hand. "We should go back."

"Not yet. Just a little farther."

Exhaustion was tugging at her limbs, and she knew she'd almost reached the limits of her endurance. The cold was seeping into her bones. She could barely feel her toes; they were so cold they felt almost hot, a strange sensation.

He turned so his broad back was toward her. "Come on, jump up. I'll carry you piggyback."

"What? No!"

He rolled his eyes at her maidenly objection. "I can't believe you're still worried about propriety. We're in a cave. There isn't a society matron in sight."

"It's not that. I'm too heavy."

He gave her that *you're being ridiculous* look she'd grown to hate. "I carted a hundred-pound pack halfway way around Europe, and carried wounded men twice your size. Come on."

He balanced the candle on a rock and bent his knees to make it easier for her. With a resigned sigh she swiveled her satchel so it was behind her, steadied her hands on his shoulders, and jumped up. She wrapped her legs around his waist, hooking them above the jut of his hips, and heat flushed her entire body as every indecent inch of her pressed to every glorious inch of him.

He juggled her weight, readjusting her to his satisfaction, and her cheeks burned as he curved his left arm beneath her bottom, to hold her in place.

Tristan had often carried her about like this when they were younger, obligingly galloping about the estate as she pretended to be a knight on horseback. But she wasn't a child any longer, and the man holding her was definitely *not* her brother.

Her entire body felt alive. Her breasts were plastered against his back, her stockinged calves rubbed over the top of his thighs, and her core was pressed indecently against his lower back. She felt shamefully exposed, with only the thin cotton of her drawers between her and his coat. The warmth of him seeped into her everywhere they touched.

It was the reverse position to the one they'd taken in the library, and for a brief, mad moment she wished he would turn around within her arms, push her up against the wall, and just kiss her senseless.

She tightened her grip on his broad shoulders as he reclaimed the candle with his free hand.

"There. Good," he murmured.

His voice was low, rougher than before, and Maddie pressed her face into his shoulder with a little feminine smile. Was he trying to ignore the feel of her, too? To test her theory she slid her palm down, over his chest, shamelessly tracing the masculine swells, and bit back a gleeful chuckle when he reached up and clenched her hand tight with his own, stopping her explorations.

"Enough of that," he said gruffly. "You'll have plenty of time to grope me after we get out of here. Take the candle."

Maddie did so, allowing him to hold her under her knees with both hands as he pushed forward. The water rose to his waist, and the current strengthened as the tunnel narrowed. Soon he fought for every step, edging forward, testing for a good foothold before he moved.

"We *really* need to turn back now. It's too deep."

Her skirts were soaking; they sagged in the water, a heavy, unwelcome encumbrance. She was in awe of his strength, his dogged persistence, but this was a fool's errand. They needed to retrace their steps to the rockfall or they'd be stranded in darkness.

"Gryff, come on. Turn around. We're running out of candle."

His growl of frustration reverberated against her chest. "All right. Fine. You win."

He stopped and started to turn, but an unexpected surge of water made him stagger and they lurched sideways. Maddie's leg hit a rock, and she gasped as she was suddenly submerged up to her chin. The rushing water caught her skirts and dragged them out behind her like a sail, and she grabbed at Gryff's shirt in desperation.

"Gryff!"

His hands tightened around her legs, but the candle hit the wall as she flailed upward reflexively. It fell with the tiniest hiss into the surging stream.

They were plunged into utter darkness.

"Bollocks."

His grim pronouncement echoed around them. Maddie groped blindly for his neck and clasped him with both arms, desperate for an anchor in the sudden pitch black.

"Oh, God. I'm so sorry! I didn't mean—"

His grip tightened. "Shh. It's all right. I've got you."

His calm confidence quelled her instinctive panic and they both stilled, adjusting to this new and unthinkable dilemma. The harsh panting of their breath mingled over the sound of the rushing water.

"Right. Well. Not an ideal situation, I'll admit," Gryff grunted.

Maddie choked back a despairing laugh. God, she loved

his humor, even in the face of disaster. Had he faced similar hopeless situations in the war with this same dry fatalism?

"I'm turning around. Keep hold of my neck."

He turned his body within the circle of her arms—first propping her sideways on his hip, as a mother carried a toddler, then bringing them chest-to-chest. Maddie hooked her ankles together behind his back and clung to him like an octopus. The reassuring strength of his arms made her weak with relief.

He had her. He wouldn't let her go.

His cheek brushed hers as he readjusted their position, and she rested her chin on his shoulder.

This was it, then. The end. There was no way they could possibly find their way back, even as far as the lake, in the dark.

An odd, calm acceptance washed over her. They'd clearly reached the end of their luck. They'd die of cold before they died of starvation. Or drown.

At least she wasn't alone.

Gryff tilted his head back and stared sightlessly into the darkness, even as he tightened his grip around the impossible woman in his arms.

Her cheek slid against his, and from the way her breath puffed against his lips he knew they were nose-to-nose, though he couldn't see her. Her skin slid against his as she angled her head and brushed her lips lightly against his own, apparently emboldened by the darkness.

"You're killing me," he groaned.

The sweet mounds of her breasts were plastered against his chest, and the perfect peach of her bottom was nestling in his hands. His cock sprang to attention, heedless of the frigid water and the fact that they'd only just made love. He leaned back, balancing them both against the wall of the tunnel as his knees threatened to buckle.

So easy. God, it would be so easy. Her legs were already around his waist. It would be the work of a moment to free himself and push into her. Heat and heaven.

The tip of his cock rubbed against the valley of her bottom and he dragged her down against him in an agonizing slow tease. She shivered. He pulled his hips back so his rod was pressed between them, first against her stomach, then lower, in the space between her legs. Her breathy gasp brought a half smile to his lips, despite the dire situation.

God, he wished he could see her, the expressions on her face.

"No," he said firmly. "The next time we make love, Maddie Montgomery, it's going to be in daylight, and we're both going to be naked, so I can see every glorious inch of you. I didn't survive all those battles in France and Spain just to die in some miserable cave. We're getting out of here. And when we do, I'm going to give you a practical demonstration of every word Johnson left out of his bloody dictionary. Are we clear?"

He felt, rather than saw her nod.

Chapter 41

Maddie let out a long, regretful sigh and pulled back a fraction in a pointless attempt to read Gryff's expression in the dark. And then she blinked, because she really *could* see his features, just slightly.

She frowned, sure she was imagining it, but the outline remained: his slant-cheeked silhouette in the darkness. "Gryff," she whispered. "I can see you."

He grunted.

She turned her head, squinting over his shoulder down the tunnel. Sure enough, the curved wall was faintly discernible in the slightest gradation of grays. "There's light. That way."

Still holding her, he turned them both.

"You see it, don't you? It's lighter over there."

He didn't answer. He simply started wading in that direction. Maddie held on to him tightly, her excitement rising as they neared the paler section. The water surged higher, up around her waist, and she felt herself grow buoyant as it took most of her weight.

Gryff was breathing hard with the effort of pushing them

both through the water, and she unwrapped her legs from around his waist and started to float.

"Wait," she said breathlessly. "I can swim. Just . . . let me get rid of my skirts."

He stopped and held her securely under the arms as she fumbled to undo the buttons at the side of her skirts. Her fingers were almost numb with the cold, and her teeth were chattering, but she was too excited by the prospect of seeing daylight to care. She managed to kick her way out of her skirts, and her petticoats, and felt them catch the current and drift away downstream like some strange jellyfish.

She was left in her bloomers and knee-length chemise, but her legs were free to move.

"Better. Let's go."

Gryff released her tentatively, waiting to see if she could manage on her own, and she pushed forward in the water, kicking her legs in the breaststroke she'd learned as a child. The chill of the water made her catch her breath, but she set out briskly toward the patch of gray.

Details of the ridged walls became more distinct. The tunnel curved sharply, and she sucked in an expectant breath as it got even brighter.

A perfect circle of pale light bounced and shimmered on the surface of the water ahead. She glanced up, and her heart skipped a beat as she realized it was coming from an aperture in the roof of the tunnel.

"It's a hole!"

Gryff grabbed her arm to steady her as he placed his feet back on the bottom. "It's better than that." He grinned, and she saw his teeth glint in the new brightness. "It's a shaft. A well."

The light was too insipid to be sunlight. Maddie couldn't calculate how long they'd been underground, but judging from the amount of candle they'd burned, it must have been several hours. Which meant darkness had fallen, and they'd been saved by a bright moon and a cloudless night.

A rocky shelf jutted out from the wall, a flat section of strata almost like a table. Gryff hauled himself up onto it in a surge of water, then reached for her hand and pulled her up next to him. She collapsed in a dripping heap, her body a hundred times heavier now that she was out of the water.

Something silvery glinted in the moonlight. She reached over and picked up a silver coin. "Look at this! A sixpence."

Gryff peered down through the crystal-clear water. Now that they were higher, Maddie could see the bottom was littered with hundreds of tiny, glittering objects. Pins and coins and all manner of metallic things.

"They were thrown into the well for good luck," she breathed in sudden comprehension. "Do you think this is *our* well? The Virtuous Well?"

"You mean Ffynnon Pen Rhys," Gryff corrected automatically. "And yes, I think it might just be."

Maddie shook her head in wonder. Only a few days ago she'd thrown her hairpin, wishing to be saved from Sir Mostyn.

She almost laughed aloud. Well, she'd certainly been granted *that* wish. So much had happened since then, she could scarcely comprehend it. A sudden thought struck her. "But the well was dry when I made a wish."

"Well, it clearly isn't dry now. Just very low. Which is good for us or we'd be underwater. The important thing is, it's our way out of here."

They both looked upward, assessing the circular hole. The circumference looked about as wide as Gryff's shoulders.

"It's a shame nobody left a bucket dangling on a rope," he sighed.

"Do you think we can climb up it?"

"I don't see why not. If we can get up there. It'll be like climbing a chimney. Sweeps do it all the time."

He slipped back into the water and waded until he stood directly beneath the hole. He tilted his head to look up. "It's worth a try. There are plenty of handholds."

He stretched his arms up to their full extent, but the entrance of the shaft was still at least three feet higher. He jumped up a few times, trying to catch the inner rim to pull himself up, but it was tantalizingly just out of reach. Her spirits dropped.

"Come here. I'll hoist you up. You can reach it if you stand on my shoulders. But take your jacket off first. And the satchel. They'll hinder your climbing."

Maddie belatedly realized she was still wearing her fitted jacket on her upper half. How ridiculous, when she wore no skirts or petticoats below. She lifted off the satchel, peeled the sopping garment down her arms, and left them in a sodden heap on the ledge.

Her white cotton shirt had been rendered almost transparent by the water, and Gryff's gaze immediately homed in on the areas where the wet material stuck to her skin. He shook his head as if trying to clear it, and Maddie sent him an amused smile.

She hadn't forgotten his words; he'd promised to make love to her in daylight. She would hold him to that promise.

She slipped back into the frigid water and swam over to him. He threaded his fingers together and offered her his linked hands as a step, as if to help her mount a horse. For a moment they were face-to-face, her hands resting on his shoulders, and as she stared into his eyes she was filled with a sense of rightness, of belonging.

Was this the feeling that soldiers had after a battle? This camaraderie, honed by shared experience? A groundswell of emotion threatened to overwhelm her. Relief. Gratitude. Love.

She blinked in shock. *Love?* Where had that come from?

There was no time to dissect the thought. Gryff straightened and she surged up out of the water, and they both wobbled as she transferred her hands to the top of his head and put her knee on his shoulder.

"Ouch!" he muttered as she tugged on his hair.

He grunted with exertion, and she had a flash of embarrassment as the apex of her legs came level with his face. She moved again, pushing up to stand with her feet on his shoulders, like a circus performer. Wobbling precariously, his fingers encircling her ankles, she flattened her palms against the rough ceiling.

"Can you get a handhold inside the well?" Gryff panted.

He moved sideways a little, and she ducked the top half of her body into the shaft. The stone walls were blessedly rough. There were plenty of places to put her hands and feet.

She braced herself against the side of the well and hauled herself up, pressing her back against one wall, then lifted her feet from Gryff's shoulders and wedged them straight in front of her, locking her knees so she was braced across the gap.

She looked down. "How will you get up?" She reached down, as if to pull him up, but he shook his head with a little smile.

"That'll never work. I'm too heavy."

"But—I can't leave you down here!"

"You're going to have to, *cariad*. I'm counting on you to rescue me. As soon as you get to the top you can lower the bucket and the rope."

"Oh."

"You can do this. Just imagine you're scaling the towers at Trellech, about to break into my bedroom and demand that shawl of yours back. I still have it."

"Well, I have your greatcoat. So we're even."

"Go on. Get climbing."

Maddie sent him a stern glance, suddenly conscious of the fact that she was dressed only in her underwear. Her bloomers had a very revealing slit between her legs. "Promise me you won't look up as I climb."

The request was ridiculous, considering what they'd just done, but she couldn't quite shed her ingrained modesty.

His lips twitched. "I promise."

She started to climb.

Chapter 42

The well was at least thirty feet deep. Maddie's limbs shook as she made her way upward, her arms and legs spread wide so she straddled the narrow shaft.

Progress was painfully slow. She glanced up constantly—mainly to avoid looking down and seeing how far she might fall if she lost her footing—and took heart from the way the small circle of light grew larger as she climbed.

"Keep going! You're doing splendidly." Gryff's encouragement echoed up from below.

Maddie willed strength into her aching limbs. She couldn't remember the last time she'd done so much physical exercise, and she forced herself to focus on finding the next handhold, then the next. One inch at a time.

When she next glanced up she caught a glimpse of the moon and the sight filled her with a new burst of energy.

"You're almost there!"

Careful not to rush and lose her hold, she made one final effort and clasped the upper lip of the well. She hauled herself up and out and collapsed on the smooth flagstones, where she lay panting and shivering in the moonlit court-yard. The mossy stone beneath her cheek and the pine-scented air of the clearing were the finest things she'd ever experienced.

"Thank you. Oh, thank you!" she breathed to the universe.

She felt as if she'd been reborn. A rush of sheer exhilaration seized her and she pushed up onto her hands and knees and peered over the rim of the well. It was too dark to see anything below, and she felt a moment of panic for Gryff, but then the echo of his shout reached her.

"Clever girl! Now find the rope and throw it down."

Maddie got shakily to her feet and staggered over to the little enclave where a wooden bucket was tied to a length of rope. The rope was secured to an iron ring set into the stone wall, and she gave it a few experimental tugs to make sure it would hold Gryff's weight. The knot was tight, the fibers fused together by countless cycles of soaking and drying.

The bucket clattered against the sides of the well as she lowered it; then the rope slackened as Gryff caught it at the bottom.

"Don't forget the satchel," she shouted down.

The rope creaked and went taut as Gryff put his full weight on it, and she prayed it wouldn't snap, but after a while she could hear his approach as he made his way up. He was much quicker than she'd been.

When his dark curls appeared over the lip of the well she caught the back of his jacket and helped haul him out. He flopped onto his back, arms thrown wide like the survivor of a shipwreck washed up on shore. His chest was heaving, but he let out a yell of pure elation.

"We're out! Thank God for that! I never want to go near a blasted cave again."

They were both making wet puddles beneath them. He sat up with a laugh and lifted the strap of her satchel over his head, dumping the sodden weight next to him. He'd crammed her wet jacket inside—the arm was trailing out the top.

He stood and held out his hand. The moonlight showed him clearly, and Maddie suddenly remembered all the other times she'd refused his assistance. What a fool she'd been. It wasn't weakness to accept help from someone stronger.

She placed her cold hand in his, and he tugged her up to stand toe-to-toe. Without thought, she grabbed the front of his shirt and pulled him down for a kiss. Her knees almost buckled when he caught her face between his palms and fused his mouth to hers.

"Christ, Maddie. I thought we were going to die down there," he admitted hoarsely.

He scattered frantic kisses all over her face: her temple, her eyelids, her cheeks. He pressed a kiss to the hollow of her throat, then wrapped his arms around her and enfolded her in a hug that was so tight her ribs protested.

She let out a breathless laugh and hugged him back.

The snicker of a horse sounded from above. He retrieved the satchel, then tugged her up the shallow steps of the courtyard. Sir Galahad and Guinevere were still waiting patiently at the edge of the clearing, tied to a low tree.

Maddie's spirits plummeted. Harriet obviously hadn't managed to make her way back this way. She glanced up at the moon. "What time is it?"

"I have no idea. But if I know Rhys, he'll have started trying to dig us out as soon as possible. We need to let him know we're alive."

"What if Harriet's still in there? Or Morgan?" Nausea cramped her stomach at the thought of Harry being trapped, or worse. All the gold in the world wouldn't matter if her cousin had been killed.

Gryff squeezed her hand. "We'll get them out. I promise."

Even if all we retrieve is a body.

The grim possibility hung unspoken between them, but she didn't doubt his word. He would be relentless in his search. He was the kind of man who would refuse to leave a wounded man on the battlefield, or a fellow soldier unburied, even if they were the enemy.

She shivered and he shrugged out of his jacket and draped it around her shoulders. The top half of it was still dry, and she caught the edges and tugged it around herself, grateful for the warmth.

"Thank you."

He fastened her sodden satchel to Guinevere's saddle and together they started down the lane.

Maddie winced at the new aches and twinges in her muscles. She was aware of her body as she'd never been before, of the chafe of wet cotton against her tender breasts, the erotic scrape of it between her legs. Of Gryff's scent, permeating the coat that enfolded her. She breathed him deep into her lungs, sneakily, like an addict.

Chapter 43

The village of Mathern was a hive of activity. A crowd of figures were clustered in the small town square; a rescue attempt was clearly under way. Torches and lanterns bobbed as people milled about, gathering horses and supplies.

Maddie pulled Sir Galahad to a halt beneath the shadowed eaves of a cottage and glanced down at her state of undress. Her boots, stockings, and the bottom of her bloomers were clearly visible beneath Gryff's jacket. She dismounted, and Gryff did the same.

"You go on without me. I don't want everyone to see me without my skirts."

Gryff nodded, then squinted up at the church clock. "It's only half past ten!"

"What? You mean we were underground for less than four hours?"

Dear God, it had felt like a lifetime.

A man dressed in the distinctive blue coat of the customs patrol stood in the middle of the square, noisily commandeering a horse and cart. "You, there. We'll need more wagons—"

He glanced up, then stilled in amazement as he caught sight of Gryff.

"Lord Powys? Good God, you're alive!"

"Indeed I am, Captain Bridges." Gryff clasped the man's outstretched hand and gestured back at her. "As is Miss Montgomery. We've had a very lucky escape."

Maddie felt heat rise in her cheeks as the captain sent her a cheerful wave. She ducked farther behind Sir Galahad's hindquarters.

"Have you seen my brothers?" Gryff asked urgently.

The man nodded. "Both well, although Morgan took a blow to the head. Doctor Williams patched him up, but he refused to stay here. He's back at the beach looking for you."

Maddie's anxiety eased a little. Gryff had lost so many friends during the war; the death of a brother would have been another impossibly cruel blow.

"And my cousin?" she called out urgently.

"Maddie? Maddie!"

All three of them turned at the shout. Maddie's heart almost gave out as Harriet raced across the square in a flurry of skirts and flung herself into her arms.

"Harry!" She returned the embrace, scarcely able to believe her cousin was real, and not an apparition.

"Dear God!" Harriet croaked. "I thought you were dead! Maddie, how?"

The tears that had been threatening sprang to Maddie's eyes. Words were impossible; her heart felt as if it might burst with relief and happiness. She pulled back, and tried to explain between shaky sobs. "We got . . . trapped. We . . . climbed up the well."

Harriet's eyes grew wide with astonishment. "You climbed up a well? With Lord Powys?"

"The Virtuous Well. Where we left the horses."

"Good heavens!"

"But what about you?" Maddie croaked. "How did *you* escape?"

Harriet gave a dramatic shiver. "When that awful man threw the lantern I threw myself onto the ground and curled up into a ball." She shook her head. "That explosion! I've never heard anything so loud. I thought my ears were going to burst. When the dust settled, the main part of the cave was still mostly intact. The only real damage was where you'd been standing. A great chunk of the roof had fallen down."

She caught Maddie's hand in a fierce grip. "I thought you were dead. Lord Powys too. And Morgan—I could see him, unconscious, near the entrance."

"What did you do?"

Harriet adopted her most formidable expression, the one she used for dealing with cantankerous customers at her father's mapmaking business. Maddie called it her *no nonsense* face.

"I climbed down from the cave, of course. And checked to see if he was dead." The hint of a smile curved her mouth. "He wasn't. Although it *was* necessary to slap him quite soundly to get him to wake up."

Despite her exhaustion, Maddie smiled. Harry and Morgan's history was just as checkered as hers with Gryff. There was no love lost between the two of them. "I'm sure you found that satisfying."

"Oh, very. It's not often one gets the upper hand over a Davies male. I enjoyed it immensely."

"Was he badly hurt?"

"Hardly a scratch." Harriet sounded almost indignant. "The man has the luck of the devil, and a skull as hard as granite. I swear, he's like a cat with nine lives. Anyway, we heard Lord Powys shouting, and while we couldn't make out the words, Morgan was very relieved that his brother was alive—even if he *was* trapped. It gave me hope that you might be back there too.

"The beach looked like a battlefield. A few of the customs men had been injured, but the smugglers were all tied up and sitting on the sand, except for their leader. *He* must have been killed; he was standing right beneath the section that fell."

Maddie shook her head, saddened by the loss of life, even if it was that of a violent criminal. Sadler had probably only hastened his own demise: the penalty for smuggling would have been hanging, but she hoped his followers would be treated with a little more leniency. Even transportation would be better than execution.

"I helped Captain Bridges bring the wounded back here," Harriet continued briskly. "But I was so worried about you. I was dreading having to tell your father what had happened." She glanced at Maddie sternly. "You look exhausted. We need to get you to bed." Her mouth curled up into a sly smile and she leaned in closer to whisper. "And in deference to your weakened state, I'll wait until tomorrow for you to tell me why you're dressed in nothing but wet underwear and Lord Powys's coat."

Heat scalded Maddie's cheeks, but then she gasped in recollection. "I can't believe I forgot! We found gold! A whole seam of it underground."

Harriet's expression was priceless. "Gold! Did you bring it with you?"

Maddie glanced across to where Gryff stood talking to the captain. Her satchel was tied to the back of his saddle. "Lord Powys has it."

"And you think you'll see it again?" Harriet scoffed. "Ha!"

Maddie shook her head at her cynicism. "Of course. He promised we'd share it, half and half, and I believe him."

Harriet still looked skeptical. "It wouldn't be the first time a Davies has reneged on a deal."

Gryff turned toward them then, as if aware that he was the subject of discussion, but a furtive movement behind him caught Maddie's eye. A slim figure with its head concealed by the hood of a cloak was slinking toward the end of an alleyway.

Gryff turned to see what she was looking at, and let out a shout of recognition. "Hoi! That's Drake!"

He set off at a run across the cobbles. The figure turned in alarm and Maddie saw that it was indeed Sir Mostyn. He tried to make his escape, but he was too slow; with a bellow of fury Gryff tackled him to the ground.

The older man's outraged bellow echoed around the square. "Release me, you oaf! I'm a justice of the peace! I'll have you prosecuted for assault."

His wiry limbs flailed within his cloak—he looked like a deranged crow.

Gryff hauled him unceremoniously to his feet. "I'm not the one who's going to be prosecuted," he panted. "You think we don't know who's been backing those smugglers?"

Drake spluttered. "Me? Are you mad? What proof do you have?" He turned toward Maddie and sent her a beseeching look. "Miss Montgomery. This is ridiculous. Surely *you* don't believe these vile accusations."

"I do," Maddie said stoutly. "Just as I believe you were responsible for sending men to silence Gryff. And myself."

Drake shook his head, but she sent him a sweet smile. "If you're truly innocent, my lord, then you've nothing to fear. The smugglers will clear your name when they're interrogated."

She took an uncharitable amount of pleasure in the way Drake's face turned an even more sickly shade of white.

The captain strode forward and seized his arm. "Considering the severity of these accusations, sir, I'm afraid I'm going to have to place you in the cells with the rest of 'em. Come along."

Drake struggled, loudly protesting his innocence, but was escorted across the square to the town's small courthouse with its attached row of cells. Maddie watched him go with no small degree of satisfaction, and turned back find Gryff watching her intently.

A self-conscious flush heated her skin. There was so much to say, but it couldn't be said here, with an audience. She needed time to process everything that had happened between them, to order her thoughts. She started to shrug his jacket from her shoulders, but he shook his head as he came up to her.

"Keep it. I'm warm enough."

She nodded dumbly.

"We need to talk," he murmured, low enough that Harriet couldn't hear. "Privately." He smoothed a strand of her hair from her temple and tucked it behind her ear. "I promised to make love to you in daylight, Maddie Montgomery, and I intend to keep that promise."

His lips quirked in that teasing way she loved, but her chest constricted as the reality of the situation reasserted itself. Gryff wasn't talking about a permanent relationship. He'd made no secret of his intent to return to London. He was suggesting an affair, a series of brief liaisons until he returned to his old life.

The thought of making love with him again was enough to make her weak at the knees, but she didn't want to be his mistress, his furtive country fling for a few weeks. She didn't want to be sneaking around, trying to snatch a few stolen moments, like Ned and Gwynn, then having to pretend she barely knew him in public.

In a flash, she realized what she *did* want. All of his kisses, all of the time.

Because she loved him.

The insight hit her in the chest like a lightning strike straight to the heart. It was the same pain, the same paralyzing shock that made it hard to breathe.

When had this happened? She couldn't pinpoint an exact

moment; the feeling had sneaked up on her, like an incoming tide. She'd always felt such extremes of emotion for him, but the fuming, bubbling cauldron of *something* hadn't been hate. It had been love.

It *was* love.

Bloody hell.

Gryff moved closer, as if to take her in his arms, but she sidestepped, supremely aware that they were in public. Her feelings for him were too new, too raw to deal with now. She couldn't allow herself the dangerous luxury of his embrace; it would be too easy to get used to it.

She nodded at his horse instead. "You keep Guinevere and find your brothers. Harriet and I can ride double."

He frowned at her sudden coolness. "All right. But I'll see you soon."

She sent him a brief smile.

"I'll take the reins," Harriet said briskly, appearing at her side. "You're almost dead on your feet."

Maddie fell into a sort of daze as they rode back to Newstead Park, lulled into a strange half-waking trance as they plodded along. A gray mist hovered a few feet above the grass like a pale blanket, hazy and insubstantial. Tiny droplets settled on her eyelashes and lent a silvery sheen to Harriet's hair.

It was easy to see why the locals believed in fairies and sprites. The moonlight cast everything in shades of black and white, but there was something magical, almost otherworldly about it. Maddie felt as if they were suspended between earth and sky.

She tried to empty her mind, to let the hush of the ancient landscape soothe her, but her thoughts refused to settle. She was in love with Gryffud Davies. But what did he think of her? *I don't hate you* wasn't the same as *I love you*.

He said he'd dreamed of lying with her, but he'd probably dreamed of bedding countless women. He wanted an arrangement, to make love to her again, but it was clear the thought of anything permanent had never crossed his mind.

Would his interest in her wane, now that his curiosity and his physical appetites had been sated? It was possible. Probable, even.

For her part, she had the sneaking suspicion that what they'd shared would have a lasting effect on her, just like the lightning. Only instead of scars upon her arm, Gryff Davies would leave an indelible mark upon her heart.

She was faint with exhaustion by the time Newstead Park came into view, and an unexpected surge of emotion brought more tears to her eyes as she gazed at the familiar outline. The house was in her bones, in every childhood memory; it would have broken her heart if they'd had to sell it.

The windows were dark; Father and the Aunts had probably gone to bed, blithely unaware of the evening's drama.

She accepted Harry's offered arm and allowed her to guide her through the quiet kitchen and up the back stairs. In her bedroom she stood acquiescent as Harriet stripped her out of her damp undergarments, and all she could think of was that this was the second time today that someone had undressed her.

Her stomach fluttered at the memory of what she'd done with Gryff, but even that couldn't compete with the bone-weariness that was overtaking her. Harriet had scarcely put her in a clean nightgown when she fell into her waiting bed and let oblivion claim her.

Chapter 44

"Keep digging! Every minute counts."

Gryff's heart swelled with pride as Rhys's frantic bellow reached him across the sand. The beach was teeming with men, horses, and carts. The few locals he passed nodded at him without recognition—they had no idea who they were looking for, only that there were souls trapped inside. As a community long sustained by coal mining, the need for haste was understood by all. A tunnel collapse or mine explosion was everyone's worst fear.

He entered the torchlit cave. A team of six or seven men were hefting rock after rock into a waiting cart with almost superhuman strength. Rhys and Morgan were at the front. Rhys was filthy, sweaty with exertion. Morgan's head was bandaged, and he had one arm in a sling, but he was using his uninjured arm to move the rubble.

The final bit of tension in Gryff's shoulders melted away. *Everyone safe and accounted for.* He'd prayed for this feeling after every battle: confirmation that none of his men had been lost. Sadly, it had been an all-too-rare occurrence.

"Tell someone we need ropes and pulleys," Rhys shouted. "Damn it, we keep going until we find them. Dead or alive."

"Glad to hear it," Gryff said with a chuckle.

"Gryff!"

Rhys and Morgan both turned in unison and charged at him. Gryff submitted to their bone-crushing hugs and back slaps with a weary laugh.

"Bloody hell!" Rhys croaked. "We'd almost given you up for dead. Morgan swore he heard you shouting, but to be honest I didn't believe him. I thought we'd move all this rock and find nothing but your mangled corpse."

Morgan glared at him, then turned back to Gryff. "Where's the Montgomery girl? Tell me she was with you?"

"She was. She's on her way back to Newstead Park as we speak, along with her cousin."

Morgan expelled a relieved breath. "Thank Christ for that."

"I hear you have cousin Harriet to thank for your rescue," Gryff couldn't resist teasing.

"Rescue! The bloody woman nearly knocked a tooth loose." Morgan put his hand to his cheek and moved his jaw-bone left and right, as if trying to click it back into place.

"You're alive, though," Rhys chuckled.

"And *she's* as annoying as ever," Morgan groused. "I swear, one of these days she and I are going to come to blows."

Rhys snorted. "If that's what you want to call it." He stepped aside and raised his voice so the other men could hear. "Stop work, lads! Here's our man, alive and well!"

A great cheer went up from all assembled, like the sound made by a victorious army after a battle.

"What about the smuggler, Sadler?" Gryff asked.

"Already found his body," Morgan said grimly. "Wasn't pretty. He's been taken to the village for burial."

Rhys eyed Gryff from head to toe, taking in his filthy shirt, bloodstained breeches, and ruined boots. "God, you look like you've gone six rounds with Gentleman Jackson. Let's get you home and have a drink."

Gryff winced as another slap on his back aggravated his bruises. He'd definitely broken a few ribs. And the back of his leg was agony. Now that the adventure was over it felt like every part of him was either bruised or broken. Odd, but he hadn't noticed any of it when he'd been making love to Maddie.

In truth, he'd been aware of little else but her from the moment they'd been trapped. Every stumble, every shiver, every sigh. He shook his head, but the image of her lying beneath him was burned onto the back of his eyes, as if he'd looked too long at the sun. He saw her even when he closed his lids.

The three of them trailed out of the cave, exchanging thanks and hearty handshakes with all those who had come to help. By the time they reached Trellech Court, Gryff was ready to sleep for a week, but he changed into dry clothes and allowed Rhys to drag him into the library.

Rhys poured three generous brandies from the decanter on the sideboard, handed him a glass, and tapped the rim of his own against it. "Here's to a miracle deliverance."

Morgan claimed his glass and lifted it to join the others. "Cheers."

"Cheers," Gryff echoed. He sent Rhys a teasing glance. "I thought you'd already be calling yourself the next Earl of Powys."

His brother looked comically offended. "Not at all! I'm quite happy being the second son, thank you very much. All the fun and none of the responsibility." He winked. "Some of us don't need a title to have women falling at our feet."

Morgan chuckled. "Amen to that."

Gryff drank deeply, savoring the burn as the brandy warmed his insides. The taste reminded him of Maddie, of their kiss at the beach, and he cursed the fact that everything seemed to circle back to her. Bloody hell, was he doomed to think of her every time he took a drink now? He was becoming dangerously obsessed.

With an effort he dragged his thoughts back to the two men beside him, profoundly grateful that they were in his life. He wished, fleetingly, that Carys could have been there to celebrate with them, but his sister was still in London, playing merry havoc with the male half of the *ton*.

Some people, he knew, barely tolerated their siblings, but the four of them had always cherished a particularly strong bond. He leaned his head against the back of the chair and took another sip of brandy.

Life was good.

Chapter 45

Maddie woke with a stiff, aching body, and her mind in turmoil. What was to be done about Gryff? She would have to
see him soon, if only to retrieve her satchel and demand her
half of the gold.

If he was right about its value, then Father could sell the
small amount they'd already recovered and settle his most
pressing debts. And then he and Gryff would have to come to
some sort of agreement on how to start retrieving the rest.

Father would hate to have business dealings with a Davies,
of course—as the proposed canal scheme had proved—but
beggars couldn't be choosers. Near-penury would have to be
sufficient motivation for making a deal with the devil.

The thought of seeing Gryff again brought heat to her
cheeks and a knot to her belly, but she knew she was playing with fire. His offer of an affair was beyond tempting, but
it would definitely be a mistake. She knew her own heart;
she wasn't someone who could switch her affections from one
man to another as easily as a butterfly flitted between flowers.

Was she prepared to wait, in a limbo of expectation, for

him to fall in love with her? For him to be ready to wed? She doubted she had the patience. And what if she *did* wait for him, and he fell in love with someone else? Her heart couldn't take that kind of rejection.

A sigh spilled out of her. Well, she certainly wasn't the first woman to fall in love with an unsuitable man. She would recover, eventually, just as she'd recovered from the lightning strike. It seemed sensible, however, to limit her exposure to him, to avoid a fatal relapse.

She would treat him as a friend. Perhaps it was cowardly, but a clean break would be in everyone's best interest. She would look back on their time together with fond memories, and only a little pang in her heart.

"Maddie, get up!" Harriet's soft knock on the bedroom door claimed her attention. "Your father wants us all downstairs."

Maddie dressed swiftly and found the whole family in the front parlor. Father waved a sheet of paper at her as she entered.

"Excellent news!" he boomed. "Tristan's home! At least, he's back in England; he sent this from Dover. He's on his way to London as we speak."

Aunt Constance clapped her hands in delight. "Oh, that's famous! Why don't we all go to town and be there when he arrives? We can throw a party to welcome him home."

Father frowned. "I told you, Connie, the town house is to be sold. We haven't a penny to waste on parties." He sank into a chair, pushed his spectacles up onto the top of his head, and massaged his temples. "Perhaps Tris can think of a way to save the estate. Because I'm at my wit's end."

Harriet shot Maddie a conspiratorial glance. "A parcel came for you, Maddie. From Trellech Court."

Father's head snapped back up, and he glared at the small brown-paper-wrapped package on the side table as if it might explode. "What's a Davies doing sending you parcels?"

Maddie felt a guilty flush creep up her neck, but she stood and pulled on the string tied around the object. It was too small to be her satchel, but her heart gave an excited thump when she saw her brass tinderbox.

Harriet leaned forward, desperately trying to peer inside as she pried open the lid, but Maddie took a quick peek and slammed the lid closed again.

She cleared her throat. "Father, I have something to tell you. Well, all of you, actually."

As succinctly as possible, she gave a highly edited version of the events of the previous day.

Aunt Connie and Aunt Prudence both listened with bated breath, while her father merely interjected with the occasional "Good God, Maddie!"

Harriet pointed at the tin. "So that's where you put the gold?"

"It is."

"And . . . is it still there?"

All four of them leaned forward as Maddie reopened the lid and tilted it for them to see. A collective gasp filled the room.

"It certainly is," Maddie said triumphantly.

In truth, it hardly looked as if Gryff had removed his half, but it had been so dark in the cave it was possible she was wrong.

"Father, this is for you." She offered the tin to her father, who took it with shaking hands. "Do you think there's enough to get us to London to welcome Tristan home?"

He expelled an incredulous huff. "I should say so. Dear girl, I'm speechless." He fumbled in his waistcoat for his handkerchief and blew his nose loudly, then dabbed at his suspiciously bright eyes. "You've saved us all."

He turned to Harriet. "You too, Harriet. Not that I condone all this gallivanting about the countryside, especially in the company of those dreadful Davies boys, but in this particular case I can see it was unavoidable. You've turned up trumps. To London we will go!"

The Aunts cheered.

"And just think, that awful Sir Mostyn was involved with the smugglers." Aunt Connie shook her gray head. "I always knew he was a bad'n. Didn't I always say so, Pru?"

"You did," Aunt Pru agreed placidly. "What a bounder. I'm very glad you didn't accept him, Madeline."

Maddie smiled. "So am I."

Aunt Connie bounced in her chair like an excited child. "Oh, I can't wait to see London again! It's been an *age* since we were there. And now we have money again, there's nothing we can't do. We're going to have so much fun!"

Maddie almost laughed at her father's aghast expression. Aunt Pru and Aunt Con taking the town by storm was something she didn't want to miss.

Chapter 46

Gryff waited with barely concealed impatience for a note from Maddie. He ached to see her again. Now that he'd learned the taste and feel of her, he was like some kind of opium addict, desperate for his next pipe.

He'd spent the best part of the morning with his brothers, assisting Captain Bridges in taking statements and depositions from the smugglers, who'd been placed in the tiny three-cell jail on one side of the village square. Now that their leader, Sadler, was dead, most of them were happy to make a full confession in the hope that their cooperation might encourage a judge to look more favorably on their crimes.

At least three of them had independently corroborated that Sir Mostyn Drake had been instrumental in helping them to avoid the customs men by providing advance warning of patrols. And they also suggested he'd acted as a middleman, storing contraband in outhouses on his estate before arranging to have them transported farther afield, to Bristol, Oxford, and London.

With such an abundance of evidence, Gryff had taken a great deal of pleasure in informing Drake of the charges leveled against him. The bastard would languish in jail until his case was brought before a magistrate.

By the time the three of them had ridden back to Trellech Court, Gryff was in a rare state of agitation.

"Any post come while we were out?" he asked as soon as they stepped in from the stables. A glance at the silver card tray in the hallway confirmed it was empty.

"I'm afraid not, sir," Beddow intoned. "Were you expecting something?"

Gryff frowned. *Yes, damn it.* He'd expected Maddie to send him a *when can I see you again* letter. Or at the very least a thank-you note for sending her that tin of gold. Even if she hadn't noticed that he'd left all of it in there for her, she could have shown some blasted gratitude.

"No, no," he muttered. "Not expecting anything."

A disturbing thought gripped him. What if she didn't want to see him again? She'd seemed to enjoy their lovemaking. She *had* enjoyed it, damn it—she couldn't have been faking her body's reactions, the tremors he'd felt when he'd been inside her—but what if he'd frightened her? Had he been too ardent in his attentions? Had he scared her?

Dear God, what if he'd put her off sex for life?

No, he was being ridiculous. Perhaps she'd just been too busy this morning to write.

Perhaps she was embarrassed.

Perhaps she doesn't like you as much as you like her, a little voice whispered in his ear.

Perhaps she was just using you to relieve her of her virginity.

Perhaps now you've shown her how good it can be, and how to avoid getting pregnant, she'll realize she can do that with any man she fancies . . .

Gryff ran a hand over his face as his stomach curled unpleasantly. The thought of Maddie with any other man made his blood boil.

Damn it, they weren't finished! He wanted to make love to her again, in daylight, just as he'd promised, with a limitless supply of contraception and a bed large enough to sleep six. He wanted to explore every inch of her. To fall asleep with her in his arms and wake with her still there. He wanted to see her rosy with sleep, pink-cheeked and drowsy after he'd pleasured her to the brink of exhaustion. He—

"Is there a particular reason you're just standing in the middle of the hallway staring into space?" Rhys demanded.

Gryff blinked and felt an embarrassed flush rise on his cheeks. He cleared his throat and cupped his hands over his crotch to conceal the semi-rigid evidence of his thoughts.

"No, no. Just woolgathering."

Morgan sent him a sardonic look. He was about to say something when the sound of hooves interrupted him, and they all glanced toward the open door. A courier clattered to a stop in the stable yard.

"Letter for Lord Powys."

Gryff's heart started to beat in double time. He strode forward and held out his hand for the folded missive. It was sealed with the Montgomery crest—three fleurs-de-lis on a shield topped with a plumed helmet—and he breathed a silent sigh of relief.

Ignoring Rhys and Morgan's avid interest, he strode into the study and slammed the door behind him for some privacy. He realized his hands were trembling as he tore open the letter.

Lord Powys, he read, then frowned.

That was formal. Not even *Dear Lord Powys*. And why was she using his title? Why not *Dear Gryff*, or *Darling*? Still, perhaps she'd been worried someone else might read the letter. Fair enough.

Please accept my undying gratitude for your assistance yesterday. I think it fair to say that it was an experience I shall never forget.

Gryff snorted through his nose. *Assistance* was one word for it. He'd never forget it either. Especially the part where she moaned his name as he drove her to a heart-stopping climax. Or the bit where she'd kissed him as if the world were going to end.

Thank you for the tin of gold. Harriet didn't think you'd surrender it, but I never had any doubts about your honor.

Gryff mentally consigned Harriet to perdition, even though he had to admit that the Davieses had a certain amount of historical form in backing out of deals with the Montgomerys.

I'm sure my father will be willing to discuss ways to retrieve the rest of the gold from the seam we discovered.

Gryff snorted again. "Willing" might be stretching it. Old Montgomery would probably prefer to have his balls roasted over an open fire than work with him, but he'd have no choice if he wanted to clear his debts and save the ancestral pile.

But those discussions will have to wait until we return from London. Tristan is on his way home, and we have decided to go en famille to welcome him.

With best wishes, and hope for your future friendship, Madeline Montgomery

Gryff stared at the final lines blankly. And then their meaning penetrated his dull brain and he slapped the letter down on the desk with an audible thump.

London. She was going to London. Away from him.

He re-read the letter, and felt his temper rise.

Friendship? Gratitude!

He didn't want her bloody gratitude! He wanted her naked in bed, under him, over him, loving him, for as long as it took to get her out of his system.

You're never going to get her out of your system.

"Shut up," Gryff muttered crossly. But his sly subconscious wouldn't listen.

You know why? Because you're in love with her. And you've been in love with her forever. Just admit it, you idiot.

Gryff raked both hands through his hair. Was it true? He tested the idea carefully, probing at it as he'd poke a loose tooth with his tongue. He blinked at the leather desktop. It didn't seem to be an unreasonable deduction.

Bloody, bloody hell.

He was in love with Maddie Montgomery, and she wasn't even here for him to tell.

A surge of righteous indignation assaulted him. The little coward, writing him a letter then running away. If she'd had enough of him, she could bloody well tell him to his face.

And if she *hadn't* had enough of him, and was merely haring off to London to avoid whatever this . . . this *thing* between them was, then he wouldn't let her get away with that either.

A striking thought came to him: In giving her that tin of gold, he'd given her the means to evade him. Well, damn it. She ought to be in love with *him*. He'd saved her from almost certain death on several notable occasions, just like every bloody prince in every stupid fairy tale. Not to mention he'd given her several orgasms, under very challenging circumstances, and was quite prepared to give her countless more, if only she'd let him.

He bloody well *deserved* to get the girl.

One way or another he was going to make her admit her feelings for him. Whether they were good, bad, or indifferent.

He couldn't believe they were indifferent. Nobody kissed the way she did, yielded so sweetly, participated with such enthusiasm, if they were indifferent.

He stood, ready to order Beddow to start packing for London, then stopped in horrified realization. He couldn't go to

London—because of that bloody duel with Sommerville. He sank back into his chair with a groan.

Rhys entered the study without knocking and collapsed gracelessly into one of the deep leather armchairs. Gryff scowled at him.

"Hung over?" Rhys asked amiably.

"No."

"Injuries from yesterday giving you grief?"

"No."

"Must be a woman, then. Nothing else puts that look on a man's face."

Gryff scowled at him some more.

"Miss Montgomery, I take it?" Rhys chuckled, unperturbed by the glower. "You looked exactly like that when you came back in from the garden at Squire Digby's. Only five minutes after *she* came in with a very similar expression, I recall."

He studied his nails, and Gryff cursed his brother's perspicacity.

Rhys glanced at the letter on the desk. "Lovers' tiff?"

"We're not—" He bit back the instinctive denial as he realized that's exactly what they had been. Heat flushed his cheeks. He wanted them to be lovers again.

Rhys raised his brows and chuckled. "Ah."

Gryff dropped his forehead to the desk. "Bloody hell."

"I spoke to one of those two lovely barmaids at the Red Dragon when we were in town," Rhys said. "Bess. Or Tess. One of the two. They said their cousin Gwynn, who's one of the maids up at Newstead Park, was off to London with the family." He paused significantly. "But perhaps you already knew?"

Gryff raised his head and ran his hands through his hair.

Rhys sent him a sunny, innocent smile that fooled him not a bit. There was a devilish twinkle in his eye. "I forgot to tell you yesterday, what with all the excitement. Sinclair wrote to me. It seems you're no longer persona non grata in London."

Gryff's heart missed a beat. "How so?"

"He said Prinny was at White's the other day, and re-marked at how dull it was without you. When Fox pointed out that *he* was the one who'd banned dueling, he said—and I quote—'Good God, Charles, half the House of Lords would be locked up if we punished everyone who dueled. My father forgave his war minister and foreign secretary when they did it. Someone tell Powys to come back before I die of boredom.'"

"Good God!" Gryff muttered.

"That's practically a royal command," Morgan chuckled, striding in through the open door.

"He only wants me back so he can ask me for money," Gryff said dazedly. "Or to beg me to forgive the loans Father gave to him. He's always short of cash."

"That's probably true," Rhys said. "But at least it means you're not banished here forever."

Gryff shook his head. When he'd ridden down here last week he'd thought of it as a punishment, as something to endure until he could return to the excitement of London. Only the promise of seeing Maddie again had made it remotely tempting.

Now she was the reason he was desperate to get back to town. He wanted to be wherever she was.

He'd never been as attracted to any other woman as he was to her. She fascinated him on almost every level. Not just the physical, but the intellectual too. She was brave, and strong, and beautiful. God, he knew of fifty men who'd have given up at the first obstacle down in those caves, but she'd soldiered on. Resourceful, determined. Amazing.

He wanted to see her, to tease her, to laugh with her, and to love her. Again. And again. And again.

A hundred times might not be enough. He was beginning to think a lifetime wouldn't be enough.

The thought made him pause. No, not a *lifetime*. That was ridiculous.

Or was it?

Filled with new determination, he pushed back from his chair and stood.

"Pack your bags, boys. We're going to town."

Chapter 47

"Maddie, you're never going to believe this. Fortune smiles on us once more!"

Maddie glanced up from her book and lifted her brows at her father's jubilant expression.

They'd been in London for almost a week now, and it was as entertaining and as exhausting as ever. Tristan had arrived shortly after they'd all unpacked at the town house in Hanover Square, and the past few days had been a whirl of social engagements and house calls to renew friendships and acquaintances.

"What is it?" she asked mildly.

"A note from James Christie." At Maddie's blank look he said, "You know, the auctioneer, over in Pall Mall."

"Oh, right."

"He sent me a list of items in his next sale. You remember that dictionary you asked me about a short while back?"

"Yeees," Maddie said slowly. Heat rose in her skin and she tried to fight the telltale blush that accompanied it. That dictionary had caused a whole heap of trouble.

She'd been trying not to think about the man responsible for that trouble all week, and had failed spectacularly.

Her friend Elizabeth Trent had told her that Gryff and his brothers were back in town, and the news had kept her on pins and needles for days. She'd jumped every time there was a knock on the door, and her pulse increased whenever the mail was delivered.

She wasn't sure if she wanted to see him or not. It wasn't as if he'd call on her here, for a social visit, but she'd been hoping he might reply to her letter.

The possibility that he might have followed her back to town to persuade her to reconsider an affair was too far-fetched to hope for. He'd probably just got bored with life in the country. Perhaps, now that she'd relegated him to the status of friend, he was looking for some other woman on whom to lavish his affections. The thought made her grind her teeth.

Father was still talking.

"Well, by the greatest good fortune, the second volume's coming up for sale tomorrow. What do you think of that, my girl?"

Maddie wasn't sure he expected a reply, but she smiled brightly anyway. "That is excellent news." A kernel of suspicion stirred in her chest. "Why would someone be selling just the second half?"

Father shrugged. "Who knows? People lose books all the time. I know *I* do. Does it matter?"

"No. I suppose not," she murmured.

Her initial thought—that Gryff was, for some unfathomable reason, selling his half of the book—was foolish. It was just a coincidence.

"Do you know who the seller is?"

"No idea," Father said dismissively. "The catalog just says 'property of a gentleman.'"

"Hmmm."

"I'm going to bid for it."

"You still have bills to pay," she cautioned. The gold from the caves had been worth more than six hundred pounds, and father had used it to pay off his most pressing creditors. That, in turn, had been enough to reassure the rest, who'd agreed to wait until the next batch of gold had been extracted for payment in full. Father had assured them it would take less than six months.

"You still have to speak with Lord Powys and agree how you're going to mine the rest of the gold," she reminded him.

He gave a petulant huff, like a child forced back to his studies on a sunny day.

"Promise me you won't bid more than fifty pounds," she begged.

"Fine."

Aunt Constance looked up from her knitting as father withdrew. "Is he talking about Samuel Johnson's dictionary, dear?"

Maddie nodded.

"Do you know, Pru and I met Doctor Johnson several times? Didn't we, Pru?"

"Oh, yes! It must be over fifty years ago now. He was vastly amusing."

Aunt Constance chuckled. "Wasn't his dictionary famous for leaving out quite a few prurient words?"

"I believe it was. Lavinia Webster congratulated him for omitting them, and Johnson said to her, 'Why, madam, have you been looking for them?'"

Aunt Connie cackled in delight. "I remember! She was such a prude. Her face went as red as a beetroot. I laughed myself silly."

Maddie shook her head at their antics, then smiled as Tristan entered the room. Her older brother was looking well, still tanned from his travels. She was glad to have him safely home.

"Everyone looking forward to Lady Belton's party tomorrow night?" he asked the room in general. "I've heard it's going to be a dreadful crush."

Maddie's heart skipped a beat. Would Gryff be there? And if so, how should she act when she saw him?

At least she had a nice dress to wear. Father had authorized new gowns for Harriet and herself from Madame de Tourville in Bond Street, and she'd chosen an absurdly flattering seafoam-green silk. It was the most daring gown she'd ever bought, but the demure styles she'd worn for her previous seasons hadn't appealed. She wasn't the same girl who'd first come to London four years ago, and she was heartily glad she wasn't expected to wear the pale, insipid colors required of the debutantes.

The question was, did she want to see Gryff or not?

Chapter 48

Christie's auction house in Pall Mall was a handsome building with iron railings and a triangular portico above the door.
Maddie had decided to accompany her father, just to make
sure he didn't succumb to auction fever and bid more than
they could reasonably afford. Tristan had decided to come
along too.

Unlike many establishments, which actively dissuaded
women, the auction rooms were open to all, and she nodded
to several women of her acquaintance, including Lady Har-
court and Mrs. Coutts, as they took a seat and waited for the
auctioneer, James Christie the younger, to ascend the rostrum
and start the sale.

Father was in a jovial mood at the prospect of finally com-
pleting the dictionary, but his brows drew together as he
scanned the room and fixed on someone across the aisle.

"What's that insufferable popinjay Davies doing here?" he
hissed.

Maddie's heart leapt to her throat, but she forced herself
not to swing around in her seat. Instead she slowly turned her

head and located Gryff, who was seated a few rows back. His sister, Titian-haired Carys, was sitting next to him, looking ravishing in a lilac silk gown trimmed with lace.

Maddie drank in the sight of him. He was dressed impeccably in a bottle-green jacket and buff breeches. The twinkle of an emerald stickpin gleamed in his perfectly tied cravat.

She jerked her head to the front again, glad he hadn't turned and noticed her spying on him. "Perhaps there's a book he's interested in buying," she said levelly.

"Poppycock! I know why he's here, the scoundrel. He's heard about the dictionary and means to bid against me."

"I'm sure that's not true. Why would he want two copies of the second volume? If anything, I'd expect him to be after the first half, to complete his own set."

"The first volume isn't in this sale. And he'd do it just to take perverse pleasure in thwarting me, that's why," Father groused. "He's as bad as his father. Even if he doesn't win it, he'll have still inflated the price. It's what Davieses *do*."

He was working himself into a fine state of agitation, but Maddie couldn't help notice the twinkle of anticipation in his eyes at the prospect of a new challenge. He was enjoying it, she realized with a start. The presence of a new foe had added an extra dimension to the task.

"I'm sure you're wrong," she murmured, but the words sounded unconvincing, even to her own ears.

Tristan lifted his brows as he caught sight of Carys. "That red-haired hellion's still scandalizing the *ton*, I take it?"

Maddie chuckled. "You could say that. Her latest escapade was a horse race along Rotten Row."

He made a disapproving clucking sound with his tongue. "The girl's always been a hoyden. Her brothers give her far too much leeway. Just because she's beautiful doesn't mean she should be given carte blanche to do whatever she pleases."

Maddie sent him a teasing sideways glance. "Oh, you noticed she's beautiful, hmm?"

"From a purely aesthetic point of view," Tristan said quickly. "Her temperament leaves a lot to be desired."

"She's turned down at least a dozen suitors since you left."

"I wonder how many of them realize what a lucky escape they've had. She doesn't need a husband, she needs a tamer."

"Now, that's mean," Maddie protested. "You have to admit she's far more interesting than the latest batch of insipid debutantes. At least she's memorable."

"*Memorable*," Tristan echoed with a laugh. "That's certainly one way of putting it."

The subject of their conversation chose that moment to lean forward in her seat and look directly over at them. Her wide mouth curved in a genuinely delighted smile. Tristan cursed under his breath as she raised her faintly curved eyebrows in silent, laughing reproof—she'd caught them watching her.

Maddie had no doubt Carys was aware they'd been talking about her. As they watched, she brought her gloved fingers to her lips and blew Tristan a teasing kiss followed by a tiny wave.

Tristan whipped his head back around and sat back in his chair, arms crossed. Maddie sent the other girl a friendly smile, then turned back to the front as the auction began.

"What lot is the dictionary?" she murmured.

"Twenty-three," Father said.

They all waited impatiently.

"Lot twenty-three," Christie finally intoned, "Dictionary, Samuel Johnson, volume two."

A clerk dressed in black held the book aloft next to the rostrum so the room could see it. Maddie shifted in her seat and forced herself not to glance back at Gryff.

"Shall we start the bidding at two pounds?"

"Here!" Father raised his hand to gain the auctioneer's attention.

Christie nodded. "Two pounds, here at the front. Any more interest?"

Maddie held her breath, praying her father was wrong about Gryff being there to outbid them, but her heart leapt as Christie accepted a bid of three pounds from behind them. She swiveled around, and sure enough, Gryff was lowering his hand. He caught her eye and a wicked grin slid over his face.

Her mouth dropped open in shock. The wretch! He really was bidding against them.

"Five pounds," Father offered.

Christie pointed his gavel at him. "Five pounds here. Do I hear ten?"

Maddie glared at Gryff, just daring him to bid. He lifted his brows, sent her a slow, taunting smile, and casually waved his printed catalog to bid ten pounds. Her stomach did a little somersault.

"That blackguard!" Father muttered beside her, pointedly refusing to turn around. "He's running me up!" He bid twelve pounds.

Gryff bid fifteen.

Father bid eighteen.

Gryff bid twenty.

Maddie gripped the back of her chair and sent her most intimidating frown across the room at Gryff. *Stop it!* she mouthed.

His answer was a wink, and a bid of twenty-five, against her father's twenty-two.

Christie seemed delighted by the heated competition. "I have twenty-five pounds, here on my left."

Father stuck his hand up. "Thirty pounds," he said belligerently.

Maddie sucked in a breath, praying Gryff wouldn't force

the bidding any higher. His gaze held hers and her pulse thumped erratically in her throat. He slowly shook his head.

"No more bids?" Christie said, rather mournfully. "Are you sure?"

When Gryff shook his head again, the auctioneer said, "In that case, sold, for thirty pounds, to Lord Lucas." He crashed his gavel down on the rostrum, and a second clerk recorded the sale in the ledger.

"Ha!" Father crowed.

Maddie slumped back into her chair, completely at a loss to understand Gryff's motives.

Was he angry at her for refusing his offer of an affair? Was this some sort of revenge?

That scenario hardly fit with his character; he wasn't the sort to play cruel, vindictive games. Even if she'd hurt him by her rejection—and she didn't think he cared deeply enough about her for *that*—he wouldn't do something so spiteful. He'd probably already found his next mistress. Why waste time punishing *her*?

And if he'd truly meant to annoy her father, why hadn't he simply kept bidding? He knew how precarious their finances were. He could afford to pay a great deal more than them. But instead, he'd let her father make the winning bid. It made no sense.

She endured the remaining half hour of the auction with barely concealed impatience, the back of her neck tingling with the certainty that Gryff was watching her from across the room. He didn't bid on any other lots, and she wound herself into knots wondering why he would go out of his way to antagonize her father—especially since the two of them were going to have to work together on the joint mining project very soon.

As soon as the last lot was sold Tristan headed outside to locate the carriage. Maddie and her father made their way over to the tables at the front of the room to collect and pay for their purchase. Since most of the other buyers had the same idea, there was a general crush of bodies as everyone converged on the hapless clerks.

Father surged forward, making his way through the crowd with a judicious use of his elbows, and Maddie found herself hemmed in on all sides, squashed between a red-faced man with round spectacles and an elderly scholar.

A large body pressed up against her from behind and the unmistakable scent of Gryff's cologne filled her nose. Her heart crashed against her ribs as for the briefest of seconds her back was pressed against his front. She almost sagged against him, then stiffened her spine.

"Step aside for the lady," he growled.

His arm came around her in a protective cage, and he pushed the red-faced man aside. His intimidating size caused a clear path to open up before her. She hurried forward to join her father at the clerk's desk, acutely aware of Gryff's commanding presence inches behind her. Her whole body tingled in awareness.

Father's smile of greeting turned to a frown as he saw Gryff. "Lord Powys," he managed stiffly.

Gryff stepped around her and inclined his head in a polite nod. "Baron Lucas." He turned to her, his eyes glittering with secret amusement. "Miss Montgomery."

She bobbed a tiny curtsy, suddenly tongue-tied. She'd been intimate with him, but now it was if they were polite strangers. A pang of regret clenched her stomach. Idiot! She could have had so much more. Why *hadn't* she agreed to an affair? It might only have lasted for a short time, but wouldn't it have been better to have loved and lost than never to have experienced it at all?

She'd been trying to protect her heart, but it would have hurt either way. Just looking at him, and yearning, was painful.

"You made the winning bid, sir," Gryff said gravely. "Congratulations."

Father seemed a little taken aback by such a sporting attitude, but he obviously decided he could be magnanimous in victory. "Thank you, Davies. I'm sure you'll find your missing half at some point."

The phrase jolted Maddie's memory; Aunt Pru had been searching for her "other half" too.

Gryff's gaze flickered to her. "Thank you, sir. I certainly hope so."

She clenched her hand into a fist and pressed her nails into her palm. He was talking of books. Not love.

Mercifully, the auction clerk interrupted them and Father accepted the volume in question. He clutched it to his chest and gave the cover a loving stroke with his hand.

Maddie froze. There was a scratch across one corner.

A rather distinctive scratch.

A scratch she'd traced with her fingers when deciding whether to steal that very same volume from Gryff's library.

She glanced up, and found Gryff watching her intently, that enigmatic half smile at the corner of his mouth. She opened her own mouth to accuse him, but he shook his head in a tiny negative motion.

"Will you be attending Lady Belton's gala this evening?" he asked casually.

"We will," Father said.

"Then I shall see you there. I have a proposition to put to you."

Maddie frowned as her stupid heart gave another jolt. He was addressing her father, referring to the joint mining project—but his gaze never left her face.

She had to stop seeing double meanings in everything he said.

Gryff raised his fingers in a jaunty salute and stepped back. "Until tonight then. Enjoy your purchase."

He strode away, leaving them both in shocked silence.

Maddie barely noticed the carriage ride home. She filtered out Father's ecstatic chatter and tried to make sense of what had just happened.

Gryff had put his half of the dictionary up for sale. And then deliberately bid on his own property against her father.

Why? To get the price up? To make her father pay the maximum amount?

That was an incredibly risky strategy. He couldn't have known when Father would stop bidding; he could easily have ended up buying his own book back again—and incurred extra fees from the auctioneer in the process.

The busy streets beyond the carriage window rolled past without her really seeing them. She wanted to scream with frustration. She knew that wicked smile. Gryff Davies was up to something, but she couldn't for the life of her imagine what it was.

Chapter 49

"Dear God, Carys, what's that on your head?"

Gryff looked up at Morgan's exclamation. Carys stood framed in the doorway of the study, having paused there for dramatic effect. She lifted one hand and gently patted her elaborate coiffeur.

It was an astonishing sight. Blue ribbons had been threaded through her natural red hair to resemble waves, and a miniature ship, complete with paper sails, perched atop them at a jaunty angle, as though being pitched and tossed in a storm. Pearl-ended pins were scattered throughout, like tiny specks of seafoam.

"It's a ship, brother dear," she said sweetly. "In honor of your safe return from the perilous seas."

"Yes, I can see that," Morgan said, his tone mystified. "Three years in the navy and I can, in fact, recognize a ship when I see one. It appears to be a galleon of some kind. The real question, I suppose, is . . . why?"

Carys's rich laugh echoed around the room. "Why *not*? Because it's so completely ridiculous. It amuses me to make the slavish followers of fashion look silly when they inevitably copy my style. You watch, after tonight ships will be all the rage."

Gryff took in the rest of her outfit. The year of her come-out Carys had endured the pale pastels expected of a debutante, but the following season she'd embraced the ability to choose richer, more provocative colors. With her creamy skin and flaming hair she could make almost any tone look good. And she always managed to add some individual quirk or detail that made her stand out from the crowd. Tonight's dress was no exception.

"Are you really going out in that?" Rhys drawled, from his recumbent position on the sofa.

Carys rolled her eyes and glanced down at the expanse of milky bosom on show. "Of course I am. Don't be such a prude, Rhys. This low neckline is *everywhere* this season."

"It's not the neckline I object to. It's the fabric. I've seen windows less transparent."

"Pfft. It's an optical illusion." She lifted her skirts. "See, the top layer's sheer, but the underlayer is skin-toned. It just *looks* like I'm not wearing anything underneath."

Rhys let out a disapproving huff.

"Almost-naked is the look we're going for these days, is it?" Gryff chuckled.

Carys grinned at him, sensing an ally. "It is. I'll be most disappointed if some stuffy old dowager doesn't faint at the sight of me. And at least I haven't dampened the material to make it cling, like Cecily Browne did last month."

Rhys turned to Gryff. "You can't mean to let her out of the house looking like that?"

Carys glared at him. "Of course he does. Stop being such a hypocrite. If a woman you liked wore this dress, you'd be delighted. It's only because I'm your sister that you're being so disagreeable."

"You look like an opera singer," Rhys growled.

Carys's smile widened. She clearly took that as a compliment, instead of the criticism he'd intended. "Oh, good. And I suppose you'd know, given how many of them you're acquainted with."

Gryff interrupted before Rhys could say anything else.

"You look lovely," he said soothingly. "Just make sure you wear a cloak or you'll freeze to death in the carriage."

He'd long ago learned to trust his little sister. Carys knew to an inch just how far she could push her outrageous behavior. She might take a wicked delight in creating a stir in society, but she'd never do something so terrible that she'd be ostracized.

She sent him a triumphant grin. "Thank you, brother dear. I'm so glad you're the oldest, and not Rhys or Morgan. They'd have packed me off to a nunnery years ago."

"I doubt anywhere would have you," Morgan muttered. "Not even if we financed a whole new cathedral."

"Just try not to have anyone propose to you this evening," Gryff said, only half joking. "I'm sick of lovestruck swains cornering me in the cardroom to 'have a word.' I want a night off."

Carys waved her hand in a dismissive gesture. "You know I do nothing to encourage them. In fact, I do everything to *dis*courage them. Just look at this hair. It's monstrous. But they're all so shallow, all they see is my pretty nose and my well-turned ankle."

"And your impressive dowry," Morgan added with a chuckle. "That's more than enough to make a man overlook your eccentricities."

Carys sighed. "It's true. I've even made having freckles fashionable. Last summer I deliberately spent weeks without my hat, hoping freckles would put me beyond the pale. And what happened? As soon as we got back to town, Simon Bainbridge declared himself 'utterly charmed,' and the next thing you know half the ladies are buying brown pencils and drawing freckles on their cheeks. I can't win!"

Gryff chuckled. "Well, there'll be at least one man there to-night who won't fall under your spell. Tristan Montgomery's back from his Grand Tour."

Carys wrinkled her nose, which made her look more like the stubborn twelve-year-old he remembered than the self-possessed young woman she'd become. For an instant he wondered at the change; halfway through her first season she'd gone from dutiful, biddable debutante to this carefree, confident creature, almost overnight.

He hadn't taken much notice of it at the time, being determined to enjoy his last few weeks before going to fight in France, but now he wondered if something had happened to cause such a seismic shift. As a girl Carys had always indicated that she would like to marry, but now that she was out, she seemed entirely dismissive of the male sex.

"Temperate Tristan's back, is he?" Rhys said, using the teasing nickname they'd given their neighbor on account of his levelheadedness.

"He is," Carys said dismissively. "Gryff and I saw him at the auction this morning. He looks exactly the same. I expect he's as uptight as ever."

"Oh, he's not that bad. You're just cross because he never reacts to your teasing."

Carys shrugged. "The man's an automaton. He needs to learn to enjoy himself more."

"Leave the poor chap alone," Morgan said easily. "Content yourself with the adoration of every other man in the room."

Carys's green eyes twinkled. "Ah, but you know I can't resist a challenge."

Gryff rose to his feet and tugged at the cuffs of his evening jacket, suddenly impatient to see his own particular challenge for the evening: Maddie.

"We should be off. I'll have Pinsent bring the carriage round."

Chapter 50

Lady Belton's ball was, as Tristan had predicted, a terrible crush. Carriages lined the streets waiting to deposit their occupants at the porticoed entrance to the Belton residence. It took Maddie and the rest of the family almost twenty minutes waiting in the receiving line until they finally stepped into the crowded ballroom.

The Aunts were all of a twitter. Father looked resplendent in a new deep-burgundy evening jacket, and Tristan looked as handsome as ever. A stickler for detail and aesthetic order, he was always immaculately turned out.

Maddie scanned the room. She spied Harriet and Uncle John at the far end of the dance floor and sent them a half-hearted wave.

She spotted Rhys Davies next, talking to a ravishing blonde near the punch table, then Morgan, whose arm was supported in a sling. Judging by the gaggle of women around him, it was clear he was attracting a great deal of feminine sympathy.

Harriet rolled her eyes as Maddie reached her side. "Do you

see that? He's matched the fabric of his sling to his waistcoat! What a charlatan."

Maddie chuckled at her outraged tone, then stilled as she saw Gryff, heart-stoppingly handsome in dark evening clothes. She looked to see who he was with, and blinked in disbelief: He was standing with Henry Sommerville, the very man with whom he'd dueled less than a fortnight ago.

The two of them had obviously decided to let bygones be bygones. Even as she watched, Gryff said something amusing, and Sommerville roared with laughter and slapped him on the back.

The beautiful woman at Sommerville's side was his wife, Sophie. It was clear from the way she barely glanced at Gryff that there was nothing more than friendship there; she couldn't take her eyes off her own husband. Still, Maddie was envious of the woman's easy relationship with Gryff. She wanted that teasing banter, that laughter.

As if he sensed her gaze, Gryff glanced over and her heart leapt to her throat as he caught her eye. His mouth curved in a smile, and she watched him excuse himself from the Sommervilles and start around the room toward her.

"I'm going to get a drink," she mumbled to Tristan.

She had no intention of avoiding Gryff, although it would have been a simple enough matter in such a crowded affair. She began skirting the room, weaving between groups of revelers, aiming to meet him halfway. His behavior at the auction this morning had been driving her mad—she *had* to know what he was doing.

They met in front of a large pedestal bearing a larger-than-life-sized sculpture of Perseus holding aloft the snake-topped head of Medusa—part of Lord Belton's famed collection of ancient marbles. Maddie thought the furious expression on Medusa's face probably matched her own. She rather wished she could turn Gryff to stone with just a look. He was incredibly frustrating.

She didn't waste time with courtesies. "All right, Davies. Out with it. What are you about?"

His smile told her he was amused at directness. "I told you, I have a proposition. For your father. I know neither of you were keen on the canal, so I've been researching alternatives. A compromise, if you will."

She narrowed her eyes, suspicious of his sudden affability. "You? Willing to compromise? How?"

"A tramway," he said, his eyes bright with enthusiasm. "Using horses or even a steam-powered engine to pull the trucks. It would be far less labor-intensive, and therefore far cheaper than a canal. And instead of disrupting your archaeological treasures, the tracks could bypass the areas you wish to remain undisturbed."

Maddie digested this information. "That does, actually, sound like a decent solution," she admitted, rather grudgingly.

"I'm delighted you think so. I'm hoping your father will agree."

"Aha!" she pounced. "So *that's* why you let him buy your half of the dictionary. You're trying to put him in a good mood."

"That's rather cynical," he mocked gently. "And only partly true."

"Well, why else would you do it?"

He glanced over at the newly forming set of dancers in the middle of the room and held out his arm. "I'll tell you if you dance with me."

"We'll cause a scandal," she said, alarmed. "I don't think a Davies has danced with a Montgomery since before the Norman Conquest."

"What's the matter? Scared?"

"Of course not."

"Then come on." He took her hand and tugged her gently into the center of the room.

The previous set had been a lively reel, but as the couples formed into pairs, rather than two long lines, Maddie realized it was going to be a waltz.

Of *course* it was a waltz. Because she had the worst luck in the entire world, apparently. She held her breath as he gave her arm a gentle tug and pulled her around to face him. Her front bumped his chest, and she sucked in a little breath.

God, she'd missed him.

From the corner of her eye she saw her father pause mid-sentence to stare at her in shock. Auntie Con, over by the punch table, raised her glass in a cheeky toast and sent her an encouraging nod.

Gryff slid his left hand to rest at the small of her back and raised their joined right hands in preparation for the dance. Her skin heated as he subjected her to a thorough inspection. His gaze lingered on the skin of her shoulder, left bare by the deep V neckline of the dress. She'd powdered her skin, but the faint fernlike scars left by the lightning were still visible.

It was the first time she'd ever worn a dress that revealed them in public, but the dread she'd expected hadn't material-ized; the only opinion she cared for was his, and he'd already seen her almost naked. And approved.

No more hiding.

"Nice dress," he said.

"Thank you. I got tired of hiding my scars."

"Bravo."

His light praise made her feel buoyant, but she reminded herself not to be swayed by his flattery.

There was no time for further conversation. The musicians launched into the opening bars and Gryff simply swept her away.

Carys Davies took a deep breath and edged closer to Tristan Montgomery, being careful to make it look as if the crowd—and not her will—was bringing them together. She kept her face averted, but she knew exactly the moment his cool blue eyes came to rest on her neck: Her entire body tingled.

He'd always made her react this way.

With one last, practiced trill of laughter she dismissed her previous dance partner and twirled around—and feigned a gasp of shock as she bumped into Tristan's solid body.

His hands shot out to steady her arms, and she allowed herself the illicit thrill of pressing her palms to his chest as if searching for balance. Heat and strength flowed into her.

"Oh, goodness! Do excuse me," she said brightly.

He stepped back, as if her touch burned him, but she still managed to inhale a heady waft of his cologne. It made her stomach flutter.

His brows drew together in a frown—his standard expression for her—and she quelled a spurt of irritation. To every other female he was courtesy itself, dry wit and easy charm personified. Why had *she* always been the sole recipient of his displeasure? Even as children he'd dismissed her as being too young and too silly to bother with.

He was so controlled, so coolly amused. It drove her mad. And his polite disapproval always made her worry that he saw right through the carefree social persona she worked so hard to project—to the lost and broken girl she was inside.

Carys blinked. Nonsense. He was just a humorless grouch.

A gorgeous, irresistible grouch.

She sent him her most dazzling smile. "Montgomery! You're back unscathed from the Continent."

He gave the briefest of nods. "As you see."

"Your Grand Tour was a success?"

A little warmth came to his eyes. "It was. Italy was a revelation. Architecture is so much better in person, rather than illustrated in a book."

His gaze flicked to her ridiculous coiffeur and the corners of his mouth twitched. In any other man it might have been amusement, but with him it was undoubtedly disapproval.

"Some things have to be seen to be believed," he said drily.

Carys felt an unaccustomed blush rise on her skin. Everyone else in the *ton* thought her wildly amusing and creative. Tristan Montgomery always managed to make her feel frivolous and faintly ridiculous. Which she was, of course—deliberately so—but it irked her to have him point it out.

Quite why she should crave his approval was beyond understanding. As Morgan said, she should content herself with her scores of other admirers.

But there was something so deliciously unattainable about Tristan. It was probably because everyone else liked her, and he was the sole anomaly. The thought of getting him to smile, or to look at her with anything other than slightly sardonic amusement, called to her like a silent challenge.

A new set was forming for a waltz. Carys glanced longingly at the dance floor, in the vain hope that he would take the hint and ask her to dance, but he merely gave her a polite nod.

"Do excuse me, I see Lord Pennington over there. I've promised to design him a new orangery." His blue eyes flicked over her face, lingering for the briefest of moments on her lips, and he gave a faint, cynical smile. "Business before pleasure, Lady Carys."

"Only in the dictionary," Carys quipped. "*B* before *P*. Unless you're a courtesan, of course. Then pleasure *is* your business."

Her heart pounded as she waited for his reaction to her deliberately provocative words. No gently bred woman would *ever* use the word *courtesan* in polite conversation.

A reluctant smile tugged at the corner of his mouth, and her heart missed a beat.

She'd made him smile!

"You say the most dreadful things, Lady Carys," he said mildly.

His gaze dropped to her lips once more and a fizzle of excitement shimmered through her blood. His tone might be cool, but surely she wasn't imagining the flash of heat in his eyes?

"Someone should stop your mouth."

Carys lost the power of speech. Before she could think of anything suitably biting to say in return—and, mercifully, before she blurted out *Oh, please do!*—he gave her a quick bow and strode away.

She let out a slow, simmering breath. Dear *Lord*. Why was it that she could flirt with a hundred other men and feel nothing but faint enjoyment, but every interaction with Tristan Montgomery left her singed. She was like a moth to the uncaring flame.

Which was stupid, because *she* was the flame-haired, passionate one, whereas Tristan was as calm and collected as a glacier.

Except for those brief flashes of heat.

Carys bit her lip. Perhaps he wasn't a glacier after all, but a mountain, like Vesuvius: deceptively snowcapped on the surface, bubbling lava beneath.

What would it take to make him erupt . . . ?

Maddie swirled around in Gryff's embrace. They'd never danced before. Not even a country dance at one of the local gatherings. But their bodies didn't seem to need instruction, and her heart soared as they turned as effortlessly as water over a mill wheel. The room blurred into a kaleidoscope of jewels and dresses as she gazed up into his handsome face.

The sensation of being in his arms, of belonging there, was so perfect that her heart squeezed tight, as if already anticipating the loss. She tried to take in every detail: the scent of him, the strength of his thigh as it slid against hers, the confident way he guided her around the dance floor. In case this was the first and only time.

When the dance ended it took a jolt from someone behind her to bring her back to earth. Gryff led her off the dance floor and she followed, unresisting, even when she realized he wasn't returning her to any of her relatives. He drew her into a relatively quiet corner, by an open door that led out onto a small balcony. Maddie was glad for the cooler breeze as she willed her pounding heart to slow.

"So, tell me about the dictionary."

He smiled. "You're relentless."

"You're prevaricating."

He leaned his shoulder casually against the wall, blocking her view of the room and creating an oddly intimate atmosphere. She tried not to notice how good he looked in evening dress.

"That dictionary," he said, "is the perfect metaphor for a successful marriage. Two halves that are incomplete. Better together than apart."

"That's very poetic."

He tilted his head and studied her intently. "It's *also* the perfect metaphor for our two families."

"Constantly divided?" she quipped.

"Better together. The Davieses and the Montgomerys need each other to be complete. Think about it: Would your father have been happy if I'd just given him my half of the dictionary?"

"Well, no. Probably not," she admitted. "He'd have been incredibly suspicious."

"And disappointed. He got far more pleasure from outbidding me, because something hard-won is always more appreciated than something that's come easily."

His intense gaze was making her feel hot and agitated.

"Well, that's true," she managed, a little breathlessly. "And I have to admit it was a clever plan, because he'll probably be feeling magnanimous enough to agree to your railway now. Especially if it helps get our half of the gold out of the ground faster."

He took a step closer. "I didn't do it so he'd agree to the railway."

Her heart began to pound.

"I did it," he said, "because he's got something I want much more than a dusty old book. Something far more valuable. I've wanted it for a very a long time, only I didn't realize it until recently. Now I don't think I can live without it. I'd give him my whole library, every ounce of gold in that mine, if that's what it takes."

Her heart clenched—she'd never expected to hear such an admission from him—but she bit her lip, determined to be honest. *Wanting* wasn't the same as loving.

"If you're talking about me, and having an affair, then I'm sorry, but I can't."

His eyes bored into hers. "Because you don't want me?"

"Because I like you too much," she admitted in a painful whisper.

He let out a whoosh of air, as if her answer had relieved him of a heavy weight. He reached out and caught her hand, threading their fingers together, and she braced herself for having to counter his arguments on why they should still be lovers.

"Do you love me, Maddie?"

She glanced away, flustered. "What does that have to do with it?"

"Everything, I'd imagine," he said drily. "Since I love you."

Her gaze snapped back to his. "What?"

"I love you." His crooked smile melted her heart. "I think it's a lifetime affliction."

She shook her head, stunned. "But—"

"I need two words from your dictionary. They both begin with *M*."

"Which ones?"

"Marry me."

All the air left her lungs. "But—"

"I'll relinquish my claim on the shared land," he said quickly. "If you think it will help your father agree."

A shaky laugh escaped her. "And end the feud? That's the *last* thing he'd want. We'd have more luck convincing him to let me marry you so I can be his spy in the enemy camp."

He squeezed her fingers. "Is that a yes, then?"

Maddie couldn't stop the smile that split her face. "Yes!" She lifted their joined hands and pressed them to the center of her chest. "Oh, why did you ask me in the middle of a crowded ballroom, you beast? I want to kiss you, and I can't."

"You're right. That was incredibly stupid."

With a quick glance over his shoulder, he tugged her through the open door and out onto a narrow balcony barely wide enough for the two of them. He kicked the door closed with his heel, whirled her around in a flurry of skirts, and backed her up against the cool wall. Her heart pounded in anticipation.

"Do you want me to get down on one knee?"

"It *is* tradition."

He shook his head but dropped to one knee and raised her hand to his lips. He kissed her knuckles. The glow from the ballroom lit the angles of his face, and Maddie marveled at her incredible good fortune. This man was hers, forever. Maybe she *wasn't* the unluckiest girl in the world.

"Madeline Montgomery, will you marry me?"

"That's a lot of alliteration," she teased. "But yes. I'd be honored."

He surged to his feet and pressed her back against the wall, and she shivered, loving the heat and the hardness of him. "You should kiss me now," she breathed. "To seal the bargain."

He smiled as he caught the reference. "Like we did at the bridge?"

"Exactly."

"My pleasure."

Maddie returned his kiss with ardent enthusiasm. With a sigh of pure joy, she flung her arms around his neck and closed her eyes, pressing herself against him.

Home.

It was at least ten minutes later when they finally pulled apart. Her lips were tingling and her blood was singing in her veins. "We really should go back to the party," she panted. "We'll be missed."

Gryff nodded. "I'll call on your father tomorrow and formally ask for your hand."

"Sir Mostyn offered two thousand pounds if I'd marry him," she couldn't resist teasing.

"I'll offer five."

"That might just do it," she said. "Especially if I tell him I don't want anyone else. I know he can be a bit cantankerous, but he really does want to see me happy. He'll grumble and stomp, but he'll agree in the end. He loves me too."

They managed to slip back into the ballroom unobserved. It was the height of torture to spend the rest of the evening keeping a polite distance from each other, but Maddie was amused to watch the other members of their families in action.

Morgan, she noted, was watching Harriet whenever her cousin wasn't looking. The odd, calculating look on his face made her resolve to have a word with Harry about being wary of Davies men with a grudge.

Better still, the sight of Carys, Gryff's vivacious, redheaded sister at the center of a gaggle of admirers, had Tristan shooting daggers of disapproval across the room.

Maddie bit back a smile. Those two really were complete opposites in terms of temperament: controlled, ordered Tristan and impetuous, laughing Carys. She couldn't wait to see them forced to spend some time together in the coming weeks.

Gryff was right: Neither family would welcome a complete end of hostilities. Hating each other was simply too much fun. She and Gryff might be making an alliance, but this could very well be the start of a whole new era of Davies-Montgomery rivalry . . .

Epilogue

Maddie descended the steps to the Virtuous Well and pulled a silver sixpence from her reticule. The water level was much higher now than when she and Gryff had escaped from it; she could see the dark ripples of water about halfway down the shaft.

She closed her eyes, muttered a wish, and tossed the coin.

A pair of strong arms came around her from behind, and with a smile she leaned back into her husband's embrace.

"What are you wishing for?" Gryff asked. His lips nuzzled the side of her neck. "I don't know what you could possibly want. You already have an amazing, attentive husband who lets you do whatever you like."

Maddie bit her lip as she tried not to laugh at his insufferable conceit. She glanced down at the wedding band that glimmered on her left hand; Gryff had used the first gold extracted from the Davies-Montgomery mine to make it.

"I was wishing for the people I love to find equal happiness," she said. "Tristan, and Harriet."

"What about my side of the family? Rhys and Morgan are

as wild as ever, and Carys is causing me endless sleepless nights."

"I wished for them too," she smiled. "And you know, I've been thinking . . ."

"Always dangerous." He pressed kiss to her ear.

"The next time a Davies has to meet a Montgomery for the equinox, who do you think we should send? Tristan and Carys? Or Harriet and Morgan?"

Gryff turned her in his arms and pressed a kiss to her lips. "I'll leave it entirely up to you, my love."

Acknowledgments

Thanks, as ever, to Patricia Nelson at MLLA and Jennie Conway and all the team at St. Martin's Press for keeping me on the straight and narrow. To Gen, Sara, and Tara for your friendship, endless support, and encouragement. And a huge thank you to every reviewer, blogger, YouTuber, and Bookstagrammer who not only read my books, but share your love of romance with the world. Thank you! Your passion and enthusiasm are so appreciated by authors like myself. Finally, to everyone who's ever left a review because you've loved my books, thank you too! I hope you enjoy this one just as much. Happy reading!
Love, Kate

Don't miss the next book in the Ruthless Rivals series
by **Kate Bateman**

A DARING PURSUIT

Coming Summer 2022 from St. Martin's Paperbacks